Honeycomb

Raymond Carras
and William Drummond

Honeycomb

Pan Original
Pan Books London and Sydney

First published 1979 by Pan Books Ltd,
Cavaye Place, London SW10 9PG
© Raymond Carras and William Drummond 1979
ISBN 0 330 25783 8
Printed and bound in Great Britain by
Richard Clay (The Chaucer Press) Ltd, Bungay, Suffolk

Contents

1 Sergeant Pryke 9
2 Eulalia 13
3 Pieter Kloot 16
4 Senhor Gonsalves Pereira 21
5 The MS *São Paulo* 25
6 At sea 32
7 John Embleton 39
8 El Palacio do Sonho 44
9 Scarface 53
10 The bet 59
11 Warning – DANGER! 67
12 Enter Philip Mitchell 74
13 Progress Report One 81
14 Lisbon – Orly 85
15 Liversedge Hall 88
16 Progress Report Two 98
17 General Ballsup 100
18 At the White House 103
19 Operation Honeycomb 104
20 Within the Maze 110
21 Horsemeat 114
22 The Hotel Shelduck 117
23 This Blessed Plot 123
24 The Smallmans 128
25 Meeting the boys 131
26 A minor detour 133
27 Not real common 134
28 Final briefing 137
29 When is murder . . . 138

30 . . . not murder – warfare 141
31 Grete *chez* Ohlsen 143
32 Off Sheerness 145
33 Hexite hesitation 146
34 The monstrous sky 150
35 An extraordinary inspection 153
36 A lesson for Lucas 155
37 Belmouth to Fleet 158
38 A good meal 162
39 Hijack 163
40 A way with rats 166
41 Enemy in need 168
42 Telephone exchange 170
43 The odds are even 171
44 Sir Hilary afraid 174
45 Plan D 176
46 Better to walk 177
47 Through Sunday city 179
48 Smoke without fire 181
49 Retreat 182
50 Choice of evils 183
51 Embleton at Leman Street 185
52 Nothing to sneeze at 187
53 Letter to a godfather 190
54 Water boatmen 194
55 Out of order 197
56 Lucas underground 198
57 The Pool of London 200
58 In Westminster 203
59 Somewhere in Bloomsbury 204
60 A case of overwork 206
61 Dublin, via Liverpool 208
62 VS Day 210

1 Sergeant Pryke

South Africa, April 1944

It was not until the second night that Lucas Molyneux was alerted. The sixty-watt bulb in the shower shed, brown with fly-dirts, was so weak that the '6' scratched on the green paint of his locker might have been chance; but on the second night there was a '9' cut deeper into the metal: 69.

As he stood under the old zinc shower, with half the holes blocked, always running either too hot or too cold, he did not worry. But he pondered. While he was down the mine, somebody was snooping round the shower shed. Well, no diamonds would be found in *his* locker. Only a moron would try that. With bloody Security Sergeant Pryke and his master key.

But what was the point in scratching numbers on a door, which was so old that there wasn't even any fun in vandalism? 69? *Soixante-neuf?* Not his fancy.

He towelled off, listening to the blacks arsing around the other side of the wall; under the same water (from the same boiler-room) but continents, centuries apart. It was cold. He put on a pullover and then his bush jacket, before going into the dusty compound. It was floodlit, like the POW cage in which the falangists had kept him for five weeks in Badajoz: the same ten-foot wire meshing, except that here the triple barbed wire at the top was on both sides, to prevent anyone getting in as well as out. It was a sort of 'Diamond Concentration Camp'. But of course it was the British who invented that triumph of the twentieth century, the concentration camp. During the Boer War – as Lucas's room mate Pieter was never tired of saying.

A pity Pieter was on the second nightshift this week. Lucas did not like drinking alone. He started up the jeep and drove to the gates. There was the same dreary routine as one guard came over with his rifle slung and the other waited, hand on the gun in his holster. 'Pass, please.'

'You know me,' Lucas said, 'or should by now.'

'But have you got your pass is what I don't.'

Lucas held the pass under the guard's torch, showing the non-descript photograph. The guard flashed on to Molyneux's non-descript face and then waved to his mate, who raised the STOP barrier.

As Lucas eased forward over the dirt road he thought what a farce it was. He might have had an arseful of diamonds; as indeed he had sometimes had. Now in the safekeeping of Mum in Stepney, until such time as this bloody war was over.

Out of the glare of the floodlights, when he was belting down towards Kimberley, night descended. The stars were like holes in the canvas of a great tent. Did the Pole Star shine as bright on blacked-out London as the Southern Cross on Kimberley?

Next evening when he clocked on, Lucas took dust from the top of his locker and rubbed it over the *soixante-neuf*. Then he put on his gear and went over to the lift hoists. He was curious to know what, if anything, would happen.

For eight and a half hours, he was so engrossed in the problems of tunnelling – at the same time as routine and as attention-demanding as driving a heavy lorry – rock formations, shot-placing, charges, fuse lengths, roof props and so on, that he did not give the mystery of his locker a thought. But on his way back from the face, going up in the lift and across to the shower shed, he found himself wondering, indeed hurrying to see if there had been anything added.

Something had. But what it was he could not be sure. It was a straight line, about twice the distance from the '69' as those two figures were from one another. (Were they really figures? or just doodles?) This line was not upright, but at an angle like the hour hand at two o'clock. It was made with the same implement – a blunt knife, the thin edge of an electrician's screwdriver, perhaps. Closer to the '69' it would have been '1'. But at this distance, it might have been a random gash.

As he struggled with the hot and cold taps, he wondered who it might be. No black would dare go into a shower shed reserved for whites. It could be any of the white staff going down on second nightshift. The obvious suspect was Pieter, who was fond of making fun of Lucas's jitteriness, which he called his 'Molynuisance'. It was just the sort of twisted joke he liked to make.

Well, two could play at that game. Before he left the shower shed, Lucas took a stub of pencil and wrote on Pieter's locker '% 2 U'. If it was Pieter, ten to one he would scratch something more on Lucas's locker when he came off-shift at ten a.m.

But next afternoon when they briefly saw each other before Lucas drove out to the mine, Pieter said nothing, and there was no fresh graffito on Lucas's door. That cleared Pieter. Or did it? Lucas had sensed that Pieter was watching him with unusual care. But was that his imagination, or his friend's awareness that he was worried about something he didn't want to mention?

It would not be true to say that during that nightshift Molyneux worried consciously. Fear was like a seed which did not germinate until he entered the cage. His heart beat faster as the crowded lift shot upwards. As the gate clanged back, he felt in his pocket for the key of his locker. He had to have a cigarette to steady his nerves. He didn't look at the door; he shook a cigarette out of the pack, lit it and took a deep draw before he glanced at the numbers. A fourth digit had been added and it was the number he dreaded, 2. 6912 were the first four of the five digits in his regimental number. Whoever scratched them knew he was a British army deserter and was threatening exposure.

Suddenly his movements speeded up. He laid the cigarette on the sand of the ash-tin, stripped off, showered, dried and dressed – as fast as someone in an undercranked movie. Then he picked up his smouldering cigarette and strolled as composedly as possible towards his jeep.

Before he reached it, a voice shouted, 'Hey, you!' Lucas turned. It was Pryke, 'the Prick'. 'The name's Molyneux, not Hey You.'

Pryke sauntered over, smacking the palm of his hand with a truncheon. 'Oh, is it? I thought it wasn't a French sort of name; more Armenian, like. Still you, being an educated bloke, will correct me if I'm wrong. A rose by any other name, says the Immortal Bard: which, vicky verser, goes for other four-letter words. Such as shit. I mean, contrariwise.'

Leucas Ramoulian was his real name. He had changed it by deed poll after he bought himself out of the army, and before he volunteered for the International Brigade. 'What are you up to, Pryke?'

'Just a routine check.' Pryke's grin was more frightening than a scowl. 'Never do to give the nigs the idea they were the only ones.' He poked Lucas in the solar plexus with his truncheon. 'Sort of good for racial morale.'

The inspection room was a combination of hospital and torture chamber. The x-ray apparatus would have shown any diamond up. But there was a probing of mouth, ears, armpits and even the urethra, culminating in the savage intrusion of an unlubricated enema. In Franco's jails, Lucas had known indignities, but nothing as deliberately humiliating. When it was over, Lucas felt as if he had been sodomitically raped. Pryke stood over him, as an assistant sieved the stool. 'Nothing there, boss.'

'Was there any reason?' Lucas was so angry he could not finish the sentence.

'You're clear, Mr Molynoo. If you've got any complaints, you know where to make 'em. Major Carlisle was in the sappers, too. Only he fought. In the First World War.' He waited till Lucas was dressed. 'Like to go and see 'im, now?' Pryke took Lucas by the elbow. (As if Major Carlisle at three a.m. was waiting in his office, not at home in bed!)

When they got outside the inspection room, Lucas freed his arm. 'You still haven't told me what all this is in aid of.'

'Let's say that it's in aid of us both: of Sergeant Ramoulian L., No. 69125, 'cos he's earning better as Mr Molynoo than fightin' in fuckin' Europe; and of me, because I can do with fifteen quid a week for keeping me trap shut.'

'Bloody blackmail?'

'Call it silence-money,' Pryke said. 'Sounds better. You know where I keep my boat, at Foster's Creek. I'll see you there Saturday evening, after fishin''; say half-past six.'

Lucas walked over to his jeep, without answering. As he put the key into the ignition and turned it, Pryke called, 'I might even give you a beer, sonny. If you're good.'

2 Eulalia

Lucas could afford fifteen pounds a week, just. But if he paid it, Pryke would increase the squeeze to twenty, twenty-five. I must not pay, he kept saying to himself, not even once. He had thirty-six hours before the rendezvous at Pryke's boathouse. But if he did not turn up for the Friday nightshift, Pryke would know he'd done a bunk and go to Carlisle. Next Monday, he was on the ten a.m. dayshift. The weekend would give him two days before he'd be missed at the mine.

But how in the name of goodness had Pryke found out his army name, rank and number? Even he himself had forgotten his army number until a couple of days ago. When he got very drunk, as he not infrequently did in this hell-hole at weekends, he couldn't remember next morning what he had said the night before. He had sometimes seen Pryke at the club, but they instinctively disliked one another; it was inconceivable that Lucas should confide in Pryke, however drunk he got.

He drove to the bungalow he shared with Pieter Kloot just off Siege Avenue in Kenilworth and parked the jeep under the lean-to. He wished Pieter wasn't on the second nightshift. He wouldn't be back until about ten-thirty a.m. There wasn't anybody else Lucas could trust in Kimberley. He wasn't sure that he could trust even Pieter. They had talked about the war in Europe, but Lucas had never told him about buying himself out of the REs, changing his name to join the International Brigade and then getting so browned off with both sides that he swore he'd never fight again for or against any political creed. Or had he, when he was drunk?

He went in by the back door as usual, took a lager and small cubes of ice out of the fridge and then, in the front room, poured himself a brandy on the rocks. There was only one person on earth whom he could trust and that was his Ma, who was in Stepney. And it was only her good faith he could trust, not her intelligence. There was no one on earth he could trust – he took a deep drink of brandy – except God, who didn't exist. He swallowed. 'But if you do, God,' he said, 'help me.' His bum felt weak. The memory of that anal assault came back, and Pryke's leering face. He swallowed the lager chaser. Pryke lived on Siege Avenue. He was married to a faded blonde who grew pot-plants which threw out roots and leap-frogged from pot to pot. She had dozens of them, even offered Pieter one; the only fruit of their marriage.

He fetched another lager and more ice. He did not turn on the light in the kitchen. He could see well enough from the light in the front room. He looked across the back yard to the gate used by the tradesmen and the hut where Eulalia slept. Blackmail, he thought – black female. He ought to go to sleep, to be ready to talk to Pieter before he went to bed after second nightshift. But how did Pryke know his name, rank and number? He poured another brandy, even stiffer, and waited while the ice melted. Where could he disappear to from Kimberley? If he asked for a transfer, experience in a gold mine perhaps, Pryke would trace him. Durban, Cape Town were out as escape ports. If he tried to get a passage, Pryke would report him to Major Carlisle and the security police would be alerted. Make his way, say, to Tanganyika and then what? Volunteer for a war which he had done all this to avoid? He went to the desk and wrote a note: 'Pieter, *V. important*. Wake me up, before you go to bed. *Must talk*. Luke.' He put it on the pillow of Pieter's bed. Then he went back to his drink.

The night was very still. The only noise he heard was the ticking of the clock. Everyone in Kenilworth was asleep. It would not be long before the cocks began to crow. Thinking of cocks, his rose. He went into his bedroom with his brandy and lager chaser. By the time he had undressed, he had finished them. Though he was still weak behind, he was very strong in front. He slipped a pack of cigarettes and matches in the pocket of his dressing gown, took his small torch, turning out all lights as he went.

He went into the kitchen and crossed the yard to the hut. Eulalia was snoring as loud as a bullfrog, but he went into the hut. She was lying on the iron bed, curled up like a baby in her mother's womb. The clothes were pulled up to cover her mouth. Only her tight black curls, the ebony forehead, and broad nose were showing. She was sleeping so deeply that despite his need he would not wake her. But then, perhaps because of the flash-

14

light on her lids, she opened her eyes. They were very large and their whites coffee-with-cream colour. She was heavy with sleep; and he was turning away when she called, 'Oh, you come. Ah hoped.' So he stopped.

She had been schooled by Jesuits and christened Eulalia. The Jesuits had taught her to love goodness, but not to hate sex. She put out her hand and held his cock. 'Hullo, darlin',' she said, looking at it as if it was a welcome guest, 'you lookin' fine to-night.' She kissed it on the mouth and then she grasped his balls, 'An' you feel fine.' She threw back the covers and addressed the bush between her legs, 'You got company, Fanny, wake up!' Then she turned to Lucas; 'Fanny's still asleep. Could you wake her up, while I play with the boys?'

Fanny was hiding in a dense, wiry bush, smelling like a vixen's hole, but with the ferreting of the tongue she soon woke up and without a word Eulalia pressed him so that their positions were reversed. She lay on her back, legs spread wide apart and he was poised above her, not kissing her lips but tantalizing her clitoris with the mouth of his urethra. It was something they had never done before and Eulalia, stretched to another expectancy, could not bear it. It was like being offered food which was never put within reach. She caught his cock and then pushed it home, with her other hand on his buttocks.

He drove into her, brought her almost to a climax, and then he began to withdraw. With each thrust inwards, he drew further outwards. She was bursting to come, but he was trying to find a way to come with her. It was terribly important for him. He had had numbers of women in England, Spain, on the boat, in South Africa and Mozambique; but though he had brought them to fulfilment, he had never had an orgasm in a woman. He was the answer to the maiden's prayer; but after being buggered by Pryke's enema, he had to come into a woman to prove himself.

After half an hour, he brought Eulalia to a climax. It was of course wonderful to bring any woman to a climax, each was different just as each time was different. (Like landing a salmon, if ever he could afford that sport.) But there he lay alongside his Bantu girl, as tense as she was relaxed. He lit two cigarettes and they smoked in the darkness. He had pretended to match her moans of ecstasy, but she put down her hand and felt his cock

15

as stiff as ever. 'No come?' she asked. 'Coming again,' he lied, laying his hand between her thighs.

He left it there until she was ready and started to move herself to him. The smell of her sweat was as rank as musk. It excited him. He wondered if his stench excited her. Certainly the stiffness of his cock did. She played with it as if it was a mouth-organ; and when she was ready, the most elaborate battle began in which she gave him entry to her mouth but denied it to her Fanny, then gave him lower access thrusting up the *mons pubis* so that her hair ground on his. She turned her head away, then suddenly took his tongue down her throat. She fought, she embraced, bit, kissed, dug nails in, climbed up, crouched, sat astride, and finally came.

He got off the bed; by the time he had arranged the covers over her, put on his dressing gown and kissed her sweaty brow, she was snoring.

3 Pieter Kloot

'I don't see, Luke man. Why you worry how Pryke knows? Is true? Isn't true? Which?' He had read Lucas's message and roused Eulalia to make breakfast, before he woke Lucas up. Now they sat on the step, having downed a glass of fresh orange juice, bacon and eggs, toast and marmalade, and two cups of coffee each.

'Of course, it's true. I want to explain ...'

'Don't, man. I understand. But what do we do?'

'*We?*'

'Hell, man, we've been sharing four years.' Pieter leant across and tapped the back of Lucas's hand with a coffee spoon. 'We've enjoyed the smooth. Now's the rough.'

Pieter was eighteen months younger than Lucas. Lucas had thrown his weight about, with his knowledge of England, France, Spain, Egypt, Palestine and the sad history of Armenia. But now he was relying on the Boer, with a lifetime in South

Africa, a family tradition running back 200 years. 'You say, Piet.'

'You've got to get out of SA, yes?' Lucas nodded. 'You want to stay neutral, *if* you can, huh?' Another nod. 'The only neutral colony you can get to is Mozambique, from which ships sail, not in convoy, to Portugal.'

'And what do I do there? *If* I get there!'

'Boats sail from Portugal to Brasil, where a man with your experience ... no trouble about a labour permit, with a little ...' Pieter rubbed the middle finger of his right hand along the base of his thumb, 'and the right contacts. You might do better there than in Kimberley. Your Portuguese is ... enough.'

'And how does a chap like me fix that?'

'You'll have to leave that to the backward Boer,' Pieter said. 'I've been thinking. People here would do things for me they wouldn't do for you. No offence, man. You understand?'

'Only too well.' The Boer clannishness and the British snobbery had relegated him beyond the Kimberley pale.

'So you must be utterly guided by me, man. Do everything I say, even if it doesn't seem to make sense. We haven't got much time to explain – if you're going to get away – because that bastard Pryke will be after you if you don't show up, and go to Major Carlisle within the hour – once he knows you've called his bluff.'

Lucas could picture it. 'I'll need money.'

'How much have you got in the bank here?'

Lucas looked in his deposit account. 'Sixty-seven quid. But I've £500 on deposit; only, that's on seven days' call.'

'I'll see what I can fix. Under no circumstances draw more than the fifteen pounds which Pryke expects to get tomorrow. You know what Kimberley's like for gossip. If you tried to clear your accounts, you might as well shoot yourself. But draw that fifteen. I wouldn't mind betting that Pryke will hear of it when he comes off-shift tomorrow morning.' Pieter stood up and emptied his coffee cup. 'Don't worry, man. I've had a feeling you've been sort of stagnating down here. I'm going out to pull some strings.'

'How many have you got?'

'More than a Jew's harp, more than a fiddle. Call it a Boer's harp; and man, believe you me, those strings don't snap.' Pieter's jauntiness surprised Lucas, until he realized that this was the first time in all these years of sharing the bungalow that Lucas had come out into the open. They had drunk, shot, fished, holidayed together, but Lucas had always kept his distance. Perhaps Pieter was pleased at being told openly what hitherto he had only guessed.

Certainly from that moment, Pieter took over control. He had been to see a friend ('no names, no pack drill') who shipped a lot of freight through Lourenço Marques, to Portugal and South America through the Companhia do Navegação Brasileira. The president of the shipping line – Dom Rosario – was, by lucky chance, in Lourenço Marques and had expressed his willingness to take Lucas on as a sinecure supercargo, as far as Lisbon and perhaps to Rio de Janeiro, out of gratitude for services rendered by his friend in Kimberley; but speed was necessary ('to which, Luke, I took the liberty of saying that you would not object'). Dom Rosario was sailing either Monday or Tuesday, depending on the turnaround; and was not prepared to delay his departure for any supercargo. 'So, man, as soon as I come off-shift tomorrow morning, I'll see you on your way.'

'What about Pryke?'

Pieter held up his hand. 'We're coming to Pryke later. First about your money. Drop a note to your bank manager to say that you wish to transfer £500 from your deposit to your current account. If you post it tomorrow, he won't get it until you are in Lourenço Marques, or even on the high seas. Meanwhile you give me a cheque, made out to cash for £500, and dated Monday week; in return for which I will give you its equivalent in sterling, escudos or krugerrands, whichever you prefer.

'Then about Pryke – it's important to keep him quiet over the weekend. He must think that you have tried to keep the rendezvous. I think it would be a good idea if you told Pryke tomorrow morning that you were going fishing on the Vaal; and when he arrives there, he finds not you, but evidence of an accident. Something he has to report to the police, not to Major Carlisle.'

It all came out so pat; Lucas said, 'What precisely do you mean, Piet?'

Pieter Kloot yawned. 'Dunno,' he said, 'I'll sleep on it. But it's an idea. Pryke wouldn't want anyone to think he'd been blackmailing. If it looked like something fishy had happened to you, I mean.'

The more Lucas thought, the more he was convinced that Pieter was right. Since he had landed in South Africa, three weeks after the Munich crisis, he had been *stagnating*, marking time until the war should end. Now Pieter was to transport him from the blackmail of Pryke to Portugal or beyond on the magic carpet of a Dom Rosario. Kimberley, which he had sought as a refuge, had come to seem a prison, or self-internment camp. Lucas felt more exhilarated than for years. Pieter had converted menace into adventure. He contemplated possible 'accidents'. Should he take the boat which they jointly owned and capsize it on the Vaal River? No: waste of time and a good boat. A car accident? He couldn't sell his jeep; to travel in it would expose his trail, when he abandoned it. Wrecked at Foster's Creek, it would mislead both Pryke and the police.

Pieter agreed with him next morning. There was a lay-by on the main road, just beyond the side road leading down to the creek. Lucas was to drive there and wait for Pieter, who would come by a different route. There would be time for Pieter to drive Lucas to Pretoria Station and double back to rig the accident before the rendezvous with Pryke. When Lucas asked how, Pieter answered, 'Leave that to me,' and counted out the krugerrands, pounds and escudos, before pocketing the cheque for £500.

Everything went smoothly until Lucas put twenty-five pounds in an envelope and said, 'Give that to the girl from me on Monday, will you?'

Pieter would not take it. 'I'll help you out of my country, Luke. But I have principles.' Twenty-five pounds was a fortune to a Bantu servant. With it, Eulalia could buy a husband. Perhaps in Pieter's eyes it was ruining to the domestic economy. Lucas did not argue. He went into the kitchen, where Eulalia was bent over the sink. 'This is for you,' he said as she looked up. 'But don't open it until Tuesday.'

She wiped her hands and took the envelope. She opened

her mouth, but she said nothing: just took the envelope and held it to the breasts which he had sucked and fondled, but never seen.

'Time to get cracking,' Pieter called.

As they were driving to Pretoria, Lucas said, 'Don't you think *I* have principles?'

Pieter drove with his eyes on the road ahead. 'Um. But a sort of cripple's.'

'What sort?'

'I suppose it's being Armenian, but not in Armenia – under Turkish, Syrian, Soviet rule; whatever it may be. You've got no sense of country.'

'How could I? Born in the East End of London. Armenian immigrant parents. The Communist International was my attempt at belonging. No more belonging for me.'

'*No man is an island.* You've got to—'

'I don't want to be an island. I'm a neutral. Like Switzerland; land of cuckoo clocks and cheese with holes in it.'

'And world banks and useful international organizations like the Red Cross. Switzerland can be neutral because it pays all sides to keep it neutral. But what have you got, Luke? Great skill as a tunnelling engineer. That's an asset which many people would be prepared to exploit. Supposing you can't get work in Portugal? You may have to take sides sooner or later.' Piet's voice was curiously dispassionate, like Wal's, the kindly political commissar in Spain who warned of the inadvisability of questioning the party line. 'Are you doing all this for me out of friendship,' asked Lucas, 'or your principles?'

Pieter Kloot took his eyes off the road ahead and looked at Lucas steadily but without emotion. 'They don't conflict, man.'

He dropped Lucas fifty yards from Pretoria station. While Lucas was humping his two suitcases to the booking office he saw Pieter's jeep disappear round a corner, heading back for Foster's Creek, to arrange an accident which did not conflict with his principles.

4 Senhor Gonsalves Pereira

Lucas had spent two vacations with Pieter in Mozambique. In Lourenço Marques, they had always stayed at the Polana Hotel, on the grounds that the best was good enough for them. But when he got off the train on this visit, Lucas decided that the worst was best for him. He deposited his cases at the station and walked down towards Delagoa Bay. Wearing his oldest khaki trousers and bush jacket, he merged unobtrusively with the blacks, whites and *mestiços* in the *avenida*. There had been no hitch at the frontier and there was no reason to think he might be followed; but he twice stepped into alleyways and waited to see if anyone turned after him or glanced in his direction. No one did. He remembered Pieter Kloot's watchwords: 'Take it easy!' He was a free man now and should not forget it.

Beside a news-stand there was a hoarding with a street map of the city. The office of the Companhia do Navegação Brasileira was in the Beco da Trindade. The legend at the side of the map indicated where the main shipping lines were. But there was no mention of the Brasilian Navigation Company and he could find no Beco da Trindade in their neighbourhood. He went into a corner café and sat at a secluded table from which he could watch the whole room. When a black waiter came, he ordered a local lager, in his best Portuguese. 'You want to eat, sir?' said the waiter in English. The table he had chosen was one of eight with tablecloths. Lucas plumped for the dish of the day, but when it came it looked like yesterday's and smelt like the day's before: a ragout of sinewy goat with yams, peppers and aubergines drowning in train oil. But the lager was ice cold. After discussion with three colleagues, the waiter told him that to find the Beco da Trindade, he must go down to the enclosure, turn right, take the sixth on the right, the first *ruela* on the left. 'You will see the church at the end of the *beco*,' he said.

As Lucas made his way there, he realized that, as it was Sunday, the office would be closed. But there was no harm in making sure where the offices were.

The Beco da Trindade was a short alley leading to a small modern church. No. 3 was a three-storey building with windows

21

shuttered and barred like a prison and large doors painted the colour of bulls' blood. The doors were closed, as was the passenger door, set into the right-hand gate. There was no knocker, no bell to push or pull.

He was turning away, when from the church appeared a figure wearing a black cassock and biretta. As he came closer, Lucas saw that the priest's features were negroid but his skin without a vestige of colour. Seeing Lucas, the priest stopped. *'Cerrao,'* he said. *'Sesta.'* He pointed to his watch and held up five fingers.

'Open on Sunday?' Lucas was astonished. But the albino priest smiled, nodded and went on his ecclesiastical way.

Two blocks away Lucas found a café bar called the Amerigo, with rooms to let. The owner looked like a capuchin monkey, and his left arm hung like a sawdust doll's. There was a stretched canvas bed, one sheet and a mosquito net without holes. 'No bugs. Very clean. Very cheap.' Lucas took it.

By the time he had brought his cases from the railway station, it was past five o'clock. The small door in No. 3 Beco da Trindade was open. Inside was a large courtyard, in the middle of which was a blue gum tree. On the walls just inside the gates, the names of a large number of different concerns were painted in alphabetical order, with the number of staircase and floor. The Navigation Company of Brasil was C-30, which Lucas found was in the far-left corner. The staircase was unlit; on the first half-landing in a corner there was something which he hoped was only *dog* shit. On the top floor there were three doors, each with clouded glass panels. The middle one read

Dr Gonsalves Pereira
Específicos Urinogenitarios (Tocar 1)
Peliculas Aphrodite (Tocar 2)
Companhia do Navigação Brasileira (Tocar 3)

It seemed as though Dr Pereira had diversified without expanding. Lucas touched the bell three times. Each time it buzzed like an infuriated bluebottle, but there was no invitation to enter. He tried the door handle and it opened. He found himself facing a wall on which was a large chart of the urinogenitary system and a calendar depicting a nude Polynesian girl drinking fruit juice through a straw, her privates hidden by a large pineapple. Seated between these two pictures was a small young woman with large ears and an enormous typewriter. She was painting the middle nail of her left hand magenta. She looked up at Lucas.

'Good afternoon, senhorita. I wish to see Dom Rosario.'

'Is not here.'

'Where can I find him?'

'He comes.'

'When does he come, please?'

'Now.' The girl used the word *agora*, which literally means now, but often proves to mean later. '*Brevemente?*' queried Lucas. 'Soon?' '*Agora*,' the girl repeated.

'May I wait?'

'As you please.' She turned her attention to the fourth nail on her left hand. Lucas looked at a chair, the caned seat of which he noted was giving way. He sat gingerly on the edge. 'Do you mind if I smoke?'

'It is not forbidden.'

As Lucas puffed away, the girl completed the fingers of both hands. It seemed to Lucas a terrible waste of time. There was a door leading to an inner office. What was happening there? he wondered. Was Dr Pereira prescribing a genito-urinary specific? Projecting an aphrodisiac film? Or was the office empty? 'Are you sure Dom Rosario is coming soon?'

'He did not come yesterday. Or the day before. So he must come *agora*.'

The logic of this argument was not immediately apparent. Lucas had smoked another cigarette before he grasped her meaning. Then he took out a five-escudo silver piece and caught it in the palm of his hand. The senhorita transferred attention from her nails to the silver piece. It was a trick she seemed to like. When he had caught it the third time, Lucas placed it on her desk between the typewriter and her nail varnish. 'For the favour of an appointment with Dr Pereira,' he said and bowed formally.

She put the coin down her blouse between her breasts, smiled as briefly as a photographer's flash, and opened the door of the inner office. There, in front of an enlargement of a motor ship, sat the albino negro. He had discarded cassock and biretta for a white tropical suit, in the lapel of which was the ribbon of some Portuguese (or perhaps imaginary?) order. His mouth was open and he was spraying his tonsils with a pink mixture.

For a moment he seemed embarrassed. Then he closed his mouth, laid down the syringe, sprang to his feet, revealing teeth less white than his complexion. 'Please to come in, senhor,' he said; and, pointing to the syringe, which lay beside an ebonite telephone which had grown green with age: 'Is good for the pharynx, the glycerine thymol. The responses strain the vocal chords.'

'You are a doctor?'

'A *doutor*,' Dr Pereira said, 'no *medico*. Of theology. Here in Mozambique, we pride ourselves on versatility. What is it Shakespeare says ... ?'

'I haven't the foggiest idea,' said Lucas lapsing into English, and then reverting to Portuguese. 'Dom Rosario. I wish to see him *agora*.' He put his hand on Pereira's desk and lifted it to reveal a fifty-escudo note.

'Is difficult.' The doctor stretched out his hand. 'Perhaps—' Lucas clenched the note. 'Now. This evening? His ship is in the docks.'

'The docks are closed. You must go through customs, emigration, the security police. This is Sunday, senhor!'

'And yet you are open!' said Lucas.

'On your behalf. Especially. At the request of Dom Rosario, Senhor Molyneux. I do not ask questions but I say to myself, he must be a very important man, this Senhor Molyneux, if he cannot wait. Or he must have good reason to be in so much hurry. Tell me if I am wrong, please.'

'My friend in Kimberley spoke to Dom Rosario, who promised to give me a passage to Portugal on a boat of his.'

'I know,' said Dr Pereira. 'That was Friday, at eleven-forty-five. Dom Rosario was here. He spoke on that telephone. He gave a promise. Englishman's word, you know. But today is Sunday. In Lourenço Marques, we are all friends. What I know, my friend knows. What my friend knows, I know. You understand. What they say in England? "One great big happy family!"'

'I do not understand,' Lucas said.

'My friend the chief of police gave me a copy of a telegram he received from Kimberley this afternoon.' He opened a drawer and handed it to Lucas. It read; 'Kimberley to all stations, SA, SWA, Tanganyika, Mozambique, Angola. Leucas Ramoulian, British deserter, holding Passport No. 19278456, under the name of LUCAS MOLYNEUX, wanted for interrogation regarding murder of Security Sergeant Albert Pryke evening of Saturday Stop Please hold, pending further inquiries. Harkness, DPC, Kimberley.'

'It's a lie,' Lucas said, 'and you know it.'

'If I did not know it,' said Dr Pereira, 'I would not agree to help you. But here in Lourenço Marques, there are many people who do not know it. Tomorrow a big reward may be announced. I understand you have only £500.'

'That's my bloody life-savings,' Lucas exploded, in English.

In English, Dr Pereira answered, 'In your place, I would say, "Take my life savings. Give me my life." You think other?'

'If you double-cross me, I'll kill you,' Lucas said.

'OK,' said the doctor of theology. 'We go to the Amerigo.' (He knew where Lucas was staying.) 'We pick up your valises. You do not trust me?' He removed a gun from his drawer, Lucas took it. It was a Colt. 'Is a good gun, loaded. I show you how it work.'

'I know; and it *is* loaded.'

'Dom Rosario is my friend and you are innocent,' Dr Pereira said. 'I don't want to make big money. You hold the gun and give me £400, escudos, esterlinas, krugerrands, no matter. Feel me.' He stood up and Lucas frisked him. 'When I take you on *São Paulo*, you meet Dom Rosario. You give me £100 and the Colt. *Inglesu palavra?*'

It was Hobson's choice; and Lucas took it.

5 The MS *São Paulo*

Few people are prepared to do something for nothing. But all the people to whom Dr Pereira spoke were willing to do nothing for something. A word at the gate of the enclosure, the passage of a note in a friendly handshake, secured an entry. The doctor took Lucas's passport, disappeared through an office door and emerged five minutes later with it duly stamped for departure. The customs officer took some rustling up, but he did not require the opening of cases before chalking them through. The police stopped them only to pocket a *gorjeta*. In little over an hour, they were climbing up the gangplank for the MS *São Paulo*, an unimpressive craft of 6,000 tons, sadly in need of paint. The after-hatches were open and the hold was being loaded by the ship's derrick. No one paid any attention to them until they reached the upper deck. Then they were stopped by some officer, whose right eye held them accusingly while the left roved in a manner which Lucas, if he had been a young woman, would have taken to be flirtatious. He seemed to want to know what or whom-the-something the two intruders wanted. Again there was a conference which ended in Dr Pereira grasping the officer by the hand warmly and the officer putting the shaken hand promptly in his trouser pocket. To see Dom Rosario personally was apparently impossible without first seeing Captain Kneller: an act of protocol which surprised Lucas since Dr Pereira was, at least ostensibly, the shipping company's agent in Lourenço Marques.

Lucas ought to have been very angry. He was being stripped of the savings of five years by a series of people whom he had to trust (though he knew they were crooks) in order to escape from the blackmail of Sergeant Pryke (who might or might not be dead, but whom he was told he was suspected of murdering). He felt like an amateur boxer pushed into the ring to fight a champion and finding that the referee was against him, his seconds untrustworthy and the judges suspect. The blows were coming too thick, too fast. He could not stand the possibility that Captain Kneller might refuse to have him as supercargo and he might find himself back in his room at the Amerigo without anything to show for £400. He produced the Colt from his pocket. 'I demand to see Dom Rosario,' he said in a loud voice. He did not flourish the gun, but he made clear that he intended to use it against someone or something.

Captain Kneller and Dr Pereira looked at him, shocked at his interruption of their ritual. It was like someone forbidding the banns in the middle of a marriage service. But then they looked away from Lucas. Lucas turned and saw that a door had opened behind him. With one hand on the knob, the other on the lintel a large man filled the doorway so that little could be seen of the cabin beyond. His sweat might have served, with vinegar, to dress a salad. His head was as round as a football – almost; because a bullet wound had produced an unnatural dimple in his right cheek. His body was like a barrel, broadest in the middle. 'Who wants Dom Rosario?' he asked, thickly. His voice, the bloodshot eyes, the way he clung to the door, showed that he was drunk.

The captain and the doctor began excuses, but Lucas cut across them. 'I do.'

'And who the goddamn are you?'

'I am a friend of a friend of a friend of yours. In Kimberley.'

'And what you want?' Dom Rosario's mood seemed as uncertain as his grasp on the doorway. 'I'd like a drink,' Lucas said.

Dom Rosario beamed. 'And why not? Why shouldn't we all have a drink. Demerara rum.' He stood aside and waved Lucas into his cabin. 'You have a rum, too, Pereira. Put some colour into those cheeks of yours.' He ignored Captain Kneller and closed the door between their two cabins. 'Sit down.' He looked at the table. 'Something missing.' Then he stared at Lucas. 'So you are a friend of Mr Van Os?'

Van Os was chief of the Suid Africa Bond. Pieter Kloot had admitted knowing him, but always swore he did not belong to the SAB, an organization which professed neutrality but was secretly pro-Hitler. 'A friend of a friend.'

Dom Rosario laid his index finger alongside his nose and winked. 'I understand.'

It was more than Lucas did, but he smiled conspiratorially, then looked round for a glass. There was only one on the table.

'Press that bell, Pereira. What has that goddamn boy done with the glasses? When he comes, I'll string him up by the testicles.'

Instead of pressing the bell, the doctor opened a cupboard and took out two glasses. Rosario chuckled and sloshed them half full of rum. '*Gasosa!*' he said pointing to the mineral water. 'You see why I made Pereira my agent. Lazy as sin, but you've only got to mention testicles and *boum!*' He emptied his own glass and glared down at three flies eating some sugar crystals on the table. 'Do you know how many goddamn thousands of children, Mr Whatsyername, die every year because goddamn flies have eaten their goddamn sugar.'

'No, sir. Call me Lucas, sir ... Do you?'

'Fair question.' Rosario picked up a leather fly-swat with a bamboo handle. 'I'll give you a fair answer.' He brought down the fly-swat and the three flies flew away. 'Goddamn millions.' He glared at Pereira. 'Testicles! Aren't you going to fill *my* glass?'

Lucas opened his eyes, saw his suitcases on top of a folding stool. There was a clatter of winches and in his head the banging of hundreds of little hammers. Closing his eyes again, he tried to sleep. But his body burned, his head ached, his tongue was parched. The air was still and humid. The wall by the side of his bunk was hot to the touch. He would have liked to die.

He was dehydrated; the alcohol burned in his blood. He got off the bunk. The carafe for drinking water beside the folded basin was empty. Glare through the port-hole above the upper bunk blinded him. Blearily he looked round until he found a bell beside the light switch. He pressed and could hear it ring. He was still wearing his clothes of yesterday. He stripped off the bush shirt, let down the basin and ran the cold tap. It was tepid and salt. The soap would not lather, but at least it was fresher than his rank sweat. He pressed the bell again. When no one came, he opened the door and looked up and down. Three doors down there was a notice: WC. As he went into it, nausea mounted at the stench. He reached the can just in time.

When he got back to his cabin, someone was inside. From the height Lucas thought it was a boy. But the face was middle aged. The steward was holding a chamber-pot. He was some sort of oriental – deeply pockmarked. He pointed to the pot. 'Captain say, no go out. Plenty tlubble.' Sam Lee seemed to have too many teeth. Speech was a sort of feat of dental juggling, which produced clouds of spray. 'Plenty policemens.' Sam Lee closed the door and bolted it. 'Me knock' – he tapped three times quickly, three slowly, three quickly – 'you open.' A smile revealed his tangled teeth. 'Other knock. No open. No speak. Savvy?'

Lucas savvied. 'Very thirsty. Plenty iced water.'

Sam Lee smiled. 'Last night, velly dlunk. Me go. You lock. Me knock.'

Lucas bolted the door and climbed on to the top bunk. Through the port-hole he could see the stevedores at work. But there was no sign of any officials. He tried to remember what had happened last night, but he could not recall a thing after Rosario had called Pereira 'Testicles'. Though Rosario was in no state to interrogate him, Pereira might have done; and Lucas had a vague suspicion that Kneller had come in at some time. Yes, he was sure; and Kneller did not give the impression of being a drinker. His head ached so appallingly that he could not concentrate. He lay down on the lower bunk, sweat beading among the hairs on his chest and trickling down over his rib-cage.

Three quick taps, three slow, three quick. He unbolted the door. Sam Lee had a tray with a litre bottle of mineral water and a glass. It was ice cold. 'More,' begged Lucas. 'Two more.' He gulped down the first glass and burped with the gas. He stirred the second glassful with his index finger, then drank more slowly. The sweat was pouring down into his waistband. He towelled himself off and lit his last cigarette. His brain was beginning to function. He could chalk up at least one thing in his favour. He was aboard the *São Paulo*. Though he had lost all his savings and was at the mercy of Rosario and his crew, they did not intend to hand him over to the authorities in Mozambique or South Africa. If not friends, they were allies.

Sam Lee tapped again. He had brought only one bottle. 'No more cold.' But he brought also a paper. 'Captain's compliments.' Lucas thanked him and asked for strong black coffee and cigarettes. He did not open the paper until Sam Lee left. Then the headline struck his eyes – 'MURDER'. Then lower down the page beneath the word 'WANTED' was a snapshot of himself, one that Pieter Kloot had taken three weeks before on a fishing expedition; luckily, like most of the pictures taken of his unphotogenic features, utterly unmemorable. '*Have you seen this* man?' he read. 'Lucas Molyneux, aged 30, medium height, average build, brown hair, brownish eyes, tunnelling engineer at the Consolidated No. 5 Mine, Kimberley, wanted for questioning by the Kimberley CID in connection with the murder of Sergeant Alfred Pryke, with whom Molyneux had an appointment at Foster's Creek at 6.30 p.m., three hours before Sgt Pryke was found murdered. See Main Story.'

The newspaper was the *Pretoria Record*, Sunday edition. The story had made the front page. 'Our Kimberley Correspondent', however, had little enough to go on. Sergeant Pryke's fishing punt had been found drifting down the Vaal River some three miles below Foster's Creek. He had been shot at close range by a sporting rifle. Half his head had been blown away. He was clearly still in his punt when the assailant killed him, perhaps in the darkness of his boat-house as he was returning from a fishing trip. Mrs Pryke had confirmed that her husband had an appointment with Molyneux at Foster's Creek but she did not know the reason for their meeting. Mr Molyneux had phoned Sgt Pryke that morning. In the vicinity of Pryke's boat-house there were tracks of a car which had recently been driven up and driven away again. There was no evidence of the whereabouts of Molyneux or his jeep. Mr Pieter Kloot had left the bungalow which he shared with Molyneux early on Saturday morning and spent the day shopping and seeing friends in Pretoria. He did not return until ten-forty-five p.m. and friends confirmed that he did not leave Pretoria until mid-evening. The housegirl stated that Molyneux had left before Mr Kloot. She was found to have the sum of twenty-five pounds hidden under her mattress, which she said had been given her by Molyneux prior to his departure that morning. She admitted that she thought that Molyneux did not intend to return to Kimberley and this was a goodbye present. '*She is presently at Kimberley Police Station, helping with inquiries.*'

Lucas laid down the paper and tried to think. When Pieter had urged him to telephone Pryke to say that he would be at Foster's Creek on Saturday evening, had he really been wanting to make sure that Mrs Pryke knew of the rendezvous? Pieter had assured him that he would go straight back and fix something at Foster's Creek: instead of that he had arranged an alibi by staying with friends in Pretoria. But why had they murdered Pryke – and how had the murderer, whoever he might be, succeeded in getting close enough to him that he could blow half his head away? They didn't need to go to such lengths to make sure that Lucas did not bolt back on his own tracks.

Then, from the night before, Lucas dredged up a fragment of memory. He recalled Rosario stretching forward and stroking the back of his hand in a manner which Lucas would have taken to be amorous if it was possible to imagine Rosario capable of sexual feelings, and saying – 'We were expecting you to come last week.' Did Rosario really say that? In this world of total nightmare, how to disentangle reality from fantasy? No, Lucas remembered drawing his hand away, astonished at the thought that Rosario was queer. It *had* happened, he thought; in which case—

Sam Lee gave his taps and Lucas opened the door. To the black coffee he had added a breadroll sandwiched around a slice of cheese. 'Policemens gone. Sail soon. But no leave cabin, please.'

When he was alone again, Lucas sipped the black coffee, which was foul. The cheese roll was fouler still, like a rubber sole inside a leather shoe. Suppose that Pryke had been given the information about Lucas's desertion on Monday by someone in the SAB, call him X ... Pryke should have notified Major Carlisle immediately, but might conceivably have tipped the wink to Lucas. In either case Lucas would have appealed to Pieter on Monday or Tuesday and made the planned getaway in midweek. Instead of that Pryke had resorted to a devious piece of blackmail. The plan had hung fire until Friday. No wonder Pieter had tried to head Lucas off from finding out how Pryke knew, and emphasized the importance of making a getaway.

Pryke's demand for hush-money had complicated the SAB plan. He had to be kept quiet; and how better than to kill him in such a way that suspicion would fall on Lucas? The murderer, probably X, had hidden in the boat-house and blasted Pryke as he brought in his punt from fishing, set the punt adrift on the

Vaal River and then driven off in Lucas's jeep, which could either be crashed in some lonely spot or parked, say in Johannesburg, to mislead the police.

It was a possible explanation. But what the hell did it matter what had happened in South Africa? What was going to happen to him aboard the *São Paulo*? The SAB did not go to all this trouble out of sheer delight in dirty tricks.

The engines had started up. He could hear the noise of hatches being battened down. He thought of Eulalia held for questioning. He prayed the buggers would let her keep the twenty-five quid.

6 At sea

When they dropped the pilot, Sam Lee came down and told Lucas that it was safe to leave his cabin. But Lucas continued to lie on his bunk. He still felt terrible and he could not face Rosario or Kneller. He smoked and drank *gasosa*, trying to think. He had got to *anticipate*, working out moves ahead like a chess player. It was something which he had never done. In his private life, he had always reacted to what had gone before: the International Brigade, prison in Badajoz, the Munich Crisis, Pryke's blackmail, Pieter's help, Pereira, Rosario – like a trained dog leaping through one paper hoop after another. Even as a tunnelling engineer, he had been only an underground man, working out what had to be done at each seam face as it was opened up; not a top man, exploring possibilities for miles and years ahead. Now he had to become a chess player, a top man.

If he was right that he was a victim of a plot, in which the SAB had induced him to flee from Kimberley to Lourenço Marques, he could infer what might happen in the future from what must have happened in the past. There must, for example, be in London someone with access to War Office records who knew that he was a deserter and had passed that information to the SAB. The SAB had used Pryke, who obviously wasn't an SAB member, to act as an agent; the same was true of the use that they had made of Pereira and his secretary. The same might be true of Rosario. This was not a tightly-knit organization. It was a loose association between political sympathizers and those who were only interested in easy money.

Pieter and the SAB were politicals; the murdered Pryke and the enriched Pereira and his secretary were, in their separate ways, mercenaries.

He lit another cigarette from the stub of the last and went over his chain of thought. It seemed to hold. What about the link with the War Office? That couldn't be connected with the British. They would have contacted Major Carlisle. So, clearly, he had been pressganged to be a Nazi agent, and – since they had gone to this much trouble – for a very important job. He got up and pissed in Sam Lee's chamber-pot. Very cloudy, but he was beginning to feel better. For the moment he was VIP, but when it was over he would be VD: Very Dispensable.

Rosario appeared to him as the only weak link so far visible in the future chain. He was surely a mercenary, not a political; and a queer mercenary at that. He rang the bell and unbolted the door. Sam Lee knocked only once this time. 'You ling, sir?'

'I'd like a plain omelette and a lager,' Lucas said. 'Here. In the cabin.' He held his stomach. 'No feel well.'

He did not leave his cabin until early the next morning. During the night his thoughts had clarified. It was no good telling himself he ought to become a chess player. He had tried playing chess, with Pieter, but though he knew the moves he had not that sort of brain. Anyway, he was not playing against pawns, knights, rooks, bishops, king and queen; he was pitted against a war machine – which tried to operate human beings like chessmen. But as he knew from the services, no war machine was infallible, and human beings moved more flexibly than chess pieces. Thank God for bureaucratic bungling and human weakness!

The promenade deck was being sluiced down, so Lucas went for'ard. On the orlop deck there was a crate of scrawny chickens, pecking at their mash and one another. To the starboard lay the green mass of Natal, emerald along the sunlit littoral but yew-dark inland where it was shadowed by storm clouds. He stood in the prow, watching the blue waves rising and falling helplessly away in white bubbling defeat. Even the wind was hot and humid. There was no refreshment as he drew it into his lungs.

He turned, aware of someone beside him. It was a short man, wearing a starched white drill-suit and a peaked navy-blue cap. He had a round white face, with a faintly pink wart at the base of his left nostril. He was standing almost at attention looking rheumily at Africa.

'Good morning,' Lucas said.

'On the mountains, it rains,' the man said. 'But here the sun shines.'

'So,' agreed Lucas, 'it would appear. My name is Molyneux.'

'I know. Mine is Grebenchick. Wolfgang Grebenchick, doctor of philosophy, Bonn and Heidelberg.'

'German?'

'I am in Wien born. Since the *Anschluss*, Austria, Germany is the same.'

'Why aren't you fighting?' Lucas asked. 'Or,' he looked round the *São Paulo*, as it might be a secret battlefield, 'are you?'

Dr Grebenchick looked puzzled, then gave a thin smile. 'I understand. You choke. I am four times wounded. In Minsk. In Smolensk. In Kharkov two times. I am on the sea for healthiness. And you, Mr Molyneux; why you are here, I wonder?'

'Me? Also the healthiness. I hope.'

Dr Grebenchick pointed to the shore ahead. The green coast-line was broken by a white splodge. 'Look,' he said. 'Durban! For healthiness, we must go below soon. When the British make examinations, they are more interested in us as in the cargo.'

'Why?' asked Lucas, as puzzled by Dr Grebenchick's logic as by his grammar.

'Portugal is Britain's oldest ally. The *São Paulo* docks at Lisbon. When copper or chromium or diamonds go to Deutschland, it is so little. It is better as to make of Portugal an enemy.' Of course, remembered Lucas, *wenn* in German means if, and *als* means than.

But *wenn* proved not if, but when. As the *São Paulo* approached Durban, a camouflaged launch put out and headed for her.

Lucas watched it through the port-hole of his cabin, feeling the slackening of the engines' speed. In the bow of the launch, a figure in white ducks lifted a loudhailer. 'Cap'n Kneller. Just comin' aboard for inspection.'

'Please to come aboard Cap'n Jones.'

A rope ladder fell as the launch eased alongside. Lucas lay so that he could not be seen. (He had bolted his cabin door just in case.) But everything sounded as jovial as could be; and after about a quarter of an hour, he heard Captain Jones say 'Be seein' you,' and as he climbed down the ladder, Captain Kneller shouted, 'Love to the missis and the kids.'

The launch swung away the moment the captain stepped aboard; and the *São Paulo* went full speed ahead.

Lucas lunched in the saloon with Dom Rosario and Dr Grebenchick. 'Captain Kneller seems a good friend of Captain Jones,' Lucas observed.

Rosario laughed. 'War is not total. Not in the Indian Ocean. Jones, he likes Havana cigars, Demerara rum; Mrs Jones – the nylon stockings from America, the good perfume from Paris.'

'A *suborno*?' He did not associate British or South African naval officers with bribery.

Rosario shook his head. 'A gift of friendship. You been tunnelling too long to understand this war, Mr Molynoo. Very simple. British Ministry of Economic Warfare say, "Deny the Axis all strategic material. Insist all ships sail in British convoy." British Foreign Office say, "Don't be bloody fool. Portugal is oldest ally. If Rosario want to sail alone, well and good. If some copper, chrome, industrial diamonds reach the Third Reich, what's it matter, if not too much. If too much, British navy torpedoes Rosario's ship and says it is the Germans." But Rosario is not bloody fool. It is not so, Grebenchick?'

'So earlier I have our friend informed.'

'And did he tell you, Mr Molynoo, that he is four times wounded?'

'In Smolensk! In Minsk! And twice in Kharkov!'

'Is that so?' There was a twinkle in Rosario's eye. He turned to Grebenchick. 'And you told me, Herr Doktor, it was in the thigh, the shoulder and twice in the bum.'

'Please, gentlemen, between these two statements, in logic,

is no contradiction made.' A bead of sweat appeared upon his wart. Dom Rosario had a fit of coughing, which may have been caused by inhaling the smoke of his Havana or by his efforts to suppress laughter.

As he took his afternoon siesta, Lucas reflected that though both Rosario and Grebenchick were his enemies, they were not friends of one another. As the owner of the *São Paulo*, Dom Rosario's presence aboard was explicable. (But unless his interests were very limited, *why* did he neglect all the others, when in Kneller he seemed to have a competent captain?) He obviously found Grebenchick a tiresome bore. So why had he taken him as a passenger?

The voyage round the Cape of Good Hope and up the Atlantic coast was leisurely. At Lobito in Angola they took on a cargo of maize. Lucas went ashore with Dom Rosario and they got drunk on lager. By that time Lucas had established a warm relationship with the Brasilian, strengthened by a mutual dislike of Grebenchick. It had begun the evening of the first day after they had passed Durban. Rosario and Grebenchick were playing backgammon in the saloon. It was a game which Lucas and Pieter had played night after night in Kimberley, when they were both on day shift. Lucas found it suited his temperament, the rapid calculation of chances which altered with each throw of the dice. He sat down and watched the two players. Grebenchick was the more conservative. He played always for safety, using the forward game. Rosario was just the opposite. It was clear he was richer than the German, could afford to lose more in the chance of gaining more. They played with the stakes automatically doubled each time a double was thrown. Grebenchick never doubled up except when he was certain of winning, but Rosario aggressively doubled to make the German afraid of losing.

When Rosario suggested that Lucas should cut in, Lucas said that it had cost him his life's savings in order to purchase his free passage. 'I'll stake you to a goddamn *conto*,' Rosario said. 'If you lose it, we forget. If you win, you pay me back.' Lucas did not know what a *conto* was until Rosario counted out a thousand escudos in notes.

That first evening, with beginner's luck, Lucas repaid Rosario's stake and pocketed more than two *contos*. Rosario did not mind. In fact he was glad to have established an opponent against whom he could play for the rest of the voyage. But Grebenchick was outraged. On the voyage out, he had won money from Rosario. That he should start to lose to an Armenian wounded him doubly, in his purse and in his conviction of the *Herrenvolk*'s superiority. Each evening the three of them had played backgammon after dinner and each evening Dr Grebenchick's winnings from Dom Rosario had grown smaller and smaller, until finally he refused to play. He retired to his cabin, saying that he wanted to read; and Rosario had then suggested that Lucas and he should adjourn to *his* cabin, where they played a game or two and then they talked, over glasses of Demerara rum and ice.

Lucas pretended to having a weak head and acted much drunker than he ever was. He never woke up in the morning with alcoholic amnesia, as he had with Pieter. He never made the mistake of probing too deeply into Dom Rosario. He developed his character, like a photographic print – using rum instead of hypo. Their careers had been very similar despite their difference in age – Rosario was almost old enough to be Lucas's father. He had been a fishing skipper in Brasil, but when the Spanish Civil War had started, his Republican zeal had led him to buy an old tub to ship arms to the *Frente Popular*. It was dangerous, but it was profitable, and he felt that he was serving the cause of democracy, until it dawned upon him that the Spanish Civil War had nothing to do with democracy. The Popular Front was a gang of liberals, communists, anarcho-syndicalists and Basque nationalists, fighting one another for power, while they were fighting against Franco, Moorish mercenaries, falangists and royalists. And the whole of this civil war was a field day in which the Nazis and the fascists tried out their weapons and tactics against the Soviet Union.

Lucas and Rosario had both become disillusioned. But whereas Lucas had allowed himself to be taken prisoner by Franco, Rosario had extended his arms-running to both sides. By the end of the Spanish Civil War, he had half a dozen ships in his fleet, running arms to Franco and bringing communist refugees to Latin America. Like many self-made men, Rosario was dazzled by the brilliance of his rise to wealth. Only one thing mattered: money. Ideologies were window-dressing for the business of power. Rosario did not care with whom he traded, provided he could extend his private empire; and, in admitting this, he was not more cynical than patriots and politicians, only more honest. 'Then why are you wasting your time on the *São Paulo*, instead of looking after your interests in Brasil?' asked Lucas.

Dom Rosario did not answer at the time. But when they were alone together in the Hotel Magnifico, Lobito, he unbent. The Nazis had lost the war, he explained. It would drag on for months, perhaps years, because of the ridiculous Allied demand of unconditional surrender, which gave the Germans no hope of peace by overthrowing Hitler. But most of them were not so mad as not to think of the future. They were making plans for escape – to the Middle East or Latin America – and were already exporting their loot from Europe: jewels, pictures, sculpture, altar pieces, *objets d'art*. When the *São Paulo* sailed from Lisbon to Rio, she would carry in her holds a precious cargo. 'I am telling you this, Lucas,' said Rosario, using his christian name for the first time, 'because I will hold this in trust until the war is over. After that, if they arrive to claim it, it is theirs, after of course the payment of my handling charges. Otherwise ... suppose they are tried as war criminals and executed ... then who will know, supposing it is well hidden? I have a site, but I need a tunnelling engineer. Someone I can trust. Like you.'

'Why should you trust me?'

'You are a reasonable man. Alone, in Brasil, without a friend except Dom Rosario, without a labour permit ... do I need to say more?'

Lucas smiled. 'I'm interested. But I'd like to read the small print.' No need to say that he had already accepted an offer which would remove him from the cockpit of Europe. It seemed too good to be true.

And so it proved.

7 John Embleton

The secretary depressed the intercom. 'Major Embleton's here, sir.' She had a freckly complexion like the underside of a fern leaf, and a plaintive smile. 'Do you mind me saying how much I liked your *Pillars of Hercules*?' she said.

It was John Embleton's worst and most popular book. 'No author minds anyone saying that.'

She gave him a little reassuring nod, before resuming her work, leaving Embleton to look at the brass-headed nails in the padded leather door of the Chief's office. He wished he could smoke, but the Chief disapproved of alcohol and tobacco except in the course of business. As a novelist, Embleton would have liked a chief more in the round. He was an officer, but wore no uniform; always a black suit with white pinstripe, Anthony Eden hat, black silk socks with dark clocks; aggressive hair seemed to be trying to invade his face; on his scalp it was cut *en brosse*, but it luxuriated from his eyebrows, ears and nostrils. On his upper lip it sprang forward as if only restrained by scissors from invading his mouth.

The buzzer sounded. The secretary nodded. Major Embleton stood up, straightened his Sam Browne, pinned his black leather swagger stick under the left armpit, clutched his leather gloves firmly and marched into the presence of the Chief, before whose desk he came to attention and threw up a smart salute, which the Chief ignored because he was bent over a file.

When he looked up, he said, 'We're not on the parade ground, Major. Do sit down.'

The only chair was so deep and comfortable that Major Embleton would have sunk some two feet below his superior officer. Embleton chose its broad leather arm.

The Chief touched the file. 'This fellow, Otto Neumann—Rather a bungle, eh?'

'If the police find a man trying to dynamite Rotherhithe Tunnel, sir, well, it's natural they should think of stopping him first. The cyanide capsule ... I mean, I gather he died in the van before they got him to the station.'

'But your instructions, Major, were to turn him in.'

'That was Monday. This happened three days later, on the Thursday.'

'Precisely. You had three days in which to scare him. In that case, he would have postponed the Rotherhithe Tunnel.'

'But I only met him the night before.'

'I have read the report. In a public house. You had "a friendly conversation" and arranged to meet there next evening. Instead of which, Herr Neumann was arrested trying to blow a hole in Rotherhithe Tunnel which would have immobilized one of the main supply routes to the invasion ports. Why didn't you insist on accompanying Neumann home from the public house? Create an incident which would have got you both arrested?'

'I'm sorry, sir, I did not realize the urgency.'

'Well, the sooner you realize that military intelligence can't lollop along like the donkeys in your peacetime thrillers, Major Embleton, the better I'll be pleased. The trouble with you – the trouble with the whole of this section – is that you've been waiting so long for the Second Front to open up by the invasion of France that you think it'll never happen. Well, it's bloody well going to. Don't ask me when, but it's any month, any week, any day, any hour now. It may be happening at this very moment. Hundreds of thousands of men putting out in invasion barges all along the coast for an operation which, if successful, will deliver European civilization from a barbarism more ruthless than Attila's or Genghis Khan's. But if it fails, Embleton, if it fails, I can assure you that the fate we feared in 1940 will overtake us. From what we think is a position of overwhelming strength, we shall be reduced to such weakness that we may be compelled to evacuate these islands and continue the struggle from overseas.'

'Isn't that pitching it rather strong, sir?'

'It is not, young man,' the Chief said. 'Those secret weapons of which Herr Hitler boasts aren't just propaganda. During this war we have seen the most amazing development of technical weaponry. But we are on the eve of a lethal revolution which will make the weapons of destruction of which we're now so proud as old-fashioned as the catapult and knobkerrie. Nineteen forty-four is the year of decision. The fate of civilization, as we know it, is being settled *now*.'

'I'm sorry, sir. Do you want to post me back to the Rifle Brigade?'

'Don't be an ass, Embleton. Take this file. Read Neumann's case history and deliver me the most imaginative report you can on what use the Nazis might have made of Neumann if he hadn't committed suicide.' The Chief handed over the file. 'I want it in forty-eight hours.'

Embleton stood up to take it. 'But you realize this is a nonsense, sir. If Neumann had blown up Rotherhithe Tunnel, they would probably not have used him again.'

'Of course,' the Chief said. 'But it's not a nonsense. It's an imaginative exercise. It'll certainly teach you something. It might even give me some ideas, for which, as your superior officer, I shall take credit in reward for covering up your bloomer about Neumann. At any rate, I'll know what sort of assignment I should give you next.' As Embleton took the file, the Chief added, 'If any.'

Beneath the bristling moustache, Embleton thought he detected the vestige of a smile. But it might have been imagination.

As he went out, he said to the secretary, 'Have you read my *Bastard in Beirut*?'

'It sounds intriguing,' she said.

'I'll drop it in the day after tomorrow. It has a sort of subtlety – which some people missed.'

Like Intelligence in wartime, Embleton thought. There was Military Intelligence, Naval Intelligence, RAF Intelligence; all burrowing away so secretly that there was no cooperation between them. Not at departmental level, anyway. Perhaps the Chiefs of Staff exchanged their information. But unlikely. They were all fighting their own little wars, with Combined Operations as a sort of fourth arm of the Services.

In Military Intelligence, MI 5 concentrated on espionage and MI 6 on counter-espionage. But where one ended and the other began was never clear to those operating in the field, though Embleton presumed that in the higher echelons of the War

Office in Whitehall and SHAEF headquarters in Bushey Park, the reports were collated and summarized to give a comprehensible picture, even if it bore little resemblance to the truth. Secrecy was self-defeating at the level of field-agents.

Writing his speculative report for the Chief, whose motto was 'Try to visualize what's happening on the other side of the hill', Embleton sketched a picture of Nazi Intelligence, translating the confusions of the Allies into German terms; the *Abwehr* under Admiral Canaris working to Field Marshal Keitel, the Chief of Staff, in association with the Gestapo; Himmler's Security Service (or *Sicherheitsdienst*), which had just secured the deposition of Canaris; the separate intelligence services of the Army, Navy and Luftwaffe. All of these, Embleton stressed, were working against one another rather than in concert. Until and unless Neumann's superiors could be identified, it was impossible to say more than that the Nazis seemed to suspect that the invasion would be launched across the Pas de Calais and further efforts would be made to disrupt communications in the lower Thames area. The London bridges, road and railway, were obviously the main targets on the supply routes. But in view of Neumann being a tunnelling engineer, he might have been later employed against strategic railway tunnels, such as Sevenoaks and/or Redhill.

It was a feeble report. Embleton felt the Chief had given him the task as a sort of punishment, like writing out 'lines' at school. He was prepared to be hauled over the coals for it. But he was not prepared for the report to be totally ignored at their next meeting. 'Ah, Embleton,' the Chief said, 'I've found a little job for you. You will be seconded to DODS, the Department of Overseas Despatch and Shipment.'

Embleton looked blank. 'I'm afraid I've never—'

'Very few people have, young man. No need to be ashamed. DODS exists under the umbrella of the Ministry of Supply. It was started after the fall of France, when there was the danger of the museums being destroyed by aerial bombardment and a high probability this country would be invaded. *Objets d'art*, priceless because unique, were stored in a reinforced underground martialling yard beneath St Pancras station. It had the advantage of being able to withstand a direct hit from any bomb then known; and of being connected via the GPO underground railway with the East End docks, if an emergency arose. DODS was formed with the primary task of maintaining the warehouse and implementing the shipment operation, should that become necessary. Meanwhile, it has played a role in the liaison between the Ministries of Supply and Transport. The Director General is Brigadier Sir Hilary Fry, a regular officer who fought with distinction in the First World War and was a director of the London and North Eastern railway after his retirement from the army. A first-class man in his day; and even now, splendid for his age. You understand?'

Embleton nodded. It sounded as if Sir Hilary was a bit ga-ga.

'We belong to the same club,' the Chief said, 'and when Sir Hilary complained that he needed a sound man for a few weeks, as, shall we call it, *adjutant*, I suggested seconding you.'

'I can't claim to be an authority on *objets d'art*, warehouse or transport . . .'

'But you'll pass muster on admin. Which is what the Brigadier wants. And you can do a security check, which is what I want, without provoking any suspicion. Not that I'm really worried, but Bodgers, I mean Sir Hilary, has scarcely had the pick of the personnel bunch. There's a railway boffin, with some bird name – Sparrow, Starling or Dunnock, I forget exactly what. He's sound enough, security-wise, I'd think. And he's got a first-rate personal assistant, Lady Virginia, poor old St Neots's daughter. You'll like her. Or maybe you won't. A better judge of hounds and horseflesh, than books. But there's been quite a turnover since 1940. And the security vetting, I'll bet, knowing dear old Bodg . . . Sir Hilary, may have been relaxed.'

For the first time, Embleton had glimpsed his commanding officer, who insisted on being known merely as 'the Chief', in the role of a human being, with friends and preferences. It was fascinating. He waited for more.

But the Chief had reverted to role: 'For admin, you work to the Brigadier. On security, you report to me. You will be interviewed by Sir Hilary tomorrow morning at Pelican House, on the Embankment just before you come to Horseferry Road, at ten a.m. This is a pure formality. But for the purposes of the interview, you will say that you have been on the Y-List, having been given leave to finish a book which is to be published in the United States to bring in much needed American dollars, and you are now seeking a posting on my recommendation. Any questions?'

Embleton stood up. 'Only one, sir. If I want to check any MI 5 record, should I do it direct from DODS or through you?'

'Through me, of course,' the Chief said. 'The security officer at DODS is Lieutenant Hampshire. He is one of the people on whom you will have to report.'

8 El Palacio do Sonho

Lisbon

Over coffee on the evening before they made the River Tagus, Dr Grebenchick turned to Lucas. 'During this sea journey I have you with much care observed. You have done well, Mr Molyneux. I have many questions asked and you have told me little. Silence, as they say, is golden. Tomorrow you will see a man who will offer you much gold. Take it, Mr Molyneux, as you have mine at backgammon taken.'

'That sounds like a job,' Lucas said, 'but thanks to Dom Rosario here, I already have one waiting for me in Brasil.' He looked to Dom Rosario for confirmation, but without success. The shipowner appeared embarrassed.

'I spoke already to Dom Rosario.'

'Sure thing,' Rosario said. 'When you've finished this assignment – don't ask me what it is, but the doctor says it won't take long – then you join me in Rio.'

'And if I say I'd prefer to sail with you? After all, passages to Brasil are not so easy with the war on.'

'Unless you accept Dr Grebenchick's offer, I am sorry but mine is withdrawn.' He stood up and left the saloon, followed by Grebenchick. Whatever differences the German and Brasilian had appeared to have seemed now resolved. Lucas was left with an ultimatum.

He went out and looked at the lights on the shore. They had

dropped anchor off Cascia. It was a good thousand yards away, swimming distance, provided the tide was not too strong. He had three thousand six hundred escudos, enough to live on for quite a time, supposing he reached the shore without detection. But supposing he was observed ... ? He remembered how quickly Dr Pereira had squeezed him of his Kimberley savings. It would be madness to try to jump ship. Portugal was crawling with foreign agents. The people who had gone to all this trouble to get him from South Africa would never let him get away as easily as that. He would have to string them along and get as much of the gold that Grebenchick promised as he could lay his hands on.

Lucas had expected that Dr Grebenchick would introduce him to his prospective employer. But it was Dom Rosario who took him in tow, with Sam Lee padding behind with Lucas's suitcases. Immigration and customs took no time. With a *Bom Dia* here and a *Como está* there, Rosario entered Lisbon as cheerily as if it was his own office. A black Mercedes Benz was parked outside. Rosario got in, produced the ignition key from a bunch on a gold chain, started the engine and waited for Lucas to join him, after he had tipped Sam Lee. Lucas was impressed. The car was better testimony to Rosario's affluence than the MS *São Paulo*.

They drove through the Cidade Baixa in silence, but as they accelerated up the Bairro Alto towards the Alcantara, Lucas said, 'In Lobito, when you offered me that job ... were you afraid I was going to jump ship?'

'Not you. Not in a dump like Lobito. No, I meant it. The job is still open, when you've finished this one.'

'When English or *wenn* German?'

'Both.'

'And who's my boss?'

'A guy named Skorzeny. If he takes you, that is. He doesn't trust mercenaries. Prefers patriots, 200 per cent Aryan. But maybe you're the only one he can find for the job.'

'Skorzeny sounds sort of familiar. But I can't think why.'

'The guy that rescued Mussolini. The only German that the English respect; barring Rommel and Lili Marlene. And he's Austrian, like Hitler. I'm doing a little job for him: a couple of Leonardo drawings *Il Duce* gave him as a token of gratitude. Thinks they'd be safer out of Europe, which is true maybe, since they weren't Benito's in the first place.'

Lucas tried to note the streets they had come through from the port. But he could not memorize them. The only thing he noticed was a bank on a corner, the Ibero-Suíço. If he got his hands on any dough, he would leave it in Lisbon; and where better than a Swiss bank? Neutral banks wouldn't be covered by any bloody exchange controls.

Almost immediately afterwards, Rosario swung the Mercedes into a drive and stopped before double wrought-iron gates, painted black and gold. He hooted long, short, short, long. Through a lodge window, Lucas could see a man peering. Then the gates swung back of their own accord. As he drove past Rosario raised his hand lazily. The man in the lodge gave the Nazi salute, standing at attention. He was not in uniform but there was a pistol in the holster on his belt. 'No worse than going back to the mine,' Lucas consoled himself, as the gates clanged back into place.

The driveway passed between leafy walls of oleanders and towering palm trees before there emerged upon an eminence a fantastic edifice of domes and turrets built in the Byzantine-Gothic style favoured by South American millionaires at the turn of the century. The decadent combination of architectural incongruity gave it a monstrous fascination, like the Whore of Babylon in old age. 'What do they call this?' Lucas asked.

'*El Palacio do Sonho*. It used to be called the Dream Palace,' Dom Rosario said, 'but Dr Goebbels renamed it the Institute for Germano-Portuguese Culture and Brotherhood. That was 1936. Of course, since the war it has changed a bit. Not so much a club any more.'

'Hence the armed guard and the barbed wire on the walls ...'

'But I always stay here when I am in Lisbon,' Dom Rosario said. 'They make me very welcome. Perhaps because I leave a sack of coffee beans.' He did not drive up to the front entrance, but into the stableyard where the buildings had been converted to garages. 'Before we go in, let me explain. I have reserved you a room on the same floor as mine. I would advise you to remain in your room until Skorzeny sends for you. You may find him rather overpowering. He is six feet seven and has a rather disfiguring scar down the left side of his face. Two things he is touchy about: the pronunciation is Skor-tsay-ny. A lot of people call him Skort-zeeny. The other thing is his rank. He used to be a *Hauptsturmführer*, or captain in the Waffen SS. After Mussolini's rescue, the *Führer* personally promoted him to *Sturmbannführer*, the equivalent of major in the army. He becomes very angry at being called "Captain". "Major" would do, but if you can get your tongue round *Sturmbannführer*, he would be very pleased. And also his decorations: there's the *Ritterkreuz*, or Knight's Cross of the Iron Cross, which was given him by Hitler, and the Gold Flying Cross, awarded by Goering. A little admiration, my dear Lucas, might come in useful. They say no man is a hero to his valet. But *Sturmbannführer* Otto Skorzeny is certainly a hero to himself.'

Some sort of manservant was waiting for them to get out. They entered the Dream Palace by a side entrance and went to the reception desk, followed by the servant with the suitcases. The clerk gave Rosario two keys, 305 for himself and 303 for Lucas, and also a letter, which Rosario opened at once. 'Good,' he said to Lucas. 'You are to go to the bar at six p.m. Someone will meet you and show you where to go.'

They ascended to the third floor in a rosewood panelled hydraulic lift which travelled at the speed of an imperial hearse. It was operated by a pageboy with large brown eyes and long lashes. He had a tight-fitting scarlet cut-away jacket and navy-blue trousers with gold braid running down the seams. '*Bom moço*,' admired Rosario, stroking the boy's buttocks. Bom bum, thought Lucas, as the boy looked mischievously up at the Brasilian. 'I show you 303 and 305,' the boy said, watching Rosario play with a five-escudo piece.

Lucas humped his own suitcases into room 303, leaving the pageboy to show Dom Rosario room 305. Room 303 had six gothic windows, looking out over the grounds, the precipitate city and the brown River Tagus to the hills beyond. The furniture was genuine Louis Quinze, looted from the Passy mansion of a marquis who had been injudicious enough to cross the Channel with General de Gaulle. Lucas tried the eighteenth-century four-poster and found that it had been fitted with a twentieth-century mattress. 'The best is good enough for me,' he muttered, 'but what a waste for only one.' It was weeks since he had blundered across the yard to Eulalia's *kaya*. For a moment he wondered what had happened to the poor kid; but then desire flooded into his loins. He went to the window, two of which opened as doors on to a balcony. Down there in the city, there must be tarts. But how on earth would he get out of this luxury prison?

He turned as something caught his attention from the corner of his eye. Three balconies away a young woman was standing, looking over the city. She was wearing a black and white swimming suit of a scantiness which was outrageous. On her head a turban bathing cap of the same material, from beneath which escaped a lock of flaxen hair. To the ithyphallic Lucas, she was desire incarnate, the bronzed limbs, tilted breast, taut belly. Her sunglasses heightened her physical attractiveness – a girl with a beautiful body, uncomplicated by personality.

For a time, it was enough just to look and admire from a distance. But then he thought, I've been told not to leave my room, but nothing about not having visitors. The prompting of his East End boyhood was to try a wolf-whistle. It was surprising the effect it had on even classy dames, the blush and the giggle or involuntary smile. But on the third floor of the *Palacio do Sonho*, something a bit more subtle was called for. He leant on the balustrade and began to whistle 'Lili Marlene', gazing abstractedly towards the far hills. At the end of the first verse, he turned and saw she was looking towards him. He raised his hand in a lazy wave.

The girl turned and went into her room. Lucas sighed. 'Love-fifteen.' Still, she was staying on the same floor, only three rooms away; a guest – someone's mistress? Skorzeny's? A prisoner, like himself? A blonde mother of the master race? He would make it his business to find out.

He went in, unpacked, ran himself a bath from the gilt dolphin taps into the deep Cambridge-blue porcelain tub. After the salt water of the *São Paulo*, he wanted to lather himself all over and wash off the brine. He tried to adjust the temperature; but he found that the hot water tap ran tepid, as did the cold. This combination of inefficiency with luxury was somehow reassuring. Perhaps the lady on the balcony would not prove as unapproachable as she seemed. He would love to see in her the tight bud blossom like an evening primrose. For him, it was the only fulfilment with any woman, the transfiguration of her public image in moaning glory.

God, his thoughts were turning to that girl again. If he was to train himself for whatever Skorzeny was planning, he needed to be fit. He put on his underpants, to curb his encumbrance, and went through the old PT exercises. Knees bend, hands on hips; arms swinging sideways and upwards; hands behind the head, elbows on the ground, raise both legs upwards and then slowly, slowly down. He could hear PT Sergeant Bulstrode at Aldershot, years ago, as he did so. 'Call that "Slowly"? Jees-us. What a shower!'

When he was doing press-ups, he rested and his eyes caught something, twined round the wire of the wooden gilded standard lamp. It was a thin plastic wire, which went up inside the standard; and just below the baton holder there was a tiny microphone. The room was bugged.

If there was one in the standard lamp, there might be others. There were. There were two in bowls of flowers (how obvious could you get?), one behind the head of the four-poster and another in the bathroom, between the cistern of the loo and the wall. It was too risky to test whether the mikes were live. But forewarned, forearmed. If Skorzeny wanted to eavesdrop, Lucas could decide what to drop on his eaves. He went back to the old PT exercises. He hadn't realized how many muscles he had unexercised; how many lessons in unarmed combat he had forgotten.

At six p.m., having taken a second tepid bath and put on his aged, but still comparatively new, Jermyn Street shoes and shirt, his Savile Row suit and his Burlington Arcade tie, he went down to the bar to meet Skorzeny's emissary. There was the same liftboy on duty. His pupils were like black olives and his eyes looked first meltingly up at Lucas's and then down at his crutch, which was for the moment detumescent. When

Hitler assassinated Roehm, he didn't end the trouble in the Reich, thought Lucas.

The bar was down a corridor past the reception desk. The floor was black and white marble, the walls of Ferrara marble red and white grained like sliced tongue. At the pillars there were festoons of flags, with the red, yellow and black of Germany in the centre, swastika flags either side and then, fanned out like a hand of cards, those of Poland, Denmark, Norway, Holland, Belgium, France, Yugoslavia, Greece and some others which Lucas imagined represented the full Balkan flush. It was quite a boast when Dom Rosario had said Hitler was certain to be beaten. The boast was repeated every ten yards until Lucas came to the bar, which was decorated in the Moorish style, with fretted woodwork and hanging brass lanterns, with red glass windows, calculated to give the minimum light with the maximum of power. The tables were of beaten brass, standing on elaborately carved legs. It was an appropriate tribute to the prophet who prescribed abstinence. No one was sitting there. But behind the bar, playing dice with himself, was an Arab in a tarboosh. He seemed engrossed.

'Faz favor,' said Lucas.

'In the patio,' said the barman. 'You will see.'

Lucas went into the courtyard. In the centre was a fountain with a green bronze boy holding up a torch which ejected irregular spurts of water. A gardener was spraying some wilting cannas. But no one else seemed there until he turned and saw at a white slatted wood table the girl from the balcony. She still had on sunglasses and the black and white turban, which was fixed through a ring above the centre of her brow. But now she was wearing a natural silk, black and white dress, with a cowl neck, cut on the slant so that the design tapered from shoulders to waist and then flared downwards, over bare brown legs. On her feet were black and white plaited leather sandals. Her lips, finger and toe nails were painted carmine. Her eyelids were darkened with kohl and there was a thin gold chain round her left ankle (which, Lucas noticed, was more shapely than her right, the joint of which was a bit red). She acknowledged his approach.

'Is it you, I—?'

She nodded. She was smoking a cigarette in one of those long cigarette holders which Myrna Loy used as a vamp, before she became William Powell's nice wife in the 'Thin Man' films, and she was drinking *pastis* with ice.

'What a pity you didn't pop down the corridor, when I saw you on the balcony,' Lucas said, sitting down. 'I could have done you and me a lot of good.' Being sort of trash, he nosed it out in others. 'What's that, anis?'

'It's genuine Pernod.'

Lucas clapped his hands and the *moço* stopped playing poker dice and came out into the patio. 'Two more,' Lucas said, 'Doubles.'

'But I have not finished.'

Lucas took her glass and choosing where the mark of her lipstick lay drained it. 'Why didn't you wave to me?'

She tapped the ash from her cigarette. 'You want to know the truth, Mr Molyneux?'

He nodded.

'I had not received my orders – then.' She took off her sunglasses. Her eyes were sky-blue, very beautiful, but no more animate than turquoise. She looked at him with a sort of cool arrogance, as if reckoning him up and finding the total inadequate.

'You only act under orders?'

'In this case.' She ejected her cigarette from the holder and stubbed it out. Then she leaned back in her chair, smiling as if she found Lucas faintly ridiculous, like a cat with a baby mouse.

'Seeing your beautiful face, I can't help wondering ...'

'What, Mr Molyneux?'

'The first name's Lucas. May I ask yours?'

'Carlson. Grete Carlson.'

'Swedish?'

She nodded. 'Wondering ...?'

'What you look like ... you are so calm now ... I'd love to see you in the moment of orgasm.'

She flushed beneath her tan. For a moment he thought she

was going to get up and leave him. But she didn't; perhaps because of her orders, or because the *moço* brought the Pernods, with a dish of stuffed olives. She bent forward to take the chit and sign it, but Lucas put down ten escudos and waved the waiter away.

Lucas raised his glass. '*Skol!*'

She stopped biting her lip. 'No man has seen that.'

'Woman?'

'No one.' Her blue eyes were fixed on his.

'You never?'

'Never.'

He passed her the dish of olives and she took one. 'Not much fun. I sympathize. From personal experience.' He raised his glass and she raised hers and they clinked. It had been a shot in the dark, but it seemed to have landed on target. 'Do you bet?'

'Bet? What is that?'

'Gamble.'

She shook her head. 'Only on certainties.'

He produced a thousand escudo note. 'I've a *conto* that says I can make you come.'

She put another cigarette in her holder. He lit it. She inhaled deeply and then blew three smoke rings. 'I take you.' She smiled again, but without ridicule. 'You are throwing your money away.'

'If I lose, it will be worth it. Let's leave this stuff and try now.'

She put out a restraining hand, looking at the protrusion of his flies. 'In ten minutes you must see Skorzeny,' she said. 'Come to room 306. At ten o'clock.'

Later she said, 'You must not think I am a whore. I am not, Mr Molyneux.'

If she wasn't, thought Lucas, she was 'under orders'. But a bunk-up, for whatever the reason, was still a bunk-up.

9 Scarface

El Palacio do Sonho had been the dream of a Brasilian rubber millionaire. But when it became first the Germano-Portuguese Institute for Culture and Brotherhood and later headquarters for branches of the *Sicherheitsdienst* and the Waffen SS, the dreams and fantasies of others were superimposed. Skorzeny's office, for example, had been made over to suit the taste of Reichsmarschall Hermann Goering. It was at the end of a long corridor, paved and walled with Ferrara marble. The door, of teak, with gilded beading, was curtly painted.

PRIVAT
Kein Eingang

On the lintel was a bell push above a glass panel and the word KLINGEN. Lucas pushed it and a bulb illuminated HINEIN. He knocked and turned the heavy brass knob. The great door swung open effortlessly, to reveal not an office but a combination of hunting lodge and banqueting hall – in which, thought Lucas, the Valkyrie might drop in for a drink with Lorelei and the Rhinemaidens after a hard day's ride. The room was so vast, the walls so crowded with the heads of bears, brown and polar, the antlers of stags, roebuck, wildebeeste, chamois and springbok, the floor so cluttered with Wagnerian furniture and animal skins, that Lucas did not notice the figure seated behind an enormous desk until he rose to his feet – a giant, proportionate to his setting. 'Mr Molyneux, please to sit down.' He pointed to a small throne, made of oak and tooled pigskin, on the opposite side of his desk. 'It is my pleasure to see you, at last.'

'*Sturmbannführer* Skortsayny?' Lucas said carefully.

'In Alcantara, we have no rank.' He waited, towering above Lucas until the latter sat down, David in Goliath's den. Though Skorzeny's back was to the light, Lucas could see the long, broad scar running from the upper cheekbone to the cleft of his chin. It passed the left side of his mouth in what looked like a smile, but the right side was depressed. Though in Alcantara there might be no rank, he was wearing his uniform.

The *Ritterkreuz*, with its swastika set in the centre of the Iron Cross, hung beneath his Adam's apple, between the badges of the Waffen SS and his rank on his dark collar. Even despite the scar he was a handsome man; cupid's-bow mouth, brilliant intelligent eyes. Though his ears were large, they were buttoned back and proportionate to the long head. Lucas would have liked him, if he had not been in his power.

Skorzeny sat down and looked at the papers in front of him. 'We have your *curriculum vitae*, but there are one or two questions I'd like to ask.' Skorzeny spoke very good English. He had an Austrian accent, but it was pleasing; and his manner was reassuring, almost like a personnel manager interviewing an applicant for a job. 'You are Armenian by birth?'

'British, by birth. Armenian by race. My father and mother were refugees from the Turkish massacres. My father was killed in the British army at Mons.'

'And so your mother, Esther Ramoulian, was left a widow to bring you up. No other children.'

'I had a baby sister. She died of the Spanish 'flu in 1919.'

'It must have been hard for your mother.'

'It was. All she could get was office cleaning.'

'And for you. Losing your father fighting for a country which was not his. Or did you feel it was your country because you were born there?'

'You mean, why did I join the army? I wanted to be a mining engineer. When I was fully qualified, I bought myself out.'

Skorzeny made a note on the file. 'But soon after you volunteered for the International Brigade; was that why you bought yourself out?'

'I couldn't get a job in civvy street. And then the Spanish Civil War. I really believed all that crap. Until I got there. Saw what was happening. If I hadn't been captured, let myself be captured by Franco, they'd have shot me – my own side would.'

'So? And when you go back to England, what?'

'I'd changed my name before joining the IB. Took out a passport as Lucas Molyneux. Back in England I was still Leucas Ramoulian; but no bloody work, except odd jobs, like barman. Till Munich, when the call-up papers came. Because

I was on the reserve, see. So I spoke to Mum; she had fifty quid saved, which got me to Durban, steerage, and up to Kimberley; as Lucas Molyneux.'

'Your reasons for this. Tell me.'

'I don't believe in war,' Lucas said. 'Any war. I've had it. Even if one side starts morally better, it makes no difference. The strongest wins, that means the most brutal. Me, I use my brains and I survive. That's my war aim.'

Skorzeny sat back and lit a cigarette. He looked up at the ceiling, the plasterwork of which was a riot of cherubs, capitals and scrolls. 'In fact, you do not care about anything or any person, except yourself and perhaps your mother?'

'That's about the size of it.'

'How long since you heard from her?'

'Not for ages. She was frightened, because of the different names. Was afraid they'd trace me.'

'So you don't know the house in Cable Street was burned down?'

'When? Is she all right?'

'She is still alive. It was a fire raid. Last November. She was glad to have a chance of writing a letter.' He looked through the file. 'It is somewhere here, but we have such a dossier on you, it is quite a business to find exactly . . .' he gave up looking. 'But you'll see it before we're through.' The right end of his mouth was smiling, like an angler's who has hooked a fish and now has only to play and land it. 'Your war aim. To use your brains and survive. One can see how this succeeded up to the time that you ran away from Kimberley, but how do you see things now, Mr Molyneux?'

'The only thing I see is that you and your friends have taken a lot of time and trouble, not stopping short of murder, in order to get me sitting in this chair opposite you. So the best thing is for you to tell me how you see my future.'

'Murder is not a word used in warfare. The man you mention paid the penalty of disobedience. If he had done what he was told, he would be alive today and your photograph would not be posted in every South African police station. The reward, by the way, has been increased to £1000.'

Lucas wanted to ask what the hell they wanted him to do

which one of their own people couldn't. But he realized that this was what Skorzeny expected; so he said nothing.

The silence became awkward. Skorzeny said, 'I do not like using mercenaries.'

'I don't like being used as a mercenary.'

'But "needs must when the devil drives".'

'When the devil drives, I demand cash down, and plenty of it.'

' "Beggars can't be choosers".'

'If anyone's begging, it's you, Mr Skorzeeny. I didn't ask to be brought here, I don't want to work for you and if you take all the trouble to send me back to South Africa, I'm quite willing to give myself up, claim the £1,000 reward and tell the court exactly what happened.'

'Here in Alcantara, we can cover up our mistakes. The grounds are large, the cellars many.' The sparring was over.

'Grebenchick said it would be a short job. How long is short?'

'Three weeks,' Skorzeny wobbled his hand uncertainly, 'maybe a month. The pay is princely.'

'How much is princely?'

'Ten thousand US dollars down, and twenty-five when it is over.'

'Then I'm kingly,' Lucas snapped. Centuries of Levantine bargaining could not be obliterated by a British birth certificate. 'Twenty-five thousand US dollars down, fifty thousand on completion. And before I learn a word about what you want me to do, I want your guarantee that I'll get out of this alive, provided I use my brains.'

Sturmbannführer Skorzeny was not used to being talked to like that by subordinates. But Lucas was not yet a subordinate. Operation Honeycomb was his brainchild: and though he was the Führer's blue-eyed boy since the rescue of Mussolini, he had enemies in the OKH, the OKW, the RSHA, the SD and especially in rival sections of the Waffen SS, who would love to see him fail. 'Impossible,' he said, 'I am authorized only for fifty thousand.'

'Which is fifteen thousand more than you offered me. Pity you didn't say that in the first place. I might have taken it. As it is, you have to get authorization for more.'

'You are insane, my friend. I give you my word that if you execute the operation properly, there is no reason why you should not survive. For you, fifty thousand dollars is a fortune ...'

'For the Third Reich, seventy-five thousand is a fleabite, if whatever you want done can't be done by your own chaps.'

'I will have to get on to FHQ.'

'Perhaps you'd like me to speak to them, for you.'

Skorzeny's scar turned white. From the file in front of him, he produced a pale mauve envelope on which was written in his mother's hand, 'To my dear Boy.' The writing was much shakier than when he had last read anything from her. The envelope was sealed. 'Open it,' Scarface said.

'I will, later.'

'Now, Mr Molyneux. I will not tell you anything, except that you will go to London. You will have new documents, a new name, a new life. For your mother's sake, read. Consider.'

'Have you read it?' Lucas asked.

'Would *you* read my mother's letters to me?' Skorzeny sounded outraged.

'Certainly.'

'Then you can understand why I have,' Skorzeny said, smiling. 'But I resealed the envelope.'

Lucas opened the cheap envelope. *'Dear Baby,'* he read, *'Every day and night I think of you & pray you OK. Such a long time you went away. Will i ever see you is what I wunder.'* Poor Mum, she could write Armenian very well, but she had never learnt to spell English properly. *'Cable Street went. It was fire bombs but before that the rufe leeked Lucky thanks to naybors, Mr & Mrs Latter, remember them, got most of the things out OK. Now I'm Wellclose Sq. 21 B, just down the passedge. Nice folk underneath she's v deaf tho Luvly panlling Real Oak but Bugs come out horible. Hopping this gets you as the man says, dearest Boy, wen will this war be over, yrs afftly Mum. P.S. I got what you sent along with yr Baby curls you know wear E.R.'* And below that there were Xs for kisses and Os for hugs.

Lucas folded the letter and put it back in the envelope. He would have burst into tears if he had not known that was what

Skorzeny wanted. If he had been a member of the Waffen SS, he would have followed Skorzeny to the death, certain that Skorzeny would do his damndest to preserve his life, if Lucas obeyed orders. But he was a mercenary and so expendable, like a cartridge case. 'No good asking how you got this?'

Skorzeny shook his head. 'But genuine.'

'Yes. The notes had better be genuine too. I'll settle for fifty thousand. Twenty-five thousand down; and the other twenty-five thousand, cut in halves.'

'Cut in halves?' Skorzeny looked appalled. 'You do not understand my finance officer, Dr Langer.'

Lucas got up. 'Your finance officer will understand me,' Lucas said. 'Will that be all for the evening?'

Skorzeny looked down at his file. 'But the plan. The tactic is difficult, but the strategy has the genius of simplicity.'

'But not the blessing of Dr Langer,' Lucas said. 'If I learnt about your plans and he did not approve ... maybe some of your *cannas* would bloom better next year. After the war is over.'

Skorzeny rose. 'You must have a drink, before you go,' he said. 'We have reached an agreement ...'

'Subject to Dr Langer.'

'A schnapps! Leave Dr Langer to me.'

'I don't like schnapps, it's too fiery,' Lucas said. 'I was drinking Pernod with cracked ice with Miss Carlson. It wouldn't mix.'

'You liked her?'

'On your instructions we got off,' Lucas said. 'After that I hope we got on.'

Skorzeny's colloquial English could not master this, but he could not resist one of his favourite anecdotes. 'This may amuse you, Molyneux,' he said. 'When I flew the *Duce* to Vienna and took him to the Hotel Imperial, he had no clothes, nothing. So I sent *Gruppenführer* Querner to get him toilet kit and pyjamas. Querner, mind you, was chief of the SS and the police in *Wien*. Tremendous fuss. Not an easy man to fit, *Il Duce*.' He sketched a pasta paunch. 'When I produced the pyjamas, he held them up. "It's unhealthy to sleep in night clothes. I never wear anything at night. I'd advise you to do the same, *Hauptsturmführer* Skorzeny." That was before my promotion – I'll never forget the twinkle in his eye. He was finished as a national leader. But he's not too old to love.'

'Nor am I,' Lucas said.

'Don't worry,' Scarface said. 'I shan't countermand. But do not expect too much. A very beautiful girl. But she cannot – how does one say in English? – *verlängern*.'

'I don't understand.'

Skorzeny's hand had been itching for the decanter and he grasped it. 'You will,' he said. 'She appears above rather stand-offish. But below – how do you say? – there is too much *Überhestigkeit*.'

'As long as you'll leave me to find out for myself,' said Lucas.

10 The bet

Grete had almost finished her toilet. On these assignments she liked to appear to perfection, not to please her visitors, but herself. She spared nothing that could artfully heighten the attractions with which nature had endowed her. Venus, rising from the foam, was the goddess she adored. Manet's 'Olympia', unadorned except by a ribbon tied around the throat, was the model she imitated. She preferred the preparations to the en-counter, luxuriating in the perfumed bath, powdering her limbs with body talc before the full-length mirror, feeling the shaved armpits, brushing the flaxen hair on her head and the brown curls of her mount, enamelling her toe and finger nails. The entry of the stranger, clumsy with drink, the laboured breath-ing, the stench of sweat, the tussling, the milky seed, spilt some-times on her skin, at others jerking home, the grunting followed by the little death, filled her with distaste. So, when the tele-phone buzzed in the bedroom, she went to answer it angry that her pleasurable preparation should be interrupted by, she presumed, the impatient tunnelling engineer.

'*Fräulein* Carlson,' a voice said in German, 'Karl Schmidt

here. I have a difficulty. Could you make it earlier, your appointment? I have another at ten minutes past ten . . .'

'You little shit, NO!' she said; and looking up at the enormous mirror on the wall opposite her double divan, she shook her fist and put out her tongue. Then she went back into the bathroom. War Combat Cameraman Karl Schmidt, Iron Cross 2nd class, personified her shame. In the elaborately scrolled border of the bedroom mirror there was a circle of unmirrored glass though which Schmidt recorded her engagements on the field of love on film, used primarily for the blackmail section of the *Auslands-Abwehr* department, but also for the entertainment of the troops in rest camps – since FHQ had decided that blue films were cheaper and healthier than brothels. When she had joined the *Auslands-Abwehr* for 'special duties', she had not known that these would involve being filmed. When she had found out, she had protested to Dr Langer, who offered her the choice of an increased salary or a release from duty, pointing out that in view of her film-work she might find it difficult to find a job in any more respectable field. She had chosen to stay on. She did not care about money, but she cared about lack of it. She was pleased when Dr Langer had told her that there was no further demand by the troops for films about the Everest Madonna, cold as ice and unscalable, because a nympho called Mitzi, whose pleasure was as manifest as her appetite insatiable, had become the forces' blue-film favourite. As for the blackmail section recordings, she was able to ignore them, except when she saw Karl Schmidt or heard his voice. When she accepted Molyneux's bet on the patio, she had forgotten about the camera. Now, as she tied the black ribbon around her neck and surveyed her desirability point by delicious point, stroking her nipples with the tips of her little fingers, the thought of being observed became intolerable.

War Combat Cameraman Schmidt knew Grete Carlson's body as well as he knew his light-meter. He was not interested in beautiful bodies. He was caught, like the Marquis de Sade, in the adolescent brambles of pleasure-pain. Unless flagellation was involved, he was bored by the work of the blackmail section. He had made his name during the thirties as a sports photographer. His coverage of the Olympic Games had been, in his opinion and that of many others, superior to Leni Riefenstahl's. He had filmed the *blitzkrieg* in Poland, Norway and France. Smolensk had been his undoing. Frostbite led to the amputation of his right leg just below the knee, a loss for which the Iron Cross 2nd Class did not compensate. He had been relegated to work behind the battle-lines. His most interesting assignment had been on the reconstruction of Skorzeny's rescue of Mussolini. A bout of malaria further downgraded him to filming for blackmail and blue movies from the converted linen rooms of the *Palacio do Sonho,* with cameras which were always breaking down and end rolls of film passed on by *Abwehr* stores. What a comedown!

His camera could only cover the divan bed; but, though Grete did not know it, the two-way mirror gave him a view of most of the bedroom. To his surprise, the Swede came out of the bathroom not in her Manet 'Olympia' rig, but wearing a heavy white silk dressing gown with black collar and facings and a black belt. She walked over to the telephone and lifted the receiver. Schmidt switched on the microphones but when she put the receiver down without speaking, he switched them off again. Tapes were precious at this stage of the war. He had indented for more every month, but every month they were crossed off the list.

The Swede went back in the direction of the hall, which led to the corridor or to the bathroom. Perhaps room 303 had arrived. But no, she had a glass of ice cubes on a tray. She placed the tray on the low table in front of the settee and brought two tumblers and a bottle of Pernod from the drinks cupboard. She placed these on the tray, thought a moment and then went back to the cupboard for two saucers and two spoons. 'The bitch,' muttered Schmidt. He picked up his telephone and dialled a number.

Dr Langer had been arguing heatedly with Major Skorzeny about the amount promised to Lucas Molyneux. So large a sum was scarcely authorized by the instructions 'a reasonable sum'. The amount must be agreed with headquarters. 'Fuck headquarters!' Skorzeny had said. 'You know what happens.

The papers go into some idiot's in-tray. They lie there a week. Then he passes them to his immediately superior idiot's in-tray, "For Consideration". Nothing happens, and meantime the occasion's passed. A mercenary is like a donkey. He needs a carrot to start him moving. Once he's on the move, you can use the stick as well.'

'But so large a carrot!'

'He knows we need him more than he needs us. It was the letter from his mother ... that's what cut him down to fifty thousand.'

'If you take the responsibility, but leave me out—' And then the telephone rang. Karl Schmidt's voice buzzed like a wasp in a bottle. '*Herr Doktor*, this is War Combat Cameraman Schmidt speaking.'

Langer motioned Skorzeny to pick up the extension. 'I am in conference,' Dr Langer said.

'I wish merely to report, sir, that room 306, when asked to advance the time of her appointment with room 303, refused and called me an obscene name. Room 305 is ready for 22.10 hours. I have only one camera, which has to be moved—'

Skorzeny cut in. 'This is *Sturmbannführer* Skorzeny on the extension. Forget room 306. Room 305 is more important. Do you understand?'

'Yes, sir.'

'Before you hang up, what was the obscene name?'

'Is that an order, sir?'

'Everything I say is an order.'

' "Shit", sir. "*Little* shit".'

Dr Langer looked grave as he hung up, but Skorzeny grinned. 'I would not call that an obscene name,' he said. 'More like a statement of fact.'

'Who is in room 305?'

'Rosario. The *Reichsmarschall* suspects his fingers are getting too sticky. The Salazar government is particularly down on paederasty and we haven't anything in archives. I shall go up to the linen room and see for myself the quality of the material.'

It was ten minutes to ten. In the restaurant Lucas had looked for Grete in vain. The meal consisted of a small red mullet with too many bones and a *wiener schnitzel* which looked and tasted like dried wet cardboard covered in ersatz bread-crumbs and fried in olive oil. The goat's milk cheese seemed made from curdled chalk. But the half bottle of *vinho verde* was good. He had thought of Pryke, Pieter, Rosario, Skorzeny, his mother and death: mostly of death. He had seen more of it than most civilians of his age. In Spain it had been a frighten-ing possibility, both in the International Brigade and the jail at Badajoz. Now it loomed up as something as inevitable as the terminus at the end of a railway line. In three weeks, a month, I'll probably be dead, he thought. So what? So would hundreds of thousands all over the earth, his age or under.

In room 303, he did not care. At ten o'clock he would go to the Swede's room. Or would something awful happen to prevent it? He had never lain with a girl of that class. He went over the girls he had gone with, counting. He gave up after thirty-seven. So many public faces – shy, proud, prim, pro-vocative, suddenly transfigured: and in all that time, he had never known the ecstasy.

It was five minutes to ten. Grete stirred her ice and Pernod. She took a sip and let it run across her tongue, around her mouth, the innocent-tasting aniseed. In Berlin she had con-sulted Dr Sigmund Ostermark, the specialist in sexual dis-orders. He had put on rubber gloves and examined her, peering at her privates through pebble glasses. Afterwards he had said, '*Fräulein* Carlson, you have wasted your sixty deutchmarks. There is nothing wrong with you. The *labia minora* in you instinctively contract. This is a reaction which ladies in certain professions have been at pains to cultivate as an art. You should congratulate yourself. You will give your man great pleasure.'

'But what about me?'

'If you will dine with me at the Tempelhof,' said Dr Oster-mark, 'in this matter I have experience.'

Grete had paid the sixty marks and fled.

She could not remember the number of faces – handsome, brutal, weak, winsome, arrogant, drunken, lascivious – which had been reduced to a composite of satisfied desire by her *labia minora* without giving her more than a sense of envy of their ecstasy and disgust at their selfishness.

War Combat Cameraman Schmidt crossed to the other side of the linen room and looked into room 305. Dom Rosario was sitting stark naked with a half corona cigar in one hand, a tumbler of rum in the other and a little ticky between his legs. Suddenly he leapt up and darted into the hall, his member rising as he did.

Schmidt swore. It was only two minutes to ten. In Portugal they had no sense of time. He lugged the camera across, feeling twinges in the foot which he had lost.

There was a gentle tapping on the door of room 306. Grete went swiftly over to the hall, passing so close to the mirror wall that she could not be seen from the linen room. She opened the door, pulled Lucas into the hall and locked the door.

Lucas was wearing a chinese silk dressing gown, embroidered with dragons in gold thread, bought in Lourenço Marques three years before. Underneath it, he was as naked as she was beneath hers. 'I must explain,' she said.

The light in the hall came only from the bedroom, very soft. 'Don't.' He kissed her lips, then held her head between his hands. 'Your eyes shine,' he said. 'I thought they were cold, but they shine!'

She put her fingers on his lips. 'Ssh!'

'Microphones?' he whispered.

'Yes.'

He opened the bathroom door and switched on the light.

'Maybe there too,' she whispered.

He turned on the cold tap of the bath. 'Come in.'

'Not here!' She had thought of lying on the floor behind the settee, out of sight of the linen room. But the bathroom, with the watercloset and the bidet, was absurd. 'At least I can see you, Grete, let me see you!' He pulled her inside and closed the door. As he did so, his dressing gown fell open and she saw his manhood standing, its head ruffled with the fore-skin collar.

He took the belt of her dressing gown and untied it. The heavy silk fell open and he held the lapels back, gazing upon the glory of her body, the breasts, the rib-cage, the tight belly and its button, the brown foam of hair which held her secret with even more wonder than she herself had felt when she had stood before the mirror in preparation. 'I can't believe it.' His voice was thick. He went on his knees and kissed her curls.

'Don't be silly,' she said, 'anyone would think I was virgin.' But she placed both hands on the back of his head and pressed his lips towards her musky secret, as he ran his hands up her thighs and held her haunches towards the explorations of his tongue.

There was a rap on the linen room door. The liftboy had come into room 305, taken a swig at Dom Rosario's rum and then started to rummage in a suitcase. Schmidt opened the door and Skorzeny came in. 'Has the performance started?'

'Just about, Herr *Sturmbannführer*.'

Skorzeny walked over to the mirror looking into room 306. 'What on earth's happening in 306? No sign of anyone.'

'If you will remember, Herr *Sturmbannführer*, I was commanded to concentrate on 305.'

Could it be, wondered Skorzeny, that the Everest Madonna was melting at last, that the Armenian tunnelling engineer, whose main physical asset was that he was the sort of man no one could remember, was succeeding where so many others had failed? If so, he might have to re-appraise the situation. Mrs Ramoulian was the only emotional hold he had on Lucas, now that Lucas had called his bluff on the charges of desertion and Pryke's murder. Perhaps if the Armenian fell for the Swedish trollop, it would be far more useful than any film for the blackmail archives or the weary troops.

They were lying on the bathroom floor, a bath-towel on the marble tiles, their dressing gowns tossed aside. With his hands, his lips and eyes, he explored her body like a virgin Eden, discovering in her pockets of pleasure known hitherto only to herself. She had so often been ravaged and trampled on by savage intruders that the delicacy with which he probed each secret and his reverence for the violated as if inviolate made her feel a fraud. 'Fuck me,' she said. 'That's what you came for.' And she put her hand down and looked at his cock, as if only that existed, not Lucas.

It really seemed to be genuine, the worship of the body which she herself had worshipped. But whereas she had adored herself in mirrors, the tilt of haunch, the taut drum of her belly, the straining of her nipples, the lobes of her ears and arching of her nostrils, his adoration penetrated inwards. She wanted to be explored within. She reared herself up from the buttocks, thrusting her mount to be tunnelled. But he only played with the tight little wrinkles round her anus. 'What's wrong with you?' she hissed. 'Can't you come in?'

Then he came in and immediately he felt the *labia* between her legs close on his penis, like a dairymaid's deft fingers kneading the teats of a cow's udder, to bring the milk spurting out. Never had he felt this wonderful embrace, and he forgot everything: the bet, the fear of not coming, the danger ahead, death almost certain. He wanted to plant his seed.

She had been so open, so longing for entry, that when he came in, she sighed with relief. But then the contraction of the lips started. She wanted to be taken. But she could not help herself. It was going to be the usual failure. She felt herself tugging at him to come.

Yet he didn't come and as he penetrated and withdrew, back to the portals and again sought the sanctum, something that she had never felt before began to stir within her. It was terrifying, because part of herself was taking over the whole. She only existed down below, where his baton was mounting to a crescendo; suddenly she could not control herself any longer and she cried out, as she caught a glimpse of heaven and his seed spurted into her, jet after jet. And there they were, lying on the floor of the bathroom, covered in sweat, exhausted, cheek to cheek.

'My angel,' he said.

'My love. My only love.'

For some time, they lay silent together. Then Lucas said, 'We both lost. The bet.'

She stroked the damp hair from his forehead. 'No. We both won.'

In the linen room, Skorzeny and Schmidt were watching room 305. The pageboy had finished Dom Rosario's rum with relish but put down the cigar. He got up.

'Roll,' said Skorzeny, unnecessarily because Schmidt needed no such instructions. Dom Rosario appeared in the bedroom from the bathroom. He was dressed as a housemaid, with cap and apron. The pageboy picked up the ashtray and emptied it on the carpet and pointed to the housemaid to sweep it up. Dom Rosario pleaded: no brush and dustpan. 'Cut,' said Skorzeny. 'Salazar isn't interested in that muck.'

Schmidt obediently cut and said goodnight to *Sturmbannführer* Skorzeny. But he remained in the linen room long enough to see Dom Rosario being caned over the bare buttocks by the pageboy before he went to bed to read another chapter of *Justine*.

'Supposing,' said Grete, 'it was just chance?'
'Come into my bed,' said Lucas, 'and we'll see.'

11 Warning – DANGER!

Lucas awoke, reached out, but she was gone. Outside, the light was brilliant. On the pillow beside him was a note in slanting script. 'Left you to sleep, dear tunneller. You must not trust OS. Trust Grete Carlson.'

He looked at his watch. It was half-past eight. He rang room service for breakfast to be served in his room, then sprang out of bed and ran a bath. He ought to tear her note up and flush it down the pan, but he folded it and put it with the banknotes in the pocket of his belt. The thought of her gave him a hard-on. They had proved three times that coming together was no fluke. As he shaved and bathed, he tried to concentrate on the meeting with Skorzeny; but he kept thinking of Grete. For the first time in his life, he was genuinely in love. The stranger he had chatted up the night before had been translated into a tender lover, as much a prisoner as he of the *Auslands-Abwehr*. She had left Sweden for Germany, hoping to make her way in films. But she had not made the grade. Cabaret, modelling, crowd-work had given her a precarious livelihood until she had got this job of 'hostess' at the German-Portuguese Institute. They confided to one another the sexual frustrations, which had made them each so inadequate with other lovers: time was too precious for reticence ... Of course he could not *trust* Skorzeny; but he had to continue with him.

Before going down, Lucas tapped on the door of room 305 and walked in. Dom Rosario was dressing. He looked angry to see Lucas. 'Don't blame me,' he said. 'I only did what I was asked. By you, too, remember.'

'That job in Rio? Is it really on, when I've finished this?'

'Of course it's on. *If* you can get to Rio.' He picked up his wallet from the bedside table, took out a card, and wrote on the back. 'This is my business card. In case I'm not there, I've written "Please assist bearer". You never know what your name might be by the time you reach Brasil.' He gave the card to Lucas and squeezed his elbow. 'No hard feelings?'

As Lucas went out, Dom Rosario called after him. '*Adeus.*' Not, Lucas noticed, *até logo* or *até à vista.* Honest, at least in that.

When the HINEIN flashed permission for Lucas to go in, he found Skorzeny with a colleague, one of those shaven-headed krauts, like Erich von Stroheim, with extra chins at the back of his neck. 'Good morning,' the *Sturmbannführer* said, wryly, 'I hope that you had enough sleep.' He was so much taller than his colleague that he could wink, without being observed.

'As a tunnelling engineer,' answered Lucas, 'I am used to odd hours. Things come up ...'

'*I* can understand.' Skorzeny implied that his colleague, Dr Langer, might not. 'But I have discussed with Dr Langer the financial proposition of last evening.'

'With which,' said Dr Langer, 'I do not agree. This cutting of banknotes into halves, *zum beispiel*!'

'But I am willing to take responsibility. I will tell you why, while we sample Dom Rosario's coffee. Of course, you drank it on the *São Paulo*. But here, I think, we roast and filter it better.' He pointed to a Kona machine bubbling away on an immense sideboard which was carved with pheasants, hares, fish and fruit. He took the seat at the head of a table and waved Lucas to sit at his right. 'If you will be so good, Dr Langer, to serve the coffee.'

As the doctor did so, Skorzeny leant across to Lucas. 'You may have been puzzled,' he said in a low voice. 'But I test any man I use for observation, enterprise, independent action and the willingness to take risks. You have done well.'

'How?'

'Fräulein Carlson was clearly our agent; but at the same time a – what do you call it? – good lie? You accomplish your ends and avoid the traps. You refuse the inviting bed and choose the bathroom floor. And then when you take her to your bedroom, you cut the wires of all the microphones, before you do anything. You would make a good SS kommando, if you can go so far without any training from Skorzeny.'

Dr Langer put a tray on the table with three horn goblets of black coffee and (out of idiom) brown sugar and cream in silverware. Lucas looked at Skorzeny, looming above him with a man-of-the-world smile on his duel-scarred face. 'Of course, Miss Carlson knew all about this from the beginning?'

'Of course,' Skorzeny said.

It was a lie so transparent that Lucas was reassured. Skorzeny was making a desperate attempt to separate him and Grete. 'She's a very clever girl,' he said. 'You'd be sorry to lose her.'

'You needn't worry. We won't.' Skorzeny poured cream into his coffee and stirred in two large teaspoonsful of brown sugar. 'I take it you are with us, Mr Ramoulian?'

'Molyneux,' Lucas said.

'Not Molyneux. He's dead,' said Dr Langer, smiling to reveal a gold cap which may have begun life on his own tooth or been removed before its former owner went to the gas-chamber. 'Haven't you read?' He passed over that morning's *Noticias de Lisboa* at the foot of which was a paragraph circled in indelible pencil, reporting the death of Lucas Molyneux lost overboard from the *São Paulo*, two days before. Suicide suspected, because

Molyneux was wanted in South Africa for the murder of Security Sergeant Pryke. 'So you see.'

'All I want to see is twenty-five thousand American dollars intact and the halves of the other twenty-five thousand.' This shutting of doors behind him merely emphasized the importance of the passport which he had in his inner jacket pocket stamped by the immigration authorities in Lisbon the day before.

'Reasonable enough,' Skorzeny said. 'Dr Langer; the money?'

Very reluctantly Dr Langer got up and went out of the room. Skorzeny raised his eyes to heaven. *Sacro egoismo!* he said *Heiliger Bureaukratte!* But thank God, it's just as bad on the other side. Without bureaucrats we could have won the war years ago. But don't worry; Skorzeny takes responsibility. He has direct access to FHQ, to the Führer himself.'

The only thing that consoled Lucas was Skorzeny's referring to himself in the third person. He must be a bit dotty; and Lucas had never felt saner.

Dr Langer came back with a portfolio. From it he produced twenty-five 1,000-dollar notes and another twenty-five cut in half. Lucas inspected them. They were in sequence and had never been issued. 'How do I know they are genuine?'

'But it's obvious.' Dr Langer and Scarface looked amazed. 'The Führer—'

'Neville Chamberlain trusted the Führer. I don't. I shall have to check these with a bank.'

'This is now a matter of urgency,' said Skorzeny. 'We have no time.'

'No time?' Lucas handed back the notes. 'Then no deal.'

Langer and Skorzeny looked at one another. 'I could take our friend to the Berliner Kreditbank.' Langer suggested. 'They would—'

'The Ibero-Suíço Bank of Lisboa has a branch just outside here. I could stroll down—'

'And away?' Skorzeny shook his head. 'You should respect our intelligence as much as we do yours.' He picked up his telephone. 'A car for Dr Langer ... Take Weissenfeld ... No, it shouldn't be long ... At the main entrance ... Transport does not matter. Anything that's immediately available.' He put down the receiver. 'I understand that as a mercenary you wish to make sure that you are being paid in good money. I hope that you understand that when you come back from the bank you will be under military discipline. You must obey your orders, or you will be shot.'

Lucas went into the Ibero-Suíço Bank, with Dr Langer on one side and on the other Weissenfeld, who had a gammy left leg and two fingers missing but was still a formidable, if battered, member of the master race. Ignoring them, he went to the inquiry desk. A bored looking counter-clerk raised his head; but when he saw the wad of 1,000-dollar notes, he came smartly to the *caisse*. Lucas wanted to see the manager. On what business? A private matter. Lucas riffled the notes. Money talks, and in a couple of minutes he was conducted to the elevator which would take him to the manager's office on the mezzanine.

To the clerk's surprise, but not Lucas's, the two Germans entered the elevator with him. The manager was waiting in a doorway at the end of the landing and would have allowed all three of them into his office, if Lucas had not asked if it was in order for 'these two gentlemen' to wait for him in the corridor outside. But of course. They were invited to sit on a mahogany settle beside a table strewn with financial newspapers. 'I don't know,' Lucas told Dr Langer, 'how long you will have to wait. But I know where to find you, if you get bored.'

Inside the office, Lucas strolled to the window. 'Nice view,' he said. There was no possibility of escape from there. 'Nice office.' There was no other exit. The manager, a grizzled German-Swiss, introduced himself as Engelhart and asked what he could do for 'Mr ... ?'

'Lucas Molyneux, for business purposes,' Lucas said, 'though I was born Leucas Ramoulian. English by birth, Armenian by parentage.' He noticed Herr Engelhart's interest in the 1,000-dollar notes. 'Yes, it's about these I wanted to consult you; first : are they genuine?'

The manager took them and, pretending to examine them, noted that there were twenty-five. 'They are in sequence,' Lucas said, 'and they continue in sequence with these twenty-five halves,' which Lucas produced from his pocket.

The manager looked intrigued, suspicious and slightly shocked. 'They seem genuine enough to me, but I will ring for our Herr Schneider who is expert in these matters.' He pressed a bell on his desk twice and then motioning Lucas into a chair on the far side of his desk, asked how the notes came into his possession.

'The gentlemen waiting in the corridor are comparative strangers to me,' said Lucas. 'They've approached me on a confidential enterprise. Their offer is twenty-five thousand dollars in advance, another twenty-five on completion, in earnest of which they have given me the final sum in half-notes.'

Herr Engelhart, who was aware of the identity of Dr Langer sitting in the corridor outside, said no more than, 'Unusual.'

Herr Schneider came in, a subordinate concealing ambition between a hissing obsequiousness. 'Interessssting,' he said, examining the notes, first for the watermark, then through a watchmaker's glass. 'Vairy interessssting!' He handed the notes back to his superior. 'Mint notes! Genuine. But the serial numbers date from 1941.'

'Were they stolen?' asked Lucas.

'Pearl Harbor was bombed, I think, 7 December 1941. Next day the United States declared war on Germany. Not stolen, captured. Would you not think so, Herr Engelhart?'

'In which case they are valid currency,' said the bank manager. 'Can we help you in any other way, Mr Molyneux?'

'You can,' said Lucas. 'To start with, I want to make a will, witnessed by you both and deposited with your bank.'

Herr Engelhart picked up his telephone. 'Send up a will form.' He put down the receiver. 'What next, Mr Molyneux?' He and Herr Schneider were beginning to enjoy themselves. Life in the Alcantara branch of the Ibero-Suíço was seldom so interesting.

'Where is your head office?' Lucas asked. 'Geneva? Basel?' 'Zürich.'

Lucas put down the wad of half-notes. 'These I want held at Zürich in a special envelope.'

'Not in safe deposit?'

'As you might securities.'

'An envelope and sealing wax, Schneider. And the rest, Mr Molyneux?'

'I want to deposit 1,000 dollars in an account in the name of Leucas Ramoulian in Zürich, if that is possible?'

'A specimen signature slip, Schneider.'

'Two thousand dollars I would like to cash and take away. One thousand in smaller US dollar notes, say five 100-dollar bills, the rest in fifties, tens and fives.'

'You have that, Schneider?'

'Yes, Herr Engelhart.'

'Of the remainder, I want ten thousand dollars placed on deposit account in the name of Grete Carlson at interest on seven days' notice of withdrawal at the current bank rate, the remainder in the same name on current account.'

'I see,' said Herr Engelhart. 'Is Fräulein Carlson aware of – er – this?'

'There would be little sense in opening the accounts if she wasn't,' Lucas said.

'I only asked,' said Herr Engelhart, 'because she banks here – a client, whom, I may say, it is a pleasure to serve.'

Lucas was able to telepathize a giggle between the bank manager and his subordinate. 'Then,' he said grimly, 'there is no need to give you a specimen of her signature.'

He signed his own specimen signatures, signed across the sealed envelope containing the twenty-five half-1,000-dollar notes. He glanced at the clock. Nearly an hour had passed. He hoped Langer and Weissenfeld were getting sore bums on the settle. 'Now for the will,' he said. 'It is very simple. All my possessions to go to my mother, Mrs Esther Ramoulian, 21-b Wellclose Square, London E1, England; or, in event of her predeceasing me, to Miss Grete Carlson.'

Simple though it was, it took nearly forty minutes to conclude the technicalities, by which time it was obvious that Dr Langer had almost convinced himself that Lucas had bribed Engelhart to contrive his escape. 'It did not take all this time to discover that the money was good,' said Dr Langer, reproachfully.

'How fucking right you are!' agreed Lucas.

As Herren Engelhart and Schneider closed the door on their new customer, the bank manager allowed himself to relax with his subordinate. 'In future, Hans, we may smile on Fräulein Carlson not merely for her beautiful eyes and slender figure, but also for her brilliant prospects and fat bank balance.'

'But, Herr Direktor,' said Hans Schneider, 'fifty thousand dollars! Someone must be crazy. But who? What is happening?'

'These are not questions which concern a Swiss banker, Herr Schneider. *Tout court*, we have a new client.'

12 Enter Philip Mitchell

'Thank you, Dr Langer.' Skorzeny did not trouble to get up from behind his desk. Nor did he ask Lucas to sit down. Lucas remembered the difference which had come over the recruiting sergeant, the moment he had signed on, years ago.

'As you know, Molyneux is dead,' Skorzeny said. 'You are now Philip Mitchell.' He touched a thick envelope on his desk, tied with white tape. 'Your dossier is here. And before you receive any instructions, you must master these documents. The real Philip Mitchell was a tunnelling engineer, like yourself, working in Switzerland in 1938. He had a skiing accident in the Austrian Tyrol. During the months he lay in coma, we made inquiries and found that he had no next of kin. So when he departed from this world in body, we kept him alive on paper. You will see from the documents that he has been a busy man, working as a freelance engineer resident in Eire, but employed more often than not in Britain.'

'A zombie?'

'A dead soul,' Skorzeny said. 'Have you never read Gogol's *Dead Souls*?'

'I saw it in the library, but it sounded depressing.'

'Your loss. It is one of the great comic novels of the world. Philip Mitchell had read it. You'll find his copy in the dossier. Glance at it, if you have time. It may help you to understand how the documents of a dead man added to a live man who would like to be officially dead is good human arithmetic.'

'You mean you kept him officially alive for me?'

'You flatter yourself. You just happen to match.' He untied the tape and produced a passport from the envelope. 'Look!'

Lucas opened the passport. There was a photograph of an undistinguished young man, and opposite it:

Occupation *Profession*	Tunnelling Engineer
Place of Birth *Lieu de Naissance*	London
Date of Birth *Date de Naissance*	3/3/1915
Country of Residence *Pays de Résidence*	UK
Height *Taille*	5 ft 8 in
Colour of Eyes *Couleur des Yeux*	Greyish
Special peculiarities *Signes particuliers*	None

'I don't look like that squirt,' Lucas said.

'Nor more would Philip Mitchell, if he were alive today. That was the photograph of a 23-year-old nonentity. He would now look like a 29 to 30-year-old nonentity. Like you.'

'My eyes are brown.'

'Who looks at eyes? You, Mr Molyneux-Mitchell, have the advantage of being an utterly insignificant man. Nobody would look at you twice, because nobody would want to look at you twice. I envy you. Skorzeny, once seen, is never forgotten. You are as undetectable as a shelled pea.' He smiled. 'Scarface has special peculiarities. You and Mitchell have none.'

'So I have to mug up being Mitchell?'

'And learn to write like him. He went to St Paul's School in Hammersmith and learnt Greek. You'll see that he wrote his e's as epsilons, his k's as kappas. Those are easy to imitate. What you must watch carefully are the pressures of the up-and-down strokes, the little flourish under the signatures. Don't copy the signature in the passport. He is eight years older; his signature, you will find, has become freer, more confident. You must continue the development. This will excuse variations. People write, as they talk, in different ways according to their moods. At St Paul's your headmaster was John Bell, but remember that he wasn't called headmaster but High Master. Mitchell was a scholar at St Paul's and he kept a little silver fish which all scholars were allowed to wear, because he was proud of being a scholar. You'll find it there, among his things. You don't need to keep it, unless you want.'

Lucas reached the end of his patience. 'I don't care a fuck what Philip Mitchell was like when he died. As far as I'm concerned, he can have hung himself with his old school tie. If you'll give me those documents, Major, I'll look at them; and anything I don't like, I'm going to chuck away. I'm not a public-school bloke and if they pick me up, they'll rumble me in five minutes, if I pretend ... I'm an engineer, not a bloody actor.'

Skorzeny stood up and looked down at Lucas, 'I recognize your limitations. For this assignment, it would not matter. Of your future, I was thinking ...'

'What about the assignment?'

'We must not be hasty. First you must become Philip Mitchell. Read the papers. Learn what you have been doing. Practise your handwriting, especially your signature. Forget Lucas Molyneux, as you forgot Leucas Ramoulian. You will report here at 15.00 hours with specimen signatures, wearing Philip Mitchell's clothes. I shall examine you on the work you have done throughout your engineering career since you left mining school. For the work ahead there is time enough later.' Skornezy handed him the envelope with his *curriculum vitae.* 'You are a quick thinker, Mitchell. I hope you are an equally quick learner. You have just under three hours. You will find your clothes waiting for you. I suggest you put them on at once. You should get used to them.'

Lucas took the Mitchell envelope and went to the door. Before he reached it, Skorzeny said, 'How big are your feet?'

'Eleven inches. Broad fitting.'

'I will send up a pair of insoles,' Skorzeny said. 'They are not so big as the dead man's shoes.'

Lying on his bed was a pin-stripe suit from Austin Reed, fresh laundered Aertex underwear, Tootal handkerchiefs. The shoes were from Dolcis. Having risen from Stepney, Lucas himself had always been a nattier dresser. Solid middle-class, Pauline scholarship boy, Philip Mitchell must have been more confident, less anxious to impress. The ties were knitted silk, or Paisley, apart from a Liberty shantung of baby's-first-motion yellow, which Lucas dropped in the waste basket. But the clothes fitted; and clothes, Lucas remembered, make the man. He put on trousers and shirt: rolled up the sleeves above his elbows. It was the usual technique, trying to stampede him so that he could not have time to think. He was damned if he was going to be hurried. He took Mitchell's passport and walked on to the balcony.

There was no sign of Grete. Unbelievably it was less than twenty hours since he had looked across at *her* balcony and been given the brush-off when he whistled Lili Marlene. Down in the grounds there were men and some women walking about; more sitting on the terrace, it being just before lunch. But no Grete.

He did not dare to knock on her door or telephone her. He was sure that the telephone would be tapped, the room under surveillance. He brought one of the Louis Quinze gilt chairs on to the balcony. (No wonder there was a French Revolution, if they couldn't devise anything more comfortable to sit on!) He sat, reading his passport. Skorzeny's chums had made a gaffe. In 1938, there was an exit stamp from Switzerland to Austria and the next stamp was an entry into Eire – 27 August 1939. But there had been so many later exit and entry stamps between Eire and the UK since that date, the document would stand up to scrutiny far longer than Lucas would under interrogation. The cover story was obvious. He had spent the war, based in Eire, but going to Britain on assignments; easy enough to counterfeit the immigration stamps. But of course the story wouldn't hold up: entering Britain with a British passport, Philip Mitchell would have been taken on one side and asked why he had not reported for military service. If the job was in London, as Scarface implied, Lucas wouldn't stand a chance of getting further than Holyhead, Liverpool or the Ulster border before awkward questions arose.

Lucas opened an envelope, typed 'MED BOARDS'. There were three exemption certificates, from Uxbridge. Owing to tuberculosis, he was graded category-C on three different occasions. There was also a letter from the Ministry of Labour, stating that Philip Mitchell, of British birth but resident in Eire, was reserved for contract service in the UK as a tunnelling engineer. It was rather grubby and well-thumbed. If not authentic, it looked as if it had passed muster often before. There were no ration cards, clothing coupons, identity or insurance cards. But if he was based in Eire, that would at least be explicable. Another envelope contained a number of references from Irish building and mining contractors. One had a brown ring, which looked as if left by the bottom of a glass of Guinness.

He looked up, hearing someone whistling 'Lili Marlene'. Grete was on the terrace below. She gave only the slightest indication that she knew he had seen her. She had come from the bathing pool and hung her damp towel over the balustrade. In order to hold it in place so that it could dry, she picked up two stones, placing one at either end. Underneath the towel, she slipped a piece of paper where one of the stones held it. She glanced up at Lucas's balcony, then down at the stone. Lucas nodded and she disappeared into the house.

He went back into the room and picked up a notebook of Mitchell's. It would give him more to copy than just his signature. Luckily the dead man's fountain pen, a small black Parker, was among his effects. The nib would help to guide Lucas. He would practise in the grounds.

The elevator was already ascending when he pressed the button. The door opened and the long-lashed pageboy stood aside for Grete to go out. She nodded at Lucas casually and as she passed said, 'Tower, I meant.'

Lucas did not know what she meant until he read the message hidden under the stone. 'Meet me in the Mirador 10-15 minutes.'

Across the lawn there was an artificial hill, planted with rhododendrons, from which rose a turret almost invisible because of the creepers which were strangling and tearing it apart. Grete was hanging her bathing dress on her balcony railing. That was it. Lucas opened the notebook and sauntered across the lawn with apparent aimlessness.

Mitchell had kept a sort of commonplace book of things that interested him. Lucas read,

The fighting man shall from the sun
Take warmth, and life from the glowing earth:
Speed with the light-foot winds to run,
And with the trees to newer birth;
And find, when fighting shall be done,
Great rest, and fullness after dearth ...

The blackbird sings to him, Brother, brother,
If this be the last song you shall sing
Sing well, for you may not sing another,
Brother, sing.'

Mitchell had written, 'Would this have been as moving if Julian Grenfell hadn't died of wounds a month after writing it?'

On the next page, Lucas read,

Language has not the power to speak what love indites:
The soul lies buried in the ink that writes.

Lucas liked Mitchell's taste in literature better than his clothes. '*Tu ne me chercherais pas si tu ne me possédais. Ne t'inquiète donc pas.*' It was a reassurance from the dead. If there really was life after death, Lucas wondered what Mitchell P. was making of all this; perhaps he had other things to think about.

He went to the mirador by a devious route, pretending to read – no, actually reading – what the dead man whose shoes he was wearing, had written in his notebook before he met his end at the bottom of a ski-jump.

Man with his burning soul
Has but an hour of breath
To build a ship of truth
In which his soul may sail—
Sail on the sea of death,
For death takes toll
Of beauty, courage, youth,
Of all but truth ...

'Thou wouldst not seek me, didst thou not possess me. So do not fret.'

The entrance to the mirador was overgrown. Since the Germans had put the barbed wire on the surrounding walls, they had no interest in a watchtower; and they were too busy on black-warfare and blue films to enjoy the view enjoyed by the

Brasilian millionaire who built this belvedere. Nature had taken over. Ivy and bougainvillaea climbed the walls, bored at the stone and mortar, entered the windows and wildly struggled for light in the dark staircase; spiders had spun webs between their yellow tendrils, to entrap the flies which rose from ordure and the small dead things on the stairs which he mounted – mice, fledglings, a bat whose heart appeared to beat with the maggots inside.

As he climbed, Scarface, Langer, Weissenfeld receded into a world as remote as the original Palacio do Sonho, the unspecified mission to London and his old mother in Wellclose Square like the menace and fulfilment of an uneasy sleep. From the top floor, he could look back across the trees and shrubs to the fantastic palace. Grete's bathing dress was like a little flag strung on her balcony, to say, 'You haven't dreamed me. I am your wonderland come true.' And then he saw her come out on to the terrace. In that perspective, she appeared minute, smaller than the green spider with a great white spot delicately walking over a leaf just beside him, engaged on business equally urgent. In his heightened awareness, he thought what a miracle it was that after the millions (or was it milliards?) of years of the evolution of life on this lucky little earth, Grete, with all that apparent aimlessness, should be homing upon him in the mirador, as instinctively as if she were an insect or a bird!

He went down to the first turn of the stairs to wait for her. She was ages coming and at the entrance she hesitated. She called – 'Lucas. Where are you?'

'Come up, my love. Don't be afraid.'

She ran up and as she rounded the turn, she tripped and fell into his arms. He held her like salvation.

They clung to each other, as if they were drowning and had found lifebuoys. At last he said, 'Why are you crying?' wiping tears from her eyes.

'I never believed.'

'Nor me!' She held his head between her hands and tried to look at him through her tears. 'I don't deserve—' She buried her eyes on his shoulder. 'Oh God!' She slid her hand down his back and pressed him in to her.

'On the top,' he said, 'it's better there.'

'OK. But let's go up together.' She opened his flies and out sprang his manhood. 'Hold me from behind.' She pulled up her blouse so that his hands were cupped on her breasts. 'Lift the skirt. I can't wait. Let's go up together!'

It was an extraordinary ascent up the wild stairway, libidinous, desperate, clumsy and yet curiously expert. They had not a moment to lose, but they did not reach the climax until at the top she turned and face to face she entered his throat with her tongue as she sucked out his seed with the longing lips beneath.

When it was over, she said, 'Lucas, dearest darling love, you musn't go with Skorzeny.'

'I've got to go, my only love,' he said. 'You've given me something to fight for.' He explained what he had done at the bank. 'You are a neutral. There is money to get back to Stockholm.'

Grete started once more to weep, and this time in a different way. 'But, dearest Lucas, I'm a Nazi whore. You cannot do this.'

'You're my woman. My wife. Fuck your past! Fuck my past!'

'Darling,' Grete said, 'have you time to fuck me?'

Lucas looked at his watch. He had. Just.

13 Progress Report One

London

TOP SECRET
Major J. Embleton DODS 17. v. '44

Having an appointment with the DG, DODS, at 10.15 hrs, I presented myself at Pelican House ten minutes early. It is a civilian building, requisitioned from the Pelican Assurance Company by the Ministry of Supply. It was constructed without regard to the requirements of Government Security. There is a porter's lodge on the right of the entrance hall and a hydraulic lift, rope-operated on the left, with a flight of stairs at the back.

There should be at all times a porter in the lodge to check passes, as well as the lift operator. When I arrived, I reported at the lodge to ex-Colour Sergeant Pickersgill, who asked to see my pass. I told him that I had left it in my battle-dress, but I had an appointment with Brigadier Sir Hilary Fry. 'Oh, well sir!' he said, 'I'll take you up.' He was, I noticed, studying the racing form in the *Daily Mail*.

'Wouldn't it be better to ring through to check?' I asked.

'I'll do that,' he said.

As he was doing so, I noticed that three people came in, to whom the porter waved acknowledgement. (DODS is on the 5th and top floor. The other floors are also occupied by the Ministry of Supply, engaged in work the secrecy of which does not concern us in this case.)

When my appointment was confirmed, the porter, without asking to see any documents to prove my identity, took me up in the lift to the top floor. As the ex-Colour Sergeant has only one arm and the lift is very old-fashioned, this took one minute and and a half. Doubling this for the downward journey, this means that for three minutes, Pelican House was without any check on entrances or exits. I asked the porter if he always had to double as liftman and he replied, 'No. But Bob's popped round the corner to get some fags.'

The lift opened on a landing which was also the head of the stair. When the lift descended, I examined the top flight of stairs before trying to enter DODS. There was on the landing of the fourth floor a wooden barrier some five inches broad on which was painted NO ENTRY, but beneath which anyone could easily stoop.

I then went back to the fifth floor. On the door, which was solid oak, was painted PRIVATE: Ring for Entry. Instead of ringing, I tried the handle and opened the door. In front of me was a long corridor, at the left of which was a glass window marked INQUIRIES; looking through I could see a girl at the switchboard of a telephone and a copy-typist busy at her machine. I passed beyond this without being noticed. On the right was door with two names on it: Mr B. Nightingale and Lieut G. Hampshire. Beyond were two offices: on the right, the DG's personal assistant, Lady Virginia Chudleigh; on the left, the deputy director, Mr J. Constantine. Facing me was the final door: Director General, Brigadier Sir Hilary Fry, KBE, MC, DSO & Bar. I took the liberty of knocking and a voice called – 'Come in.'

Before I could do so, the door was opened by Lady Virginia, who appeared to have been taking dictation from Sir Hilary. I could not help thinking, as I entered, that if I had been an enemy agent, impersonating myself, and carrying a lethal weapon, I could have held up Sir Hilary and his personal assistant without a murmur and have effected my escape with the connivance of the porter – especially if I could give him a tip for the 2.30 at Thirsk.

Lady Virginia looked at me askance, but Sir Hilary called, 'Major Embleton? Come in.' Then, turning to Lady Virginia, he asked her to stay during the interview.

When we were seated, Sir Hilary said that Pickersgill had called him from the lodge. 'I was rather surprised that you weren't carrying your pass,' he said.

'And didn't report to reception,' Lady Virginia added.

I handed the brigadier my pass. He looked at it. 'Found you hadn't left it in your battle-dress, eh?'

'I thought you might be interested to know how far someone could get, sir, just on the strength of an officer's uniform.'

For a moment it looked as if Sir Hilary was going to explode. Then he turned and said, 'Ginny, ask Mr Hampshire to come in, there's a dear.'

While Lady Virginia was out of the room, Sir Hilary explained to me that she was 'an absolute brick' and he didn't know what he would do without her. Apparently, she is his god-daughter and was engaged to Sir Hilary's son who was killed on the outskirts of Dunkirk during the evacuation. As you probably know, he has no other children of his own. It seems a sort of father-daughter relationship, as Lady Virginia lost her own father, the last Earl of St Neots, in 1937.

She came back with Lieutenant Hampshire; he's about twenty-five, short, I'd say five feet four, Ox & Bucks Light Infantry. A territorial. He was a shipping clerk in civvy street. Badly wounded, chest and pelvis, at Calais. Now C-3. When Sir Hilary made me recount my entry into DODS, Hampshire grew red in the face and looked very uneasy. I tried to tone things down, but I couldn't help being pretty damning. When I'd finished, Sir Hilary asked Hampshire if he had any excuses. 'I can only say, sir, with the pressure of the operation—' Hampshire started. But Sir Hilary broke in, 'Major Embleton here is joining us as my adjutant. One of the first things he will do is to tighten up security precautions.'

'I shall be relieved to hand over—' Hampshire said eagerly.

'You will not hand over.' Sir Hilary was firm. 'But you will be working under Major Embleton. So the sooner you get your security files ready for his inspection, the better.'

After Hampshire left, Sir Hilary outlined my other duties. There was no interview. It was just taken for granted that I had been offered and accepted the job. My main duties will be to act as liaison with other government departments. I gather that Sir Hilary is rather taken aback by the revival of an operation which had been dreamed up at the time when this country was threatened with invasion. 'Now that we are threatening France with invasion,' he said, 'it is very difficult to secure the manpower and facilities needed for what appears, even to me, I confess, a purely defensive measure.'

Sir Hilary himself is a personal friend of many of the high-ups in the War Office, the Admiralty and even the Chiefs of Staff Committee. But I gather from him that the revival of what they call Operation Serpent comes not from the Chiefs of Staff, but from Number Ten itself; and those who consider it ill-advised are trying quietly to sabotage the operation by non-cooperation. The target date has been set for 28 May. My job will be to endeavour to secure at middle levels the cooperation which would be refused at superior levels with the exception of the highest. In plain English, by-pass the generals and admirals in order to implement the orders from Number Ten.

The main weapons are tact and diplomacy. But Sir Hilary thinks that the rank of major does not pack the necessary weight, and proposes to recommend my promotion to the rank of acting lieutenant-colonel. I agree with him, though I assure you that the suggestion did not come from me.

I hope to send you my second report very shortly. I suspect that there may have been some laxity in security and would appreciate if approaches to MI 5 can come from you rather than from DODS.

14 Lisbon – Orly

The only thing Lucas was allowed to take with him was Molyneux's passport. His clothes, shoes, papers and even his shaving
kit was packed in his suitcases and surrendered with his keys
to Dr Langer, who apologized for not being able to give him a
receipt. His gold Dunhill lighter and cigarette case he had already presented to Grete. But after an argument, he was allowed
to keep his watch. With its luminous hands and its stopping
mechanism, it was superior to Mitchell's. There was nothing to
identify it with Molyneux; and being Swiss made, dating back
to 1938, it might very well have been bought by Mitchell.

Looking at himself, hair lightened by the barber, wearing
Mitchell's Austin Reed lightweight Prince of Wales suit, Lucas
felt a different man. Molyneux had ceased to exist, Leucas
Ramoulian had become merely a name in an Ibero-Suíço bank
account.

The Mercedes Benz took them out to the airport. Weissenfeld
sat in front with the driver, Lucas with Skorzeny beside him in
the back. 'Isn't it time you told me what all this is about?' Lucas
asked.

'You will learn that when I think fit, Mr Mitchell,' Skorzeny
said. 'Meanwhile I want to ask you a few questions. When were
you born?'

'Look in my passport.'

'*Dummkopf!*'

'I was born in London. I went to St Paul's School. I won a
scholarship for which I was given a little silver fish ...'

'And you don't even know your date of birth! That is the
first thing—'

'With all due respect, Herr *Sturmbannführer*, it is my life,
not yours, which depends on my becoming Philip Mitchell con-
vincingly. And I'll go about it my way. I've got to feel myself
into him. Birthdays are low down on my list. Far more important is his fountain pen; the way the nib's worn is like a
fingerprint; it almost writes for Mitchell, when I hold it lightly.'

'There is ink in the pen?'

'Of course.'

'Then empty it at the airport. The air pressure in the plane will ruin your best suit otherwise, Mr Mitchell.' He was an odd chap, Scarface; retreated when attacked, then countered from a different angle. Having won a point, he said nothing more during the car drive.

Weissenfeld followed them into the departure lounge. There were three tickets for the flight to Paris (Orly). Weissenfeld seemed to be Scarface's batman and strong-arm man rolled into one. He carried the *Sturmbannführer*'s bags, apart from a despatch case, and went ahead. Lucas followed with a suitcase in either hand, with Scarface close behind. Lucas expected that when he had had his Molyneux passport stamped SAIDA, Scarface would demand its surrender. But, for the moment, he was in possession of two passports: Molyneux's, testifying that he had left Portugal that day; Mitchell's, that he had entered Eire a month before.

The plane was a civilian Junkers. Skorzeny told Lucas to sit on the outside, with a view through the porthole of the left wing. Skorzeny sat beside him on the gangway. Weissenfeld, after talking to the stewardess, about the stowage of the bags apparently, came and sat in the seat behind Lucas. They were taking no chances.

There were so many passengers that all seats were taken. Though Skorzeny was not in uniform, he was recognized by everyone. One or two spoke to him, others nodded and smiled. But Skorzeny did not seem pleased.

When they were airborne, he put down the tray in front of him and wrote, 'Please to sign your name.' He passed the paper and pencil to Lucas, who wrote, imitating the handwriting of his dead namesake as best he could: 'My predecessor believed in life after death, do you? P. Mitchell,' and returned the paper.

'Pay more attention to your up-and-down-strokes. The line of letters like l, t and h should be six not three minutes past the hour. Yes, I do. S.'

'It's this damn pencil. If you do, do you think he's interested in you and me?'

'You are not signing your name. The angle is better but the loop of the l and h should be longer and thinner. I think he might be. But I love my fatherland. S. And my good name.'

'This Philip Mitchell should live up to the other Philip Mitchell, you mean? But would he be where I am?'

Skorzeny read this and wrote 'Compare your writing with the notebook.'

Lucas took out Mitchell's notebook and opened it. He read, 'Every man likes the smell of his own farts. Icelandic Proverb.' He pointed this out to Skorzeny, who said, 'He uses two different sorts of s, one with a loop which follows on to the next letter, one like a printed s. Why?'

The stewardess came round, taking orders for drinks. Skorzeny chose a bottle of Münchener Löwenbräu, Lucas asked for cognac.

When they were brought, the stewardess opened the beer and placed the bottle and glass on the table before Skorzeny; but the brandy, a generous double, had already been poured. Looking across the gangway, Lucas saw that a man who had ordered schnapps had been given a miniature bottle.

Skorzeny raised his glass of beer. *'Prosit!'* Lucas clinked glasses with him, but did not drink. He held the glass to his nostrils and inhaled the aroma. It smelt good enough, but when he held it to the light, the spirit was curiously cloudy and in the bottom of the glass he saw white specks. He had never known spirits to be served on a plane except out of miniatures and he remembered Weissenfeld talking to the stewardess.

'You do not drink, Mr Mitchell?'

'I like my cognac straight.'

'You have not tasted it.'

'You try it.'

'I like beer better.'

Lucas pressed the bell for the stewardess. *'Bitte?'* she asked. 'Ask her to taste it,' Lucas said.

'You like beer too?' Skorzeny asked, ignoring the request.

'With the top off in front of me,' Lucas said.

When the stewardess had taken the brandy away, Skorzeny said. 'I think you are a man full of suspicions, Mr Mitchell.'

'I think I have every reason to be, Herr *Sturmbannführer*.'

'Why should we wish you ... ?' He broke off. 'In a civilian Junkers. You have an imagination, Mr Mitchell, remarkable for a tunnelling engineer.'

Lucas felt that his fears had given him a form of persecution mania. Over the Pyrenees he had another Löwenbrau, and four more before they touched down at Orly. It was only when he was going down the gangway that he felt squiffy. 'That beer, it seems so mild,' he said as Skorzeny relieved him of one of his suitcases and took his arm. 'But it must be very strong.'

'It is like the German people,' Skorzeny said.

'Gawd!' muttered Lucas. It was not the moment to listen to a homily on the master race. 'Where are we going?' Everybody else was walking towards the customs building.

'For us there is no need of these formalities.'

A black Citroën appeared from somewhere and stopped by them. Weissenfeld opened the rear door and Skorzeny helped Lucas in. Someone was sitting in the far corner. All Lucas registered was a pair of hornrimmed spectacles and thick pebble lenses which made the eyes bulge from their sockets.

'This is Dr Einzig,' Skorzeny said, getting in after Lucas.

'Vairy pleased to meet.' Dr Einzig grasped Lucas's hand and shook it, as if this was a pleasure to which he had been looking forward for years.

Lucas tried to take his hand away, feeling the greeting had lasted long enough. Dr Einzig was holding Lucas's right arm and at that moment his left arm was pinned by Skorzeny.

'What the hell ... ?' Lucas did not finish the protest because at that moment something was clamped over his mouth and nose, and his temples began to throb.

15 Liversedge Hall

Lucas opened his eyes. There were three long windows. Outside was half-light. Daybreak? Dusk? Big bed. Hard mattress, horsehair. Fucking big bolster, ditto. Raised himself on elbow. Strange room. Huge black wardrobe, dressing table, chest of drawers. Head weighed a ton. Throbbing. Throat parched. Toothglass of water by bedhead. Stretched out, drank, tepid, put glass down. Closed eyes. Veils of sleep fell, thin lace curtains stifling his yawns.

He heard the door open. A light was switched on. He lay in the bed with his back to the door. He kept his eyes closed.

Footsteps came closer. Somebody was bending over him. 'Mitchell!' Skorzeny said. 'Mitchell, wake up!'

Lucas lay like a log.

Skorzeny lifted Lucas's left eyelid. When he saw the eyeball rolled upwards, Skorzeny grunted. Then he slapped Lucas on the cheek.

Lucas moaned, but he did not open his eyes. He turned over, apparently in a deep sleep and lay with his back to Skorzeny.

'Gott in Himmel!' Skorzeny muttered and walked quickly out of the room. He was scared.

He had not turned out the light. Lucas looked at the date on his watch. It was 20 May. It had been 17 May when they touched down at Orly. They'd kept him out for three days. He closed his eyes, but his mind was alert. If Skorzeny wanted to use him, he would have to nurse him back into tip-top condition.

Then Skorzeny came back with someone else to whom he was talking in German angrily. The other person tried to calm him down, or so it sounded.

Lucas was turned on his back. He wondered whether he should turn his eyes up if they tried to examine him, but decided against it. Instead, he opened his eyes of his own accord and stared fixedly at the man who was sitting on his bed. It was Dr Einzig. 'Who are you?' asked Lucas.

'Calm yourself, please,' the doctor said. 'How do you feel?'

'Who are you? What's wrong with your eyes. You look mad.' Then he turned to Skorzeny who came forward. 'Hullo. Who's this mad chap, sitting on my bed.' Lucas looked round the room. 'Or is it his bed?'

The doctor felt Lucas's pulse, while Skorzeny said he ought to apologize, or rather to explain, the unconventional way in which it had been necessary to bring Mitchell to this place. There were good security reasons why mere blindfolding would not have been enough. 'I do not need to tell you that you are now in the Irish Free State. Exactly where is not your concern. When you start on your mission, you will be blindfolded for a certain distance. But I can assure you that there will be no need to render you unconscious.'

The doctor was exploring Lucas's chest hair with his stethoscope. 'For Chrissake,' Lucas said, 'if you want to listen anywhere, stick it on my belly. It's rumbling.'

Dr Einzig discontinued his examination. 'Already,' he announced, 'we are in rude health.'

It was too late for a cooked meal but Lucas, who insisted that he was too weak for conversation, managed to wash down three cold sausages, two thick slices of home-cured ham, a hunk of home-baked bread and some matured Irish cheddar with the aid of a pint of Guinness.

As he did so, he tried to figure out what sort of a person could have furnished the room in which he found himself. Judging by the proportions of the room, it was part of an eighteenth-century mansion. The size and number of the windows confirmed this. But there was no elaborate plasterwork on the ceiling or in the cornices. They were modern and so was the wallpaper, ornate but not impressive. The marble fireplace was original, but it was discoloured by fire. The penny dropped. It was obviously one of those gracious homes built by the Anglo-Irish gentry; burned during the troubles and now refurbished by some Irish *nouveau riche*. And perhaps not so *riche* as all that, because the furniture, made for large rooms, was the sort of massive junk knocked down at auctions for a song because it was so unwieldy that the modestly affluent could not house it in their modern rooms, and so hideous that no one with large mansions would want it. The Turkish carpet was good of its kind, but not a kind in fashion. Apart from the ebony bedroom suite, there was an American varnished oak rolltop desk, an engraving of 'The Monarch of the Glen' and a stuffed bear. All of which was pretty useless info, but it showed Lucas that he was not so dopey that he couldn't use his eyes and nut. He prised up the edge of the carpet. The floorboards were modern; but they were oak! And to judge by old nail-holes, secondhand. What was the betting that the *nouveau riche* was a building contractor? If he was pro-Nazi, he was probably a member of the IRA; but if he had made a pile of money, he must be a secret member – working on contracts not only for the Eireann government but also perhaps for the UK. One of the contractors for whom Philip Mitchell was supposed to have been working since 1939?

The effects of the drug had not worn off. He went back to bed as soon as he had eaten and fell asleep at once.

It was early dawn when he awoke. He felt a new man as he walked over to the windows. The sky was overcast with milky grey clouds and from the ground below a steamy mist was rising. No sun shone but in the east there was a silvery sheen.

He raised one of the windows and immediately he could hear, like the roar of hungry lions, what must be waves breaking on rocks. But he could see nothing because on the far side of the misty lawns and terraces, there loomed a barrier of trees. Apart from the din of distant breakers, the only sound was the dawn chorus – the cooing of pigeons, the clear song of blackbirds, a cuckoo calling.

To the right there was a line of low buildings, the stables probably, broken in the middle by large double gates. Immediately below, leading from the terrace towards the far woodland was a flagged promenade, flanked by balustrades with plinths set at intervals, on which had once stood statues, or classical urns containing flowers perhaps, but now nothing. Halfway to the wood the promenade broadened into a circle, from which similar promenades branched off at right-angles, one towards the gates in the stable walls, the other leading towards an impenetrable pool of mist. At the far end appeared a miniature temple, a garden refuge in the classical style. There was no sign of human life; the whole place seemed abandoned to weeds.

Lucas went to the door of his bedroom. It had been locked from the outside. Inside were heavy bolts at top and bottom. He slid them home. He slipped on trousers, a shirt and pullover and chose Mitchell's lightest shoes with crepe soles. He examined his belt. The money was still in the zip pocket. He did not intend more than a recce, but to be on the safe side he put Mitchell's passport in his hip pocket.

To the left of the window there was an old wisteria, a huge twisted vegetable rope just within reach, but growing so close to the wall that it would be hard to get one's fingers round it. He took Mitchell's thick working gloves and chose only the right-hand one. There were side-shoots on the wisteria where a bare hand could get a better grasp. The bugger would be getting out of the window and transferring one's full weight on to the vine.

Then he saw that higher up, where a sort of plinth ran round the building, the wisteria bulged outwards and gave an initial handhold. If only he could get outside and stand on the window-sill, he could reach up to it. The sill was pretty wide. But how to stand up on the sill without falling backwards? It was impossible.

If he tore up the sheets and knotted them, they would adver-tise his escape to the first person who went into the grounds or looked over from the stable block. He tried the upper window. It moved easily. But even standing on the bedside commode, though he could reach up to the gap between the plinth and the wisteria, he could not pull himself up by his arms and swing his body outside without smashing panes of glass, which would alert anyone sleeping close.

Then he remembered that there was a belt among Philip Mitchell's things. He fixed it round the wisteria and inserted the latchet pin in the last hole. It held his weight, even when he tugged. He pushed it outside, lifted both the windows and leaned out. He could reach it without difficulty. Within a minute, he was standing on the overgrown terrace, his back against the wall between two windows.

Either side of the main promenade leading to the classical temple were flights of stairs. He ran across the terrace and down the left-hand flight. From there he could move under cover of the terrace, unseen from the main house or the stables.

The dew had been heavy. By the time he reached the end of the terrace, his shoes, socks and trouser cuffs were sopping. But the sun was beginning to penetrate the cloud, like melting but-ter. He was standing at the south-east corner of the house. To the north-east the entrance drive was marked by an avenue of enormous elms. That way, there could be no hope of escape. The lodge gates would certainly be guarded and ten to one there would be a high wall, built to keep the peasantry beyond the pale and now reinforced with wire, barbed or electrified. More promising was a grassy walk between two broad beds of perennials flanked by pergola roses. He walked alongside one of the pergolas. That way he would be less conspicuous, and it would seem from his leisurely pace that he was just going for an early-morning stroll.

When he looked back, he saw smoke rising from a chimney at the far end of the main building. The cook, he guessed, had lit the stove or boiler. But there was no other sign of life.

The grassy walk ended at a green door in an old red-brick wall. Above the wall, he saw fruit trees in blossom. He tried the handle. It was locked. Unlikely that there would be another door to an orchard. He walked down the wall in the direction of the wood. When the wall ended, a tall yew hedge took its place. Or rather it should have been a hedge, but it hadn't been trimmed and was running ragged. When he came to a gap, he went in and found that it was the beginning of a maze, with passages running to left and right.

There was no point in going further, because the whole object of a maze was to reach the centre and then to find your way out again.

It was rapidly getting lighter and the mist merely lay on the ground knee deep. He could see clearly across to the house and stables and be as clearly seen. He ought to get back if he was to climb into his room without being discovered. But before he did so, he wanted to explore the wood, the fringes of which were massive rhododendrons with evergreen holm oaks, bare ashes, beech and elm in young leaf all behind. He quickened his pace.

But before he reached the rhododendrons, a voice bellowed across the park. Lucas stopped; by the gates of the stable block, he saw two men waving.

He began to walk towards them but, when he had gone a few yards, he saw two great hounds streaking from the stables towards him, leaping and bounding and baying as they came. The men just stood still.

Lucas turned and ran for the wood. He found a path between the rhododendrons, but suddenly it gave out. The bushes hadn't been pruned for years. The long, rope-like branches were meshed like a huge net. He turned his back and shoved himself against them so hard that when they fell away, he was on his back. As he pushed himself up, his right hand caught on a thick dead bramble which stabbed his palm and the ball of his thumb. More brambles tore at his trousers, the mesh of his pullover, one cheek.

He could hear the baying hounds getting nearer. A clearing with only dead ferns gave a moment's respite. But the hounds were in the wood now. He could hear them crashing through the undergrowth. There was a stake, lying by a fallen oak, the outer wood rotted away, leaving a rock-hard core, a jagged spike end. He picked it up. No good against two hounds, except for a moment.

The leader, an Irish wolfhound, burst into the clearing. He looked round. There was a beech tree, a network of branches, easy to climb. He dashed towards it, but the leading hound was gaining on him. There was no time to climb.

He turned at the foot of the beech. The great hound leapt at him, jaws open. Lucas held the oak spike like a sword. The hound's impetus jerked it from Lucas's hand; but the spiked end had thrust down the beast's gullet and stuck there.

Lucas caught hold of a branch, swung himself up. The second hound leapt. He reached as high as Lucas's foot, would have taken it off at the ankle if his jaws had met. But the toe of Lucas's shoe caught the hound in the throat and he fell back on his fellow.

Lucas climbed and climbed.

He was tree'd, but for the moment safe.

Lucas remained up the tree for over an hour. After the first ten minutes, he regained his cool. Neither of the Irish wolfhounds tried to climb up after him, though the tree was so easy to climb that it was possible that even the wounded one could have succeeded. They had obviously been trained, and instructed, to pin their man. Hence the delay in any attempt to rescue Lucas. The hounds had been set on him to teach him a lesson. As he smoked a cigarette, Lucas settled down to draw his own conclusions. It was a mistake for them to leave him plenty of time to prepare himself.

Three men eventually made their way to the tree. The handler was a jockey-sized chap whose riding breeches emphasized his bandy legs. He swore when the wounded hound loped over with tail between its legs. 'Fucky nell,' he said, opening the beast's jaws, wiping the bloody slaver from its chops. 'You bastard!' he shouted up at Lucas.

'I didn't do anything,' called Lucas. 'It tried to swallow a stake instead of me.' He lighted another cigarette from the stub he had been smoking, but made no effort to come down.

The other two men stood at the foot of the tree. One was a tall, heavy fellow with the squashed nose and cauliflower ears of an ex-pug. His cord trousers were tucked into wellingtons and he had a dirty white pullover. His name, Lucas later learnt, was Macdonald. The other man, whose name was Dacey, was the boss. A shorty beside Macdonald, Dacey made up in authority what he lacked in inches. He looked like a cavalry officer, with his twill riding breeches and nigger-brown hacking jacket. 'Wouldn't you like some breakfast?' he called. The accent was Irish, overlaid on something, perhaps German.

'Will you send it up?' Lucas asked, 'or would you prefer to take those bloody ratcatchers away?'

At a word from Dacey, the handler called the hounds, put them on leash and walked them off.

'Sorry about the hound,' Lucas said, when he reached the ground, 'but he was asking for it.'

'You, too,' Dacey said.

'Because I went for an early morning walk?'

'The door was locked.'

'If it had been open, I wouldn't've had to climb out.'

'It was for your own good. You wouldn't want electrocution. So I'm warning. Don't try again.'

'That's a true word,' Macdonald said. 'No one gets out of Liversedge Hall, except the Boss says so.'

'And you keep your plug-ugly trap shut,' snapped Dacey.

They made their way back to the house, Macdonald leading, Dacey bringing up the rear. It was becoming a sort of drill; Dr Langer and Weissenfeld conducting him into the Ibero-Suíço bank, Skorzeny and Weissenfeld into Lisbon airport.

When they reached the terrace, Dacey marched ahead and

halted at the foot of the wisteria. 'You will want,' he said, surveying Lucas from tangled hair to sodden shoes, 'to change before breakfast.'

'It might be nice.'

'Then you will have to climb up to your room the same way you climbed down.'

There was only one thing which Lucas disliked more than discipline for discipline's sake and that was sadism for disciplinarians' enjoyment. 'Send plug-ugly for a ladder,' Lucas said.

Dacey's mouth twitched. 'I say, you climb.'

Lucas turned and tried the door at the head of the terrace. Luckily, it opened. He went through what must have been originally a ballroom into the great front hall. There was no one to be seen, but standing on a large Victorian table with oedematous legs was a pair of teak Burmese dancers, supporting between them a bronze gong. He took the striker that hung from one of the dancer's wrists and sent out three echoing booms.

In a moment a nice slatternly-looking girl with ginger hair and freckles appeared, wiping her hands on a grubby apron. 'Was it you boomed?' she asked.

'Yes, dear,' Lucas said. 'I'm hungry.'

The girl looked at Lucas's dishevelled clothes. 'You jest wait here,' she said, 'I'll be asking Sir John.' She went into another room, closing the door behind her. There was a mumble of voices and then she returned and said, 'You're to come in.'

Sitting in a straightbacked armchair at the head of the table was a red-faced chap with a shiny black cowlick of hair over his forehead. He wore braces and his striped flannel shirtsleeves were rolled up to the elbows. His hairy forearms were tattooed, the left with a mermaid, the right with a merman. His mouth was full and in front of him was a plate of black tripe. He waved Lucas to a chair at the table beside him. When he had washed his food down with a draught of Guinness, he said, 'You'd be Mitchell, I s'pose. Proper muck-sweat, you're in.'

When Lucas tried to apologize, his explanations were swept aside. 'Connell's my name. *Sir* John Connell. What's that for a laugh? For "services rendered to the construction industry". Like tripe?'

'No.'

'Good. I told Kitty to do you a pork chop with kidney in. You know you're working for me now?'

'Not with Dacey and Macdonald?'

'They're the Major's boyos,' Connell said. 'No, I'm loaning you to some old pals of mine in London. Maybe you know them. Holiday & Greenwood, maintenance engineers. Hibbert's the man you'll be dealing with. Holiday's dead; and Greenwood's what you might call a sleeping partner, sleeping it off when he's not pouring it down.'

'Skorzeny knows about this?'

'The Major? Sure. It's to oblige him, as well as helping Hibbert out. Just for a couple of weeks or so. It seems his foreman's dad in Dunnamaggan is dying of the crab and he wants to see the old man before he goes.'

'Tunnelling?'

'From what I gather Holiday & Greenwood do maintenance for the London underground. Their own lads are in the forces, but Hibbert draws on Irish labour. I'm one of his recruiting agents, as you might say. One of me side-lines.' He winked. 'I scratch your back, you scratch mine. That's Connell's motto.'

'Well, if I scratch your back, Sir John,' Lucas said, 'could you get one of your men to climb up a ladder into my bedroom and unbolt the door.'

Sir John looked surprised, but he didn't look more surprised when Lucas told him about being tree'd by the wolfhounds. 'Let that be a lesson for you, Mitchell. Ireland's a terrible country for prying and snooping. No privacy. Mind where you go. It's not just the live-wire – which would make your hair stand on end if I told you what it cost – but it's the man-traps, the hounds, the trip-wires. If you've complaints to make about Dacey, speak to the Major. But here comes Kitty with your breakfast; and if you'll pardon me, I'll get one of my boyos to open your room.'

16 Progress Report Two

London

Major J. Embleton, DODS 21. v. '44

In accordance with your instructions, I will try to resist my temptation to novelize. I arrange my report under heads.

Personnel

At the time DODS was set up, high priority was given to staff. Since then, there has been dilution. Of the original team only Sir Hilary, his personal assistant Lady Virginia and the technical expert Mr Bernard Nightingale survive. The original 2-ic was recalled to his regiment for more active service. His replacement, Mr Constantine, is frankly a placeholder. He held some minor diplomatic post in France up to the time of the Fall. He is violently anti-Soviet; some of his best friends in France were Nazis. He frankly told me that he thought it was a great mistake not to negotiate peace through Hess when he landed in Scotland. As deputy director of DODS, he is no more use than as a signatory of letters. But I do not believe that he is a security risk. If he had been pulling his weight, there would have been no need to second me to DODS. But to discharge him at the present moment would be to give him an excuse for opening his silly mouth to Mrs Constantine, who might indulge in careless talk, if her husband was suddenly out of a job. My policy, if you approve, is to give him the routine business which DODS has been carrying on since 1940 as a means of keeping him out of the way.

Lieut Hampshire is a nice young shipping clerk in uniform. His chief interest in his job is that it enables him to live nearby in Great Smith Street with a pretty redhead from the Ministry of Economic Warfare whom he has just married. He could be useful on the actual day of the operation, but meanwhile I propose to shunt him off into the Constantine siding in order to clear the main line. But he can also be responsible for observing the security procedures I have instituted. I won't burden you with these, but I assure you that no one will be able to walk in as I did the other day. Our friend Ken vetted them for me and approves.

From Hampshire I gathered, after much pestering, that none of the staff, administrative, secretarial or cleaning, had been referred by him for security clearance. I attach a list of their names and addresses for your attention. This ought to have been done before they were engaged. It is for you to judge whether it can be done satisfactorily in the time available. The original date for Serpent has had to be abandoned, but it's a choice of very soon or never. The latter, if the Chiefs of Staff get their way.

Reading over what I've just typed, I see that I have included under Personnel most of what I mean to put in my second section.

Security Precautions

I found that the wastepaper bins contained a great deal of material which in any decent outfit would have been shredded. When I pointed this out to Sir Hilary, he said that shredders were in short supply. Lady Virginia volunteered to undertake the responsibility of collecting all Top Secret bumph and either flushing it down the ladies loo or locking it away in a filing cabinet until after the completion of the operation. She has *noblesse oblige*. When I joined DODS, my bourgeois instincts made me distrust her aristocratic presumptions to authority. But each day I recognize more clearly that without her DODS would have ground to a halt years ago. I think she welcomes my assistance as much as I do hers.

Modus Operandi

As soon as I had studied the proposed Operation, I realized that the only chance of executing it was by slimming it so that there was no need to call on services pre-empted by SHAEF. Number Ten had laid on the service personnel at the docks to cope with the onloading and transhipment. Our problems were confined to loading from the NL Warehouse and transport. Luckily C., who was at school with me, is working at the Min of Transport. His passion in life, like Bernard Nightingale's, is playing with trains. He is bored to tears with the paperwork in his office. He was the only person I could think of who could lay on the packers and loaders we needed to assist the skeleton maintenance staff.

You would have been amused at the evening which I spent with him and Nightingale at my flat, working things out. Talk of tact and diplomacy! Here was I, trying to reconcile Bernard Nightingale, who (believe it or not) had worked out this complicated operation on his model railway in the attic of his house in Foot's Cray, with C. (who had the means of putting it into operation) but would only do so if he could operate the controls! I thought of SHAEF, of Eisenhower and Montgomery. Why not C. in supreme command,

I suggested finally, with B.N. as his second in command? And so it has been agreed.

Forgive me. I have ended by novelizing again.

17 General Ballsup

Liversedge Hall

As he was finishing his breakfast, Lucas was summoned by Macdonald to see 'the Boss', who proved to be Skorzeny. The *Sturmbannführer* was in the library, the shelves of which had been filled with complete sets of the novels of Sir Walter Scott, Dickens, Thackeray, George Eliot and other space fillers. 'So!' he said. 'You have already begun to take your exercise. That is good. You must be fit, strong.' Skorzeny did a hands-on-hips, knees-bend. 'Dacey will take you for training.'

'I don't like Dacey,' Lucas said.

'You don't have to like Dacey. Enough you obey him.'

'Connell says I am working for a man called Hibbert in London; and I'm one of his boyos, but Dacey's one of yours.'

'You will see when the time comes. Now please sign your name.' He pointed to pen and paper on a desk.

Lucas sat down and wrote his name as Philip Mitchell.

Skorzeny looked at it. '*Schrecklich!* You must do better.' He tore the paper into four bits and dropped it in the wastepaper basket.

'Isn't it time you told me what the job is? All I know is I'm deputizing for a foreman whose old man is dying.'

'Later I will brief you. First become Philip Mitchell, strong.'

'If I do, will you keep those hounds off me? I signed on as a tunnelling engineer, not a dog's dinner.'

'I think you have learnt your lesson. You may go now.'

'One moment, one thing hasn't been discussed. When I've finished this job, whatever it may be, from whom do I collect the other halves of those 1,000-dollar notes?'

Skorzeny lit a cigarette. 'You must take my word. You will be paid.'

'By you?'

Skorzeny exhaled. 'By me.'

'Then you have them here. I want to see them.'

'And if I say no?'

'No job.'

'Things could be for you ...' he shrugged, 'not nice!'

'I believe in you, Herr *Sturmbannführer*. You will guard my life, as if it was your own. Until the job's done. But those half-notes are still in Dr Langer's safe in Lisbon, aren't they?'

'By an oversight ...'

'Then they must be brought here.'

'And how would you suggest ... when there is no time?'

'To a man who brought me all the way from Kimberley, that should be easy.'

'How?'

'In Lisbon you gave instructions to a Swedish lady to entertain me ...'

'Which she did to your satisfaction, eh?'

'There are planes from Lisbon to Dublin. Instruct Dr Langer to give the money to Miss Carlson. She can bring them here; or show them to me in Dublin. In the German Embassy, if you like. But I demand to see the dough, before I go to London.'

Skorzeny smiled. 'You do not, I hope, cherish romantic illusions for a young lady who has received the silver *Hackenkreuz* with Oak Leaves for erotic services rendered?'

'If you prefer another courier, that's up to you. Perhaps Dr Langer himself could be spared ...'

'A gambler should not overplay his hand, Mr Mitchell.'

'He can't,' Lucas answered, 'when he's nothing to lose but his life; and will probably lose that anyway.'

Skorzeny stubbed out his cigarette. Lucas felt very calm. From the moment he had made his will in the Ibero-Suíço bank, he had given his life in pawn. He did not expect ever to redeem it. Weak as he was, he needn't fear Skorzeny. Not until the mission was accomplished.

Skorzeny kept driving his right fist into the palm of his left hand, over and over again. He opened his mouth to speak and then he closed it again.

There was a discreet tap on the door. *'Hineinkommen!'*

They both turned towards the door as a man, wearing blue serge trousers and a navy-blue sleeveless pullover, came in with an envelope, which he handed to Skorzeny. The *Sturmbann-führer* took it over to the desk, tore it open and read the contents. 'So!'

The messenger stood at attention. On his biceps was tattooed 'IRMA' and on his triceps a swastika.

'Perhaps, Mr Mitchell – I do not promise – but something may be arranged. Please, now go to your room and practise writing. Dacey will take you for exercises later.'

As Lucas left, he wondered what there could have been on that paper which made Scarface seem to change his mind.

When the door closed, Skorzeny re-read the cypher from London, received 11.03, decoded 11.24. 'SERPENT DELAYED COMMA PERHAPS SCOTCHED COMMA BY GENERAL BALLSUP STOP HOLD HONEYCOMB TILL FURTHER NOTICE STOP RAINBOW.' Then he sat down and wrote out two cablegrams. The first was to Dr Langer with instructions to send Carlson airborne German Embassy Dublinwards soonest with all half-notes. The second was to Rainbow, London: 'WHO IS BALLSUP QUERY'.

18 At the White House

'It's awfully decent of you, John, to drop in,' said Lady Virginia. 'Now what'll you have?' Her one-roomed flat in the White House, thought Embleton, had been furnished throughout by Heal's in Tottenham Court Road, in predictably good taste. But the cupboard that she opened revealed an array of bottles undreamed of in the fourth year of the war. 'What *haven't* you got?' he asked.

'I *am* rather lucky.' She looked at him mischievously. 'But when there's room in a diplomatic bag – who am I to complain if an old friend pops in a bottle?' She held up a bottle of Keo Brandy. 'It's Cypriot; but as Patrick says – forget about cognac, and it goes down well with ice.'

'Thank you, Lady Virginia.' It was obviously what she intended to give him, though Embleton would have preferred the Canadian Club, Glenlivet or Gordon's gin he could see in the cupboard.

'Call me Ginny, please!' She poured half a tumbler and topped it up with ice. She was equally generous to herself and they raised glasses.

Embleton waited for his hostess to disclose the purpose of an invitation which was clearly confidential. She seemed to have no hesitation in coming straight to the point. 'I want to say how glad I am you've joined us, John. I don't mind admitting I was getting pretty desperate.'

He just nodded.

She opened a silver box, with Chesterfield cigarettes in one half and Passing Cloud in the other. When they had lighted up, she asked, 'What do *you* think? Will it come off? Or will it go on being shelved?'

'Your guess is as good as mine.' Embleton sipped his brandy. Whoever Patrick was, he was right to say – forget about cognac. 'I can imagine other things taking higher priority. Does it really matter?' It was a question he was in fact asking himself, but he repeated it to Ginny. 'Does it? Will it make two pennyworth of difference to the outcome of this war?'

She returned his gaze for a moment, then she turned away. 'No. No, I suppose it won't.'

'Then why worry?'

'I don't know, really. Perhaps it's Bodgers. And Mr Nightingale. All the years they've put in, the planning.' She smiled at Embleton. 'You must think me a sentimentalist.'

19 Operation Honeycomb

Four days passed in general training. Before breakfast every morning, Dacey, Macdonald and a man called O'Leary took Lucas for a run round the park. After a hefty breakfast, Lucas had a session with Skorzeny, going over his handwriting and details of Mitchell's career. Then an hour in the gym, which had been rigged up in what had been one of the main assembly rooms with horse, ropes, parallel bars, the medicine ball. A hefty lunch and more study of Mitchell's lifestyle, while the others, from the sound of firing, were having target practice; then an hour of physical training and so on.

Though Lucas learned to work with the other three men, he remained an outsider, the one member of the team who was not fully trusted. Though he spent hours with Skorzeny, Lucas got no nearer to finding out whether his demand for the missing halves of his bank-notes would be conceded, or what would be his mission in London. 'Later,' was all Skorzeny would say. 'All in good time.'

Then, presumably because the OK had come through from Lisbon, Skorzeny greeted him with a smile after breakfast on the fourth day. There was good news. Lucas would meet Miss Carlson in Dublin next day with the half-notes. He could set his mind at rest and give all his attention to Honeycomb, his mission in London.

'As you know,' said Skorzeny, 'the enemy are planning an invasion of the French coast across the Channel. This has been forced upon them by the Führer's strategic withdrawal on the

Eastern front. The German High Command plan to allow the enemy expeditionary force to land on French soil and then cut them off from their English bases and use their invasion barges for our counter-invasion.

'British Intelligence has discovered our vast installations of secret weapons – hidden along the French coast – which will paralyse the enemy's strategic centres, lay waste their cities, immobilize their ports and regain for the Third Reich the supremacy of the air.

'Anticipating the defeat of their invasion, the Anglo-Americans have contingency plans for the evacuation of the British Isles and the transfer of the seat of government across the Atlantic. The first phase of this withdrawal consists in transporting bullion, gems and art-treasures to the safety of the Dominion of Canada, in order to avoid these falling into our hands ...'

Lucas could not prevent the flicker of a sceptical smile. Skorzeny noticed it. 'You are wondering what this has to do with your going to work for Holiday & Greenwood? Let me show you.'

He went over to a wall and drew down what looked like a blind cord. It revealed a map of London on the scale of twenty-four inches to the mile. It covered St Pancras to the north, St James's Park to the west, London Bridge to the south and the King George V dock to the east. Certain landmarks were emphasized by heavy lines. There was the War Office, the Admiralty and, close-by, a round building unfamiliar to Lucas, which Skorzeny explained was the Mall HQ, built since 1939, reinforced to withstand a direct hit by a 1,000-pound bomb. Beneath it, Skorzeny explained, was among other things the control room of the underground railway connecting the north London warehouse at St Pancras with the King George V dock, where the treasure trains were to be offloaded for transport to Canada. A key point in this railway system was the Tower Hill junction where the railway line from the Mall HQ station split into two, the southern branch ending at St Katharine's dock. 'Your task,' he said, 'will be to hijack the train between the Mall HQ and divert it to St Katharine's dock.'

'And how precisely do I do that?'

Skorzeny turned to the bottom left-hand corner of the chart.

This was an enlargement of the underground railway lines and station at Monument. 'Holiday & Greenwood are contracted for the maintenance of the London Underground,' he said. 'If you go fifty metres up the number two tunnel running east to Tower Hill, you see that the tunnel casing is very close, some two or three metres from this main drain, the Belmouth outflow. A hole blown in the tunnel casing gives you, and your party, access to the drain and sewerage system running beneath the whole of London. By using ventilation shafts and laterals you can reach a grille in the tunnel of the military Underground only eighty metres from the east end of the Mall HQ platform.'

'How?'

'Later, I will show you. Now,' Skorzeny pointed to the top left-hand corner of the map, where there was another enlarged diagram and also an architectural elevation of the Mall control room. 'The trains are operated electrically and controlled automatically by the operator of the panel in the Mall station. You will enter to the south-east of the station, but you will have to walk along the west platform, keeping close to the wall which is out of observation from the control room. In the north-west, here, you see there is a siding in which is kept a diesel-driven maintenance engine. You and one of the others will man this engine and wait until the first treasure train has passed through. (You can start it up while the train is going past, so that the noise will be inaudible in the control room.) Then, you give – shall we say? – five minutes for the train to approach the Tower Hill junction, before you drive the maintenance engine through the Mall station . . .'

'And what happens when they start shooting us up?'

'A moment, please. Before you go to the station . . . in fact immediately after you have entered the military Underground through the grille, you will lay a charge large enough to block the tunnel after the maintenance engine has taken you past it . . .'

Lucas opened his mouth, but Skorzeny held up his hand.

'*Also*, before you drive the maintenance engine out of the siding, you will have started smoke bombs. In this way, they will not see you clearly from the control room as you pass through. But if they do not see you at all, they will see the smoke later. It is important that they should cut off the electric current, so that you can change the points to push the train into the St Katharine's branch, using the diesel engine.'

'You make it sound too easy. How d'you know that there won't be an armed guard on the train, for example?'

'We have full details of Operation Serpent on microfilm. Skorzeny is daring, but he is not a bloody fool.'

'Well, I want to see it. Then I'll draw up a list of further questions and tell you what my requirements are. What about this route from Monument to the Mall?'

'You sound as if you have at least a professional interest.'

'I'm interested in surviving.'

'Come over here then.' Skorzeny went to his desk, where there was a replica of the Mall to Monument section, showing only the subterranean strata of railways, drains, sewers, shafts and laterals. Drains discharged themselves into the Thames by the nearest route, he explained, sewers ran into the main sewerage outflow, ending on the north bank of the Thames at Barking; so the direction of their flow was eastward. Over this subterranean map he placed a celluloid rectangle on which he had marked in chinagraph pencil his suggested route from Monument to the Mall, showing ascents, descents and horizontals by different colours. 'What do you say, Mitchell?'

'If you want a snap judgement,' Lucas said, 'I'd say you're crazy. Have you been over the ground? Have you any idea how long it would take? Are there any grilles or doors not marked on this map? You've mapped this out like snakes and ladders.'

Skorzeny was puzzled. Ladders, yes. Rats, perhaps. But not snakes.

'How do I blow a hole from Monument tunnel into a sewer?'

'*You* do not blow the hole. You lay the charge.' He sighed. 'I will get Kitty to bring us some good Irish Guinness, yes?'

He came back and snapped up the wall map. 'Dr Goebbels does not drink or smoke. But to my mind alcohol is to a man as petroleum to a Volkswagen.' He opened a packet of Sweet Afton and they both lit up. Tension relaxed between them. Lucas asked how many besides himself would be in the hijack team.

There were only three, Sean Dacey, Macdonald and the man called O'Leary, who had been with them on their physical training. Dacey was OC Tunnel Detail. O'Leary had had experience as an engine driver. Macdonald was an electrician. Only Dacey had worked underground, training in the sewers of Berlin. But the other two had had experience in cavework. All three were good marksmen and first class at unarmed combat.

At this point Kitty brought in a great earthenware crock of draught Guinness with two pewter tankards (one, Lucas noted, from Mooney's, the other from the Ballybunion Arms). 'Thank you, Kitty,' Skorzeny said. 'We only asked because we wanted to see your pretty face.'

'Pardon?' the girl said. When Skorzeny explained, she blushed with pleasure or embarrassment, and edged awkwardly out. Skorzeny poured a Guinness which was nearly all froth and handed it to Lucas.

'Yours,' Lucas said politely and taking the jug poured himself a generous measure by holding the tankard nearly at right angles to start with. 'Prosit!' he said.

'Prosit!' Skorzeny's large nose emerged covered in froth.

'If *I* don't blow the hole in the Monument tunnel, who does it for us?'

'The Germans and the English in cooperation,' Skorzeny said, having wiped his nose. 'With your men from Holiday & Greenwood, you inspect the tunnels. You take the number two tunnel running towards Tower Hill station, working on your own.' He pulled down the map again to demonstrate. 'You place here a charge which will blow an entry into the Belmouth outflow. Then you go back forty metres and place another charge in the roof of the tunnel, heavy enough to bring down the roof and conceal the debris caused by the other explosion. The detonators of both these charges you connect with wires to the air-raid siren on the railway platform, which you will find placed here.' Skorzeny marked the position with a cross. 'Then you report that you have found a serious fracture, which cannot be repaired immediately, but will be dealt with as soon as possible. You arrange to return later. But during the night, before Operation Serpent, there is a German air raid on London. An alert is sounded. The siren in Monument station detonates both the charges. You drive to Monument station. There you are joined by Dacey, Macdonald and O'Leary. You are all wearing respirators, for fear of escaping gas. They will be able to go down as members of your maintenance gang. You climb over the debris of the fallen roof, make your way into the Belmouth outflow, unpack weapons and begin the operation.'

'Just like that?'

'Perhaps not just like, Mr Mitchell. This plan I have discussed with military and engineering colleagues. But your expert advice ... this might modify—'

'What's the thickness and tensile strength of the tunnel casing at Monument?'

'Of that we are not sure.'

'So how the fucking hell do I know what charges to lay?' Lucas smashed his fist on the table.

Skorzeny took a draught of Guinness, a pull at his cigarette. Then he said, 'In your position, you know what I would do? Go back to Monument station, report the defect and ask the thickness and tensile strength of the casing. Then I would lay the charges appropriate. Remember your cover story, Mitchell. You are replacing a foreman who has gone to visit his dying father. What other questions?'

'God knows. I've got to think it through. It'll take time.'

'You have reason. Take the map on my desk and the chinagraph to your room. Study it.' He went to the desk and opened a drawer. 'Here is a list of equipment which we consider necessary. It is in German, but there is an English translation. I hope it is accurate. If not, I can explain.'

Lucas took the map and documents. Here was something definite to work on: and work against. 'How long can I take?'

'Tomorrow morning. At ten hours. With Dacey.'

'Not the others?' By raising doubts, Lucas might demoralize O'Leary and Macdonald. 'Ought they not to be in the picture?'

'*Their part* of the picture: that is enough.'

Skorzeny was quite right. When Lucas took all the papers back to his room, he felt a professional interest in what Skorzeny had told him. He knew the possibility of nuclear explosives. When the British had blown up the heavy-water plants on the Lofoten Islands, they had been trying to destroy the Nazi nuclear experiments. Had they succeeded, or had Hitler evolved some sort of atom bomb which would wipe out the supply bases in Britain when the Anglo-American invasion forces had landed in France? It wasn't implausible.

Whatever happened, Lucas had to examine operations Serpent and Honeycomb very carefully to discover their respective flaws. The British had obviously worked their plan out carefully; but probably without any idea that it might be sabotaged in London. Their fear would be that a security leakage could lead to submarine attack on the treasure ship. Lucas concentrated on the practicalities of the hijack plan: personnel, equipment, loads, timings, routes. It was not easy for a tunnelling engineer, trained to military sapping and graduated to diamond mining, to visualize what was involved in Honeycomb. And, to distract him, came thoughts of Grete. Had she been told that she would fly to Dublin? Was all that had happened in the Palacio do Sonho an illusion?

When he looked up from his calculations, he saw Skorzeny walking with Dacey down the promenade towards the classical temple. From their gestures, they appeared to be arguing heatedly. He went to the window and opened it quietly. He could not hear what they were saying, but it sounded as if they were talking in German.

'Why ask the Englander?' Dacey was saying. 'Our own experts have checked and counterchecked. Suppose he makes objections, can we trust him? Money is all he is interested in.'

'Like any mercenary?' Skorzeny smiled, condescendingly. 'But like any mercenary, he wishes to survive. What he has to say, up till the changing of the points at Tower Hill, *could* be useful. Remember, he wants to see his mother. So he will go to London. Once there, he will have to continue. For reasons we have agreed. So! Even if what he tells us does not help the operation, it will show us how to handle him.'

They passed the classical temple and disappeared into the wood. When Lucas lost sight of them, he returned to his calculations. He had to shake their confidence. Demand more men, more time; or less equipment, fewer complications. Examine the pitfalls.

'I cannot like this Mitchell,' grumbled Dacey. 'Against him I feel like a terrier with a rat.'

'Feel like a cat with a mouse,' Skorzeny said. 'It plays with it as long as may be, but it does not let the mouse escape in the end.'

'I will try,' said Dacey, 'but I do not feel very playful. And he is no defenceless mouse.'

Out of the corner of his eye, Lucas saw to the far left the figures of Skorzeny and Dacey emerge quickly from the wood and then vanish into the entrance of the maze.

Dacey went ahead and made his way without hesitation – left, right, second left, straight on, third right. 'You seem to know the way by instinct, Hans.'

Dacey stopped at a turning. 'I use my eyes, Herr *Sturmbannführer*.' The maze was made of trimmed yew. Dacey pointed to three red yew berries. Skorzeny squeezed them. They were glass. 'I shall remember on my way back.'

At the centre of the maze was a clearing about twenty-five feet in diameter containing what looked like a round gardener's shed, with small and dirty cobwebbed windows and a heavy door with large hinges and a massive lock.

Dacey opened the door with an outsize key and switched on a forty-watt electric light. Then he bent down, pulled aside a bundle of old sacks, caught hold of a ring and lifted up a trap door. He switched on another light just beneath the trapdoor revealing a new and solidly made flight of steps. The steps had been renovated by Sir John Connell, but the maze and the passage leading to the smugglers' cave were the work of Roger Liversedge, 1st Earl of Ballybunion, who objected as heartily as any commoner to paying excise duty on wines and spirits. The long tunnel was now brilliantly illuminated (though Dacey, O'Leary and Macdonald had practised earlier negotiating it in darkness as well as by the light of their helmet lamps). It ran for over half a mile to a cave, which, with Connell's connivance and materials, German technicians had enlarged and equipped as a submarine base, with three pens – one with facilities for sophisticated repairs.

While Dacey supervised the packing of his equipment in the subterranean arsenal, Skorzeny was taken on a tour of inspection of the specially stripped U-45 by its commander Leutnant Heinrich Lustige. Leutnant Lustige could not conceal his distaste at the conversion of his highly armed 517-ton *Unterseeboot* into a submarine troop-carrier or his scepticism about the possibility of taking it up the Thames beneath the 3500-ton merchant steamer *Coonamara* without being detected by enemy radar. But orders were orders, and these had come directly from the *Wolfsschanze*, or Wolf's Den, as the Führer's headquarters 'somewhere in East Prussia' was code-named. The choice lay between certain death before a firing squad for insubordination and almost certain death for the Fatherland, with promotion and a *Ritterkreuz* in the unlikely event of success. 'According to our information, Operation Serpent will take place some time on 2 June,' *Sturmbannführer* Skorzeny said. 'This means that you must be in position to pass through the boom at the Thames estuary on the night tide on 1-2 June.'

Skorzeny did not trouble to inspect the Waffen SS platoon detailed for the holding of the dock. He trusted *Obersturmführer* Adrian von Foelkersam implicitly. He had recruited him from the Brandenberg Division after he had won a *Ritterkreuz* for a smart piece of work in Russia in 1941. Von Foelkersam could be relied on to fill in the tactical detail, given the strategic objective and an appreciation of the situation. Skorzeny talked the scheme over, sipping schnapps with von Foelkersam and Lustige in the captain's cabin, until a detail came to inform him that Hans Dacey was ready.

They finished their glasses, shook hands, gave the Hitler salute '*Auf wiedersehen.*' '*Auf wiedersehen*, in London.'

The arms and equipment had been packed in tarpaulin and sewn with creosoted pack-thread. Two sailors manhandled them to the bottom of the steps, where Skorzeny and Dacey took over.

It was dark when they got above ground. The plastic yew berries were not luminous and it was hellish difficult to find them with the aid of their torches, weighed down as the two men were, by tarpaulin packages which had no rope handles. They lost their way several times and Dacey kept swearing, both in German and English.

Lucas had finished his calculations but not the Guinness which he had persuaded Kitty to bring up for him. He sat by the window as the darkness fell, sipping Guinness and rehearsing the plan for Honeycomb, not to see whether it was feasible as he had done while making his calculations, but at what points after they had all entered the Belmouth outflow he might give the others the slip. If he succeeded, he could hide himself in the labyrinth of the subterranean workings until the deadline for the hijacking had passed. Then somehow or other he would find a way out.

Suddenly he noticed two lights from the direction of the maze. They shone for so brief a time that he thought he was mistaken. Then they both came on again. One went out. Then both went out. It looked as if two people were lost in the maze. Lucas swigged his Guinness and waited.

Then a single light appeared shining almost directly downward. This time it did not go out but began to move, jerking as it might if the holder was walking. The two men were not returning through the wood. They walked along the edge of it to the classical temple, then turned towards the house. But they only came halfway and then branched off at right angles to the stables where, after some time, the light disappeared.

That seemed to be that. But a couple of minutes later a light appeared again at the stables and began to move more rapidly towards the house. When it came closer, Lucas could see that there was only one figure; and from its height, Lucas knew that it must be Skorzeny.

Dacey had been left behind in the stables to do something.

21 Horsemeat

In the time of the Earls of Ballybunion, the stable block of Liversedge Hall had been used to house all the animals and attendants essential to the wellbeing of a great family: draught horses, hunters, race-horses, carriage horses; hounds, gun dogs, sheep dogs; grooms, ostlers, drivers, jockeys, kennel men; stalls, haylofts, sleeping quarters and even an abattoir.

But under Sir John Connell, the emphases had changed. The stud which he acquired was trained in the neighbourhood of the Curragh. The stables were converted to garages and workshops; the haylofts to storage rooms for diverse materials; and the abattoir was enlarged and equipped with an adjacent cold-storage room. Grooms, ostlers and jockeys gave way to mechanics, handlers, lorry drivers and other persons employed on Sir John's diverse enterprises.

The trade in horsemeat had flourished even before the war, providing choice cuts for continental restaurants and material for the producers of pet foods in Britain. But with the fall of Belgium and France, the horsemeat trade had been concentrated on the English market. London served steaks which had gone previously to Brussels and Paris.

The abattoir had had a busy day. A dozen flayed carcasses hung from hooks along the steel rail. Paddy was flushing the floor with a hose, while Mick brushed the blood into the central drain. They were wearing white linen overalls and skull caps, red and rusty with gore. They looked up as Dacey and O'Leary came in. 'Nice work,' Dacey said. 'We'll be loading tonight. But you and Mick slip along to the kitchens for a jar.'

When the slaughtermen had left, O'Leary went out and brought in the tarpaulin packages, while Dacey unhooked the end carcass and lowered it with hook and tackle until the beast's breech was level with his hips. As it was hanging from the hind legs, the anus was tight closed. 'Jaysus,' O'Leary said, 'if you shove yer arm in, you'll never get it out again.' But he made no effort to take over.

Dacey had never disembowelled anything bigger than a hare.

114

O'Leary said he'd only gutted chickens. 'But you gotta hold the legs apart an' sorta turn it inside out like a glove.'

They tried lowering the carcase further, but the body buckled. O'Leary raised the bloody neck and lifted the head with its teeth bared in a grin towards him, so that the rump was resting on the slaughterhouse floor and the hindlegs could be parted. But by then Dacey had to go on his knees to thrust his arm up the horse's arse. A post-mortem fart blew shit into his armpit and over his singlet. '*Gott in Himmel!*' he muttered.

'Carter,' O'Leary said. 'Carter knows horses inside out.' Then realizing the implications, he sniggered, 'As you might say.' Carter was a meat porter, who had regularly made the trips to the Port of London and delivered the carcasses to the pet food factory.

Dacey withdrew his arm. Carter knew nothing about Operation Honeycomb. Ought Skorzeny to be consulted? If so, he might lose confidence in Dacey. The *Sturmbannführer* was hot on tactical initiative. Dacey went over to the sink and washed the shit off his arm and cleaned his singlet. '*Augenblick,*' he said and went out into the stable yard.

Carter was talking to the lorry driver, who was filling the radiator. Dacey drew him on one side. 'You want to earn a fiver?'

'If someone asks me that,' Carter said, 'then I know it's worth a tenner.'

'It might be, when it's over,' said Dacey.

'What is it?' Carter asked.

'It's something I want to go to London,' Dacey said, 'inside a horse.'

'Sounds more than a tenner, if I've got to get it through the customs. More like a pony.'

'You do not understand,' Dacey said. 'Some presents for a friend, in one of the dead horses.'

'A pony is twenty-five quid,' Carter said. 'And cheap at the price.'

Dacey was outraged. 'Ridiculous.'

Carter shrugged. 'I didn't ask you. You asked me.'

Dacey did not give in, but he did not go away.

'I could do with a lot more money than that, being at this

moment, as you might say, hard pressed. But I know the price for a job, Mr Dacey.'

'Fifteen.'

'Twenty.'

Dacey took Carter by the elbow and steered him towards the slaughterhouse. 'My friend does not like blabbers.'

'Don't worry, Mr Dacey,' Carter said. 'It's not a loose tongue but an empty purse yours gratefully is suffering from. And if you or your friend ever want a great deal more for a great deal more, you know where to come.'

Watching him work, Dacey and O'Leary were forced to admit that Carter was an artist at removing the viscera of a horse, loading its abdomen with military material plus a packing of straw without damaging the anal sphincter, the long bum gut or the animal's appearance.

'It looks just like the others,' Dacey said admiringly. 'But in London, how will you know?'

As they hung the beast aloft, Carter took his jack knife and slashed an X on its left fore-hoof.

'Fine! Fine!' Dacey said.

Carter waited until O'Leary turned his back and then rubbed his thumb against his forefinger. Dacey had forgotten that the meat convoy was leaving that night. 'I'll be back.'

He went over to Skorzeny's office and explained what had happened in a way that excused himself and O'Leary. The *Sturmbannführer* was not worried about the twenty-five pounds so much as the possible leakage of security. 'You've got to keep his mouth shut.'

'I've thought of a way,' Dacey said. 'When we were carrying the weapons ... I was thinking ... they are heavy, there is other equipment, supposing something happens, are four men enough? Carter wants money.'

'You know I do not like mercenaries.'

'We don't have to employ him. We keep his mouth shut by the promise of employment. If he does this job well, then fifty pounds down and fifty pounds when the job is over.'

'*Sacro egoismo!* Do you know what my contingency account is?' Skorzeny asked. 'It is not the Führer's fault, but those financial *dummkopfs*.'

Dacey apologized.

'But,' said Skorzeny, 'he is not used to underground work.'

'He is a meat porter,' Dacey said, 'he must be good at carrying things.'

'And there is a good chance he won't reach the St Katharine dock! If he does, then an extra fifty pounds will not matter, even with *finanz*! Yes, Dacey, promise him a further job for a hundred pounds if he delivers the goods, and that will keep his mouth shut.'

'There is another thing. With Carter to help carry the equipment, the rest of us can keep a closer eye on Mitchell.'

22 The Hotel Shelduck

Lucas slept fitfully. In his dreams he was already underground in London, living a nightmare in which no one could be trusted, since he was everyone's enemy. He would wake, see the moonlight through the uncurtained windows and think, Don't be silly, it was just a dream. It may not happen that way ... But it might happen, even worse.

He woke early with the dawn chorus. He shaved, bathed and did his physical exercises. He was fit, fitter than he had been for years. And he needed to be.

Kitty gave him early breakfast and he was debating whether to go for a run, when Skorzeny came in. 'Good. You have thought?' he asked, helping himself to coffee and home-baked bread and butter.

'The plan won't work,' Lucas said. 'You need more men for the equipment you've shown me. I don't know what weapons they will carry. You haven't told me that.'

'It is not your concern.'

'My concern is success. Why no portable oxyacetylene?'

'Not enough men, Mr Mitchell. As you say.'

'And not enough time, either. This is worse than any assault course. There may be casualties. We don't know what snags we may come up against.'

'Please, what is snags?'

'Rust. A hinge that has rusted up. A broken rung. Someone slipping in a sewer. A sprained ankle. Any sort of accident.'

'I will give you one other man, Mr Mitchell. But I know you will succeed.'

'What makes you think that?'

'Because there is one thing in which you believe: and that is that to stay alive is good.'

'I believed that,' said Lucas, 'until I met you.'

'You should start packing, Mr Mitchell. Mr Dacey will be driving you to Dublin in –' he looked at his watch, 'thirty-two minutes from now. There you will have evidence that Skorzeny is true to his word. But I warn you. Be true to yours.'

Skorzeny was wrong. Dacey sounded his horn in twenty-nine minutes. But Lucas was already going downstairs. He gave Kitty a kiss on her freckly nose, which surprised her, and a pound note, which surprised her still more. Sir John Connell called to him when he reached the front door. He held a dead hare by the hind legs. 'With my compliments to Mr Hibbert,' he said, 'and there'll be a hamper waiting for you at the Shelduck from O'Grady, the finest butcher and grazier in the city. The rump-steak and the butter is for you, seeing you'll be without ration cards, and a couple of dozen fresh eggs. The other dozen Mr Hibbert will appreciate, with *your* compliments.' He gave Lucas a knowing wink and squeezed his elbow.

'Thank you, sir. And you, Kitty.' Though he had not precisely enjoyed himself, Lucas was sorry to leave: where he was going, he would certainly enjoy himself less.

Skorzeny came out of the study. 'No last questions, Mitchell?'

'None you could answer. How do I say goodbye in German?'

'*Lebe wohl,*' Skorzeny said. 'In that case it will be *auf wiedersehen*. If not, *Adieu.*'

Dacey was sitting at the wheel of a Ford delivery van, with Macdonald beside him. Macdonald got out and opened the doors at the back, but he made no effort to help Lucas encumbered by the hare as well as his suitcases. A tin cup was suspended over the hare's muzzle to catch the blood. Lucas carried it down with one of his cases. He handed the hare to Macdonald, saying 'Sir John wants you to string this up.'

'Fuck him,' Macdonald muttered as Lucas went back to take the other suitcase from Kitty who was humping it down the steps.

'You two travel in the back,' Dacey shouted.

There was a plank fixed to either side of the van and a rexine back-rest. But there were no windows. The two of them were in darkness when the doors were closed. 'Fuck this for a lark,' Macdonald said. He lit a cigarette, but he did not offer one to Lucas. The hare began to swing as the van moved off; when they turned a corner, the suitcases slithered across the floor. Their movement was the only indication of whether they were going up-hill or down, turning to one side or the other. Each time Macdonald took a draw, his face was illuminated, the battered nose, a ragged upper lip. When he breathed, he made a noise like *herp-hup*. But every so seldom it was *hup-herp*. Not the most stimulating of companions.

After about ten minutes there was the noise of the tyres rattling over rollers – a cattle grille, Lucas guessed. Soon after, the van stopped. Voices. The scrape of gates. Then the van moved forward, this time gathering speed. They had passed out of Sir John Connell's demesne. But though there was room for all three in front, Dacey was taking no chances of Lucas deducing where he had been held.

After they had been travelling for about forty minutes the van suddenly shot forward. There were shrill screechings, as if a chicken had been run over. But the noise continued until Dacey stopped about a mile further on. Macdonald kicked aside a suitcase and peered through a chink in the front of the van. 'Fucky nell,' he said, 'look at that.' He stood aside so that Lucas could see.

Dacey had descended from the cab and was taking a Rhode Island rooster from between the bonnet and the off mudguard, where it had become wedged. He grasped its head and wrenched it off. Then he carried the bird with him into the cab, flung it on the floor and drove on.

'That Dacey!' Macdonald chuckled. 'Judy in Parnell Street. *Herp-hup*. Some bunk-up! *Hup-herp*.'

Lucas gave him a cigarette. They lit up and began a desultory conversation. Having broken his silence, Macdonald became talkative. Lucas might have learnt much, if he had understood what Macdonald was saying. But apart from 'Fucky nell', 'Jaysus', 'Cross me heart' and 'Call me a liar?' Macdonald's words were unintelligible. 'How right you are!' Lucas would say, or, 'That's a true word.' This seemed to keep the ex-pug happy until after a very long speech (was it? or anecdote?), Macdonald clutched Lucas by the knee. 'An' what would *you* say to that, man?' he demanded. As he had given up listening minutes before, Lucas thought for some time and said, 'I'd say it was a case of the pot calling the kettle black.'

'Fucky nell, *herp-hup*, Jaysus,' Macdonald said. 'Couldn't have put it neater meself, cross me heart.' Then he fell strangely silent and Lucas, sensing something wrong, struck his lighter. Macdonald was looking strange, clutching his left wrist with his huge right hand.

'You all right?' Lucas asked.

Macdonald's head twisted towards his left shoulder and Lucas thought he was going to fall. But suddenly the fit passed and seeing Lucas holding out his lighter, Macdonald said. 'What? A fag? *Herp-hup*. I wouldn't say no.'

When they reached Blessington, Dacey stopped and unlocked the back of the van; from there on, all three rode in the cab, with Lucas in the middle. Dacey said, 'I will leave you at the Hotel Shelduck, while I do my own business.' (Macdonald looked at the dead rooster on the floor, nudged Lucas in the ribs and winked.) 'But do not think, Mr Mitchell, you can run away. We have our people at the Shelduck.'

This was quite plain when they stopped outside the hotel. The commissionaire came forward to open the door of the van with a readiness which showed their arrival was expected. Macdonald and Lucas got out and Dacey drove off.

Macdonald went through the swing doors first, then Lucas, the commissionaire in the rear. Lucas stood in the foyer, guarded on either side, until the receptionist came over and said, 'Mr Mitchell? If you would be good enough to wait in the Parnell Room, I'll tell your friends you are here.'

'I want to pee,' Lucas said.

The receptionist raised an eyebrow and a green uniformed porter shambled over. 'Help this gentleman to excuse himself, Mr Phelan.'

'I don't need help, supposing you show me where it is,' Lucas said.

'It would be no bother to join you, sir,' Mr Phelan said, taking Lucas and Macdonald down a corridor to a door on which GENTS has been painted in gilt some years before. There was only a small window, giving out on to an airshaft: no possibility of escape.

Mr Phelan led them back through the hall into a small room marked PRIVATE. It was almost entirely filled by a table, covered with a green baize cloth, and six chairs, two single either side and an armchair at each end. There were mats for glasses and ash-trays advertising Jamieson's whiskey. 'And what would be your fancy?' asked Mr Phelan.

Macdonald chose a tankard of Guinness, Lucas a coffee with cream. Lucas did not believe it possible that even if he had succeeded in getting Grete to Dublin he would be allowed to meet her, let alone talk to her, but he still held the ace of trumps. If he was indispensable to Operation Honeycomb, he would make his terms. Macdonald was a thirsty man. He was on his third pint of Guinness, before the German Embassy representative arrived.

Herr von Brandentür was a sort of Baby Moussec version of Herr von Ribbentrop, the ex-champagne traveller turned Nazi diplomat. He was only five feet four, with long blond hair combed back to cover premature baldness. Lucas's first impression was 'the smaller, the more concentratedly nasty'. He came in, clicked his heels, shook hands, clutching a black calf-leather portfolio under his left arm. He sat down in the armchair at the opposite end of the table to Lucas. Then he turned to Macdonald. 'You go, please,' he said.

Macdonald got up. The Guinness was working. 'If you want me, you'll find me in the bar.'

'So,' said Baby Moussec, 'you want to see these other half-notes.' He opened the portfolio and passed them along the table to Lucas.

Lucas did not touch them. 'How do I know that they are the other halves of the notes which I left in Lisbon?'

'Herr Mitchell. You look at the numbers. Please!'

Lucas took them. He flicked them through. 'The numbers are the same. But are they forgeries?'

Baby Moussec was exasperated. 'In the middle of the greatest war in the history of civilization, do you believe that the Third Reich has time to forge thousand-dollar notes?'

'The Führer is founding a civilization to last a thousand years,' Lucas said. 'Forging a few thousand-dollar notes must be easy.'

'Do not let us trifle, Herr Mitchell. We are not funny people.' Baby Moussec was not only angry, but also getting out of his depth. Lucas thought of saying, 'You ought to look in a mirror.' Instead he took hold of the half-notes again and said, 'If Fräulein Carlson told me that these notes are genuine, then I might believe.'

'I can assure you that these are the notes which Fräulein Carlson brought from Lisbon.'

'I don't want you to assure me. Grete must.'

Baby Moussec's bubbles stopped sparkling. 'What you say ... how can we trust you after this?'

'You can't. Any more than I can trust you. You want a job done. I want to be paid for it. I'm genuine. But are you?'

Baby Moussec looked round. There was no telephone in the room. 'I cannot act. You wait, please.' He went out of the room.

Lucas went to the door as soon as Baby Moussec left. He asked Phelan to bring him a pint of Guinness. As Phelan went off to the bar, he saw Grete sitting in a chair in the hall. She noticed, but did not acknowledge him. She got up and carelessly threw a cigarette pack in the wastebin by the tobacco kiosk. Lucas went over to the kiosk and asked for a pack of Sweet Afton and matches and, as the girl turned to get them, he salvaged Grete's empty pack and pocketed it. He was back in the private room long before Baby Moussec returned, but did not do more than abstract the note inside the discarded pack. He just sat, hugging it in his hip pocket and exulting in the look Grete had given him.

Baby Moussec brought Grete with him. 'I have been authorized by the Embassy,' he said. 'Fräulein Carlson will give witness.'

Lucas looked at her. She was the most beautiful girl he had ever known. He wished he could say, 'Let's leave this twerp and go up to bed.' 'They *are* genuine,' she said.

'But will I ever get them to match the other halves, Herr von Brandentür?' Lucas picked up the half-notes and gave them to Grete. 'How long does it take to drive to the Swedish Embassy?'

'Fifteen, twenty minutes,' Baby Moussec said.

'I'll phone you in thirty minutes, darling,' he said. 'At the Swedish Embassy. Don't try to phone me. Herr von Brandentür and I will be drinking to your health, meanwhile.' He put his hands on her shoulders. 'And to our wedding, when this little job is over.' He kissed her lips. 'That's if you'll have me.'

She clasped him to her and whispered, 'Yes, even though I think I've got your baby.'

'What shall it be?' asked Lucas, when she left. 'Champagne?'

'For me, please,' said Herr von Brandentür, 'a Baby Moussec.'

23 This Blessed Plot

Dacey saw Lucas aboard the ferry at Dun Laoghaire, but to Lucas's surprise Dacey and Macdonald themselves took the Dublin boat to Liverpool. 'You trust me?' he asked.

'You want to see your mother and earn your money,' said Dacey. 'Better we shouldn't meet until Monument.'

'And so someone else will keep an eye on me?'

'So you might guess,' said Dacey.

Lucas kept his eyes open during the voyage and going down the gangway at Holyhead, but he saw no one particularly interested in him.

The customs shed was placarded with posters about careless talk losing lives. The careless immigration control took a cursory look at his passport photograph and added a genuine stamp to the pages littered with false records of exits and entries. At customs he declared 200 Sweet Afton and a bottle of Paddy's Power, which he had bought in Dublin. 'Lucky you,' grinned the officer, seeing the steak, the hare, the eggs and butter. 'Spare a half?' Then seeing Lucas's hesitation, he added, 'Only joking, mate.'

As Lucas walked to the train, he thought that after four years of total war, the British could still learn a security lesson or two from the Kimberley diamond mines.

The sun was up and Holyhead Mountain was bathed in light. Then they were rolling across the green isle of Anglesey to Llanfairpwllgwyngyll and over the Menai Strait to Caernarvon. Lucas had forgotten how beautiful Britain was in early summer with the trees still bud-brilliant-green. Welsh voices gave place to English as they crossed the border, the compartments and the corridors filling as they moved towards London, servicemen and women with packs and kitbags, civilians reduced to a sort of uniform drabness, women wearing trousers. The countryside was at peace, but the people were only too plainly at war; and Lucas thought how much friendlier they were than the depressed and frightened people whom he had left at the time of Munich, despite the shabbiness and the smell of feet and armpits.

He was exhausted by the time he reached Euston. For the last three hours he had stood, having given his seat up to a harassed young mother with a screaming baby and a whimpering toddler. He went into the corridor and stood close to a window which gave him fresh air. He listened to conversations, but did not speak to anyone. There were strange words like 'prang' and 'spamwich'; catch-phrases like 'It's bein' so cheerful that keeps me goin'', 'Can I do you now, sir?' or 'I don't mind if I do'. He would have to be careful.

There were no porters at Euston. He cursed Connell's hare in the straw fishbag, which he had to carry in the same hand as one of the suitcases. He humped his baggage to the front of the station, where there was a long queue waiting for taxis. It was three quarters of an hour before his turn came. He had seen bombed towns in the Spanish civil war, but he was not prepared for the post-blitz life of London: lavatory pans and staircases still clinging to the walls of gutted houses, loosestrife growing out of cellar floors and in the cracks of steps leading to nowhere. The address he had been given for lodgings was 24 Bolsover Street, near the Angel. But when he got out of the taxi with his suitcases and fishbag, the place looked uninhabited. One pane of the downstairs window had been replaced with cardboard and through the others, crisscrossed with brown gumstrip, he could see drawn curtains. The bell-pull was broken, and when he hammered the iron knocker on the blistered brown door no one came in answer. Remembering the East End of his childhood, he put his hand through the letter box and found a piece of tape at the end of which dangled a key.

Lucas looked round guiltily and saw an old woman shuffling towards him. She was wearing plimsolls and a gor-blimey cap. In her hand she had a newspaper parcel out of which she was eating chips. When she reached him, she stopped and said, 'If you want Mrs Sullivan, you better try the Bolsover. Put yer bags inside, young man, and try the Snug.' She pointed a long chip towards the pub on the corner. Then she let herself into the house next door.

'What's she look like? Mrs Sullivan?'

'You won't miss 'er. Dyes 'er 'air,' the crone said. 'One o' the ruins Cromwell knocked abaht a bit.'

Lucas took his things in and left them inside the blacked-out parlour. It had been the 'best room', used only for company; but there had clearly been no company for ages.

From the outside, Lucas could see that the Snug of the Bolsover was only big enough for a few bugs in a rug. He went into the saloon bar; a man in shirt-sleeves and bowler hat viewed him with obvious suspicion from behind the counter. 'What might you be wanting?' the man asked.

Lucas looked at the empty shelves behind the bar. 'What've you got?'

'There's mild and there's bitter. And then there's mild and bitter.'

'Bitter. A pint,' Lucas said. 'Please.'

The serving counter was shaped like a horseshoe, so that one person could serve all bars. Lucas could see into the Snug, where towered over the bar the head and shoulders of someone who might have been an empress of the Roman Empire when declining to its fall. 'Could you ask Mrs Sullivan if I could have a word with her in this bar?' asked Lucas, as he paid for his drink.

The bowler hat whispered to the empress, who took a squint at Lucas and lifted her glass. Bowler hat came back and said, 'She'll be over after she's relieved herself. You never said you was a friend of Madame S.'

Lucas waited for the arrival of his welterweight landlady. 'What would she be taking, would you think?' he asked.

'Seeing as it's you,' said the bowler hat, 'it would be a tonic water special.' He bent down and poured a large gin under the counter into which he put a split Schweppes.

The door opened and through it squeezed, thanks to her corsets and body belt, a lady of heroic proportions. '*You*,' she said, advancing with her hand extended too high to shake but low enough to demand the most obeisant of kisses, 'must be Mr Mitchell. 'Ow clever of you to track me down.' She took her gin and tonic. '*Salute!* as the Spanish sergeant said.' She was wearing a black silk dress, which must have been superbly sewn not to have burst at the seams. 'So you're what Johnny Connell's sent me now.' She looked him over. 'I'll drop him a p/c to say you'll do.'

'I'm afraid I've left my bags in your front room,' Lucas said.

'You look quite properly dressed to me,' she said. She burst out laughing, dug him in the ribs, and repeated the conversation to bowler hat, whom she called 'Charley'.

'You mustn't take any notice of Madame S.,' he said. 'She was a comedy duo with her late, and she's looking for a feed.'

'What a dish!' she said, pinching Lucas's cheek. 'I could eat you all up, you gorgeous man!'

'I just wanted to say that I want to pop down to see my mother in Wellclose Square,' Lucas said, 'but I'll be in by ten, if that's OK.'

'If you're in earlier, you won't find me there – will he, Charlie? But you sleep first floor back and pull the black-out before you go. 'Spect Johnny told you the terms? Fifteen bob a week b-and-b, with ration card; twenty-five without. Paid in advance.'

126

'No cards,' Lucas said, 'but I've got steak, butter and eggs.'

'Say fifteen bob the first week then. It's a deal?'

Lucas gave her a fiver.

'Take for two tonic specials out of that, Charley. There's a pet.'

'I must see my Mum,' Lucas said.

'Oh, come orn ...'

'Drink it for me, love. I haven't seen her since she was bombed out.'

'That's different.' Mrs Sullivan passed him his change and added his drink to hers.

By the time that he had moved his stuff up into the first floor back, unpacked and loaded up the fishbag with butter, eggs and steak for his mother, it was dusk. He pulled the black-out, pocketed his torch, shoved the remaining meat and butter in Mrs Sullivan's pantry. He was lucky at the bus stop. An Aldgate bus hove up immediately.

He walked down Leman Street in the twilight. There wasn't a house untouched; but most were still standing, still lived in. He turned into Cable Street, where he had grown up immune to the clatter of heavy lorries morning, noon and night, the screams and fights and vomitings when the boozers closed. Mum's house and those either side, where the Pearlmans and the Cohns had lived, were just shells. The fish and chip shop was boarded up, but had a notice STILL FRYING. He turned down Fletcher Street into Wellclose Square. The school in the middle was still standing, protected perhaps because the houses round were so much higher. He had forgotten the numbering and flashed his torch up at a door.

'Put that bloody light out!' From Grace's Alley emerged an ARP warden, like an irate bloodhound picking up a scent after months of idleness.

Lucas put off his torch and waited. Of course, he hadn't put any coloured paper over the glass. 'Brought the wrong torch,' he apologized. 'I'm looking for 21b. Mrs Ramoulian.'

'You won't find 'er there,' said the warden. 'She's gone away.'

'When? I had a letter from her after she was bombed out.'

127

'Dunno when, exactly. Mr Smallman told me in the boozer. But you can't ask him, because he's baking. And *she*'s so deaf you wouldn't make her hear; and so scared, she wouldn't open up, even if she did. Best thing, come round tomorrow morning, before you go to work. Mr Smallman's back about six a.m., and you could catch him, before he takes his kip.'

24 The Smallmans

Lucas did not feel up to revisiting Mrs Sullivan at the Bolsover. He cooked himself a piece of steak in her kitchen and washed it down with a couple of stiff glasses of Paddy's Power. He left half a pound of butter on the table, with a note to tell Mrs Sullivan that he was tired and had to get up early next morning. Please to help herself to some steak, with Sir John Connell's compliments.

He slept badly and by half-past six in the morning he was back in Wellclose Square, knocking on the door of No. 21, with the fine bronze dolphin which had probably been fixed there a century and a half before. He could hear sounds inside, but nobody opened the door until he had hammered three times, as hard as he could. Then the door opened as far as the chain would allow and a wispy little woman with a yellow duster knotted over grey hair peered out. 'What do *you* want so early?' she asked. 'The rent ain't due till tomorrow.'

'It's about Mrs Ramoulian,' Lucas shouted.

'I'll get Mr Smallman,' she said and shut the door.

A couple of minutes later Lucas heard the chain pulled back and the door opened. Mr Smallman had half a slice of bread and marg in his left hand and a tea-towel tucked in the neck of his collarless shirt as a bib. His hair was white with flour. 'Mrs Smallman is a little hard of hearing,' he said. 'Is it about the gas?'

'It's about Mrs Ramoulian,' he said. 'She wrote and said she'd moved here after she was bombed.'

'And what would you be wanting her for?'

'Don't you remember me? I'm her son. I used to buy jam-puffs at Blakey's when I was a boy.'

'A bit of fun?' asked Mrs Smallman. 'Get stuffed?'

'I can't remember what you looked like,' the baker said. 'Any-way, come into the kitchen.' Then he bent down and shouted in his wife's ear, 'Edith, get yourself plugged in.'

'You do it, Ernie,' she said. 'You know what I'm like.'

They all went into the back kitchen and Ernie Smallman took a mug out of an oak cupboard and placed it on the tray, beside a large brown teapot, clad in a knitted cosy. Then he connected his wife up to a box on the table. 'She don't like listening to the war,' he said.

'It ain't just the bombs,' Mrs Smallman said, 'it's the noise of everything. Couldn't hear a thing after the measles when I was six; not till I got this dratted box. Bliss, it was.' She poured Lucas a mug of tea.

'You remember, Edith – Mrs Ramoulian's boy? What was in the army; and went to Spain in the Brigade; and then he run off before the war.'

'What she's gone off with that chap to see, of course I do.'

'Well, what did he look like?'

'Look like? Well, he didn't look like anyone very much. Not like Clark Gable, or Ronald Colman. But I do remember, he used to pick his nose and eat it. And he had cotton wool ∶ his ear.'

'Did 'e look like this gentleman 'ere?'

Mrs Smallman shook her head. 'Anyway, she's gone away with this feller what called, Wednesday, or was it Thursday? Said he was going to take her to see her boy.'

'It was Tuesday,' Ernie said, 'because I'd just got my ounce of Dark Flake.'

'It must've been about ten in the morning . . .'

'More like half-past,' said Mr Smallman, 'and I called up and Mrs R. came out on the landing and . . . "What is it?" she calls, leaning over the banisters . . .' A shriek came from the box and Mr Smallman said, 'You're oscillating, Edith,' and switched his wife off, so that she wouldn't interrupt. ' "What is it?" she asks, as Edith said, and I told it was about her son and she said,

"Oh, no!" as if it was something awful. But she asks this chap up and he was up there, maybe half an hour. Anyway, time for me to get my Dark Flake, and there Mrs R. was, coming down the stairs with this chap carrying her things in a wicker hamper, and she says, "Mr Smallman," she says, "I'm going away for a few days, but I don't know how long."'

'And I called out –' Mrs Smallman had managed to switch herself on again '– an' I called out, "Ernie, ask about sending letters on and what about the rent collector?"'

'That *is* true,' Mr Smallman said. 'So she pulls out four quid to settle up with the milkman and the rent and "Mr. S.," she says, 'don't bother about sendin' on no letters, seein' there won't be nothin' special, and if I'm away longer I'll send some more money".'

'And the man, what was he like?' Lucas asked.

'I seen him in the hall, so the light wasn't too good,' Mr Smallman said. 'He was wearing a fawn trench coat with a belt and shoulder strap things. And a brown, furry sort of hat, maybe like beaverskin, pulled down over his eyes. Couple of inches taller than me, I'd say, about five foot five, burly, hunched his shoulders, had both hands in his pockets.'

'Had a moostarsh,' his wife cut in, 'like a nail-brush.'

'To the best of *my* recollection,' said Mr Smallman in a voice which left no doubt whose recollection he considered better, 'he was clean shaven. But with sideburns. Sort of mid-ear length, the colour of overbaked bread.'

'The voice – what sort of voice?'

'Soft spoken,' Ernie Smallman said. 'Irish. Not Ulster. Maybe Dublin, but I'd say County Cork.'

'Which is where I've just come from,' Lucas said. He produced the steak and a packet of butter. 'I brought these for Mum; but seeing she's gone, I'm sure she'd like you to have them.'

They looked at the steak, which was about a pound in weight. 'We could never eat all that!' Ernie Smallman said. 'It's two weeks' ration. Or more.'

Lucas stood up and thanked them for the tea. He was already late for his appointment with Hibbert.

'When Mrs R. comes back,' Mr Smallman said, 'where can she find you?'

'I'll keep in touch,' Lucas said. 'I can't tell you where I shall be. All I can say is that I am engaged on very important work. Hush-hush.'

'What did he say, Ernie,' asked Edith, whose battery was fading.

'Hush-hush!' Mr Smallman shouted.

'There's no need to hush me, Ernie. I was only asking.'

25 Meeting the boys

As he went into the yard of Holiday & Greenwood, Lucas saw a gang of men, standing outside the room marked STORES. One immediately came over to him. 'Are you Mitchell?' he said. Lucas nodded. 'I'm Dooley. Got to catch the nine o'clock from Euston. We bin waitin'.'

'Sorry about your Dad,' Lucas said. 'But my Mum's been kidnapped. Where's Hibbert? Over there in the office? OK. Off you go. I'll introduce myself.'

'It's got to be done proper,' Dooley said, taken aback.

'Catch your train.'

'I'm not sayin' ...' Dooley trailed after him to the office. 'Only cuttin' it fine.'

Lucas realized he was being bloody, but he was so sorry about his mother, he had to take it out on someone. 'Mr Hibbert?' he said to the man sitting behind the desk. 'Mitchell. Sorry I'm late. I gather Mr Dooley wants to catch his train. Shall I meet the boys first?'

'Do that,' Hibbert said. 'At least you move quick.' He nodded to Dooley. 'Hope it goes well, Pat.'

''Fraid the sooner, the better,' Dooley said. 'Poor old bugger.'

The only 'boy' was a youth with red hair, freckles and bat ears. The other three were men in their fifties. Dooley put his hand on the shoulder of a grey, curly-haired chap with a deep barrel chest. 'Pascoe Lovelace,' Dooley said, 'my second. Trust him as I do meself.'

Pascoe had round blue eyes and a grip like a vice. 'If you're half as good as Pat, you'll do for me,' he said, in a voice of extraordinary depth and purity. 'You get along, chief, and catch your train. And God go with you!'

As Dooley hurried off, Mitchell said to Lovelace, 'Why get me as stand-in, when they got you?'

'It's a question I ask myself, chum,' Lovelace said. 'Except the doctors say I'm a schizophrenic with cirrhosis of the liver, the poor ignorant bastards.' Then he turned to the others. 'This is Mr Mitchell and we don't know what's wrong with him yet. But this here is Al Farmer, which despite the steel gig-lamps and his being bald as a billiard ball is a good old cock.' Al Farmer winked as he shook Lucas's hand. 'And now let me introduce Jimmy Biggs, with the flattest feet north of the river. He looks like a crook and acts like a crook, but, don't you believe it, he's as straight as a bloody die. And finally, there's the young'un Freddy Cronin, who's got a wee spot on his lung, but otherwise is as sound as a cracked bell.' Freddy blushed at the mention of the spot on the lung, but shook hands bashfully. Lovelace had a manner which could make *rigor mortis* sound as mild as acne. 'Where d'we go, boss?'

'I'll have a word with Mr Hibbert.'

'Him!' Lovelace cleared his throat and shot a gob accurately into a drain.

Lucas went back into the office. Mr Hibbert looked up from his books, with a smile which might equally well have been conspiratorial or complaisant. 'I have a hare, sir,' Lucas said. 'From Sir John. It's in my digs. I'll bring it round. It isn't very high yet. But I'm afraid some of the blood spilt. On the boat. And the train from Holyhead.'

'I hope not on your trousers.'

'On a kitbag, luckily.'

'How is the old rascal?'

'Wh—?'

'*Sir* John.'

'I don't know how he usually is,' Lucas said. 'But "flourishing" is what I'd say.'

Mr Hibbert grunted with laughter. 'I might add "as ever". Where do you want to start?'

'Monument station might be a good idea.'

'Splendid! Splendid! I'll ring Stainton, the engineer. He's been on at us for months, as they all have. You know, I don't know how we would have survived without all you neutral chaps from Eire. You don't want to use Dooley's ration books, I imagine?'

At Monument, Lucas had only to mention Hibbert's name to be greeted by Stainton as warmly as a St Bernard by a mountaineer engulfed in an Alpine snowdrift. He inquired after Pat Dooley's father ('Terrible terrible, cancer. Hope I don't go that way.'), and was issued with a pass without question. 'We've been waiting for you chaps for weeks. The casing's very dodgy in places on One and Two either way.'

'It's only a look-see.' Lucas said.

'But of course,' said Stainton. 'Lucky we're coming up for the weekend.'

26 A minor detour

The normal route for the G.G. transporter van was straight down Jamaica Road. But this morning, if there had been an observant policeman – which there wasn't – he would have noticed with surprise that it turned left off Jamaica Road, and third right along Chambers Street. Two small boys did observe that it went up Llewellyn Street, which was a dead end, but when it stopped just beyond the entrance to Goodright's Yard, which had been deserted since the blitz of 1940, and a man descended from the left-hand side of the driver's cab, they assumed that he was merely helping the driver to turn and rectify his mistake, and they continued their way to school, kicking an old tin which served as a football.

If they had lingered for a moment, they would have been surprised to see Carter hammer twice on Goodright's double gates and the transporter half disappear into the yard before turning. Carter did not get back into the cab when, less than a minute later, the transporter returned up Llewellyn Street, turned right at Chambers Street, right again at Bevington Street and then left into Jamaica Road, resuming the usual run to the G.G. Foods processing plant in Clack Street.

During that moment of backing, four bloody packages sewn up in tarpaulin were passed from the back of the transporter to Carter and from him to Macdonald and O'Leary who carried them into the surviving end of Goodright's warehouse. As the transporter drove off, Dacey closed the gates, thrust down the bolt and refixed the retaining bar, before following the others.

For a quarter of an hour, they worked slitting open the packages, assembling the contents on a workbench and checking them against Dacey's list.

During this time, Carter became gradually aware of a sound, which he did not at first identify. But at last, he became quite certain that it was a human voice: someone crying. 'Listen,' he said. 'What's that?'

For a moment they stopped working and talking. Then Dacey nodded to O'Leary.

O'Leary swore. 'I hope she hasn't shat herself *again*,' he muttered as he went towards the door of a room marked OFFICE.

27 Not real common

Stainton himself had examined the Monument tunnels – One and Two. There was nothing, at least up to the last inspection a month before, which was downright dangerous. But there were cracks in the casing caused by earlier bombings and aggravated by rust and seepage which needed attention. 'Lucky today's Saturday,' he said. 'You could come on tomorrow morning, say a quarter to one. Could you do a ten-hour shift? We'll suspend the services till noon, if you're game.'

'The boss pays the overtime,' Lucas said.

Stainton looked at him curiously. 'It's cost-plus.'

'Oh – you know I'm only standing in for Dooley. Then I'll have a word with the boys. If it's OK with them, it's OK with me.'

It was not OK with Lucas to put in a long shift and then at short notice to have to carry out the gruelling Operation Honeycomb. But he knew how to manipulate a gang as well as any shop steward. 'It's entirely up to you, boys,' he said. 'But the way I see it, while Pat's away, we want to put in as many hours a night as we can. But Sunday night-Monday morning'll get us most overtime. What you say, Pascoe?'

'Never said a truer word, chum.'

So it was fixed they should work only an eight-hour shift Sunday morning; and back they went to Holiday & Greenwood having clocked on three hours for sweet f.a. 'Mind if I take the the van to get the hare, Mr Hibbert?' 'What else is it for, Mr Mitchell?'

Mrs Sullivan was out, but Lucas let himself in with the letter box key. He went into the kitchen. There was a note propped against an almost empty jar of Golliwog Marmalade. It read,

Mr Mitchell, Miss Rainbow rang soon after you went out. Says not to worry. Will ring again about one. Thanks for the stake, says I, not she. Scrummy, scrummy, scrum. Stevie (Mrs Sullivan).

Lucas looked at his watch. It was ten to twelve. By the time that he had given Mr Hibbert his hare and walked back to Bolsover Street, it was 12.59. The telephone rang at 1.01. Lucas picked up the receiver. The operator said, 'This is a personal call for Mr Philip Mitchell. Could I speak to Mr Mitchell please?'

'Mitchell speaking.'

'Please go ahead caller.'

A voice, audibly pre-recorded, said, 'This is Rainbow speakin'. You don't need to trouble about your muvver. She is in very good hands. And you will see her when it's all over. But you must understand, you've got to wait and do what you've been told. Now here is your muvver just to make you sure she's on

135

your side and on our side. Here she is, (*sotto voce*) Blast!' Then his mother's voice came, 'Darling boy, please don't be worrying about me, but do what you got to do, whatever it is, your mother will understand, oh and yes, I am very well and I am waiting. I am waiting to meet you, darling Lu—' There was a pause and then the first voice, a woman's, said, 'So you see, your mother is alive and well. You must do what you've already been told to do and await instructions for what comes after. But just so you might think your muvver can't talk to you no more, just ask something what she and you only know and she will answer and we'll give you her reply, in her own voice, yes in her own voice. Be ready about six this evening to take a call. Now ask your questions. But make them snappy.'

Lucas strove to think as he talked. 'Darling Mum,' he said, 'Know that I love you and I've always loved you and always will. Tell me about the fambly fox and something only you and me know.'

Suddenly the line went dead. Lucas replaced the receiver and then called the operator. He gave his number. 'I've just taken a personal call. Could you tell me what number it came from?'

'Was it a transfer-charge call?'

'No.'

'Sorry, sir. We keep no record.'

He went down to the Bolsover Arms and opened the Snug door. Mrs Sullivan was not there, but he caught sight of her in the saloon, talking to a man with very black hair and a wattled woman with very gold hair. He went round to the saloon. Mrs Sullivan's behind was perched on a bar stool with the flexibility of a sack of tripe, but her upper decks, encased in stays, were as upright as a Spanish galleon while Drake was still playing bowls.

'Mrs Sullivan,' he said.

She turned. 'Oh there's my steak and butter boy!' she said. 'Meet Neville and Trixie. And do please call me Stevie.'

'That phone call,' Lucas said, 'from Miss Rainbow. Was it a real person? Or a recording?'

'Not a recording,' Mrs Sullivan said. 'But it wasn't a real person, neither. It was like a lady what had never had to clean her own shoes trying to talk common. It wasn't genuine, not real common.'

28 Final briefing

Lt-Col John Embleton looked up at Big Ben. The time was 1.57. He had eighteen minutes before the meeting in the DG's office. It was the first time since his seconding that he had paused to think how much had changed in the last two weeks. He no longer thought of himself as working to 'the Chief'. Indeed, it had been made clear that there was no future in Military Intelligence for Embleton except at major's rank.

It wasn't the rank which Lt-Col Embleton enjoyed so much as the authority he had found. Sir Hilary had delegated not merely the execution but also the planning to his adjutant. And thanks to Bernard Nightingale, his old friend Desmond Carstairs in the Ministry of Transport and to Lady Virginia, he had salvaged Operation Serpent from what at one time appeared to be utter failure.

Embleton didn't blame the Services. It was obvious that the greatest invasion in the history of mankind was imminent. On Sunday 28 May, they had been allowed a run-through. Indeed, they could have executed the operation if preparations had been completed at the warehouse and the King George V dock. Everything on the railway and the HQ control room had worked without a hitch: except that the speeds, estimated by Nightingale and Carstairs, could not be tested with the loads. When Embleton had observed that there was a maintenance diesel engine in the siding north-west of the HQ station, he had suggested that it might be manned to provide a boost to the first train. But since there were five trains, the experts overruled him. It would complicate the movements of the other four. Anyway it was not speed, but uninterrupted movement which was important.

So by that Sunday, the feasibility of Serpent had been proven.

The loading of the trains had been completed by Wednesday 31 May. But during the week the railway was in use for armed and civil service despatch twenty-four hours a day. Sunday was customarily reserved for maintenance and Carstairs had contrived a waiving of maintenance for the afternoon of 4 June. Then, suddenly, from somewhere on high there came a total ban on DODS having the railway. It was pretty plain to all of them that the invasion was being planned for the night of 3/4 June. But of course no one would say so. On Thursday 1 June, Operation Serpent was indefinitely postponed.

Embleton accepted defeat, but Lady Virginia showed her breeding. 'No harm in Bodgers casting a line,' she said. And on Thursday evening, Sir Hilary gave dinner at his club to a small group of friends, the main course being a fine capon with leaf spinach and the entrée asparagus, all provided from Shepton Mallet, by Lady Fry.

On Friday morning Sir Hilary announced, 'At least, I've gained a concession. We're on standby. We won't know anything until tomorrow afternoon. But I'd like to see you all at two p.m.: just in case.'

Embleton felt the envelope in his pocket. It was addressed to the DG, DODS. But he had been told in whispered confidence.

Operation Serpent was on Sunday 4 June, at 15.00 hours.

29 When is murder . . .

At the first ring Lucas lifted the receiver.

'Can I talk to Mr Mitchell?' The woman's voice sounded as if through a cupped hand.

'Speaking.'

'You wanted an answer from your muvver, Mr Mitchell. Here she is.' Then there was a pause and his mother's voice said, 'The fambly fox is under my bed at 21b. Now this is something just us two know: when we was at Cable Street and you was only five you said "I want my porridge" and Dad said "It's on the stove" and you felt up and took the saucepan handle and it fell all over you and you was so badly scalded you was in bed for a week. You remember. Now do be a good boy and do what they say or else I mayn't never see you, son, which I do want more than anything, if only just once.'

There was another pause and then the first voice came on again. 'This is Rainbow again. Listen very carefully. You must complete Phase One by 03.15 hours tomorrow morning. You must be ready for Phase Two at 04.00 hours. You must be ready for Honeycomb at 15.00 hours. D'you understand me?'

'But this is quite different from what was planned,' Lucas said. 'I've arranged for the boys to work an eight-hour shift.'

'It is not different. They will be working elsewhere. *Only you* will leave at 03.15, explaining that you must get something or other back at the yard.'

'But it's murder.'

'It is warfare, Mr Mitchell. Murder is a word which might apply to your muvver.'

'*Listen!*' shouted Lucas.

The telephone went dead.

Blind instinct drove him into the street and to the bus stop by the Angel. It was only after waiting ten minutes in vain that he thought how futile it would be to go to Wellclose Square. The amount of diamonds his mother might have in the 'fambly' box was nothing to what he would make if he brought Honeycomb off. He had proved what he wanted to prove, that she was still alive. But was the price of keeping her alive to hazard the lives of Pascoe and his boys? He went back to 24 Bolsover Street and found Mrs Sullivan unpacking her shopping in the kitchen. 'Always wait till the market closes Saturday night,' she said, flourishing a weary cauliflower. 'Look at that. Tuppence! Have it for dinner tomorrow, we might, with my cheese ration. Chou fleur au grattang was my late's favourite.'

Talk of the morrow reminded Lucas that by the time Mrs Sullivan was cooking her cauliflower, he would be underground; and if he ever saw daylight again, it would be dangerous to come back to Bolsover Street.

He fetched Paddy's Power from his bedroom. There was only a quarter of a bottle left. Between them they killed it and 'Stevie' suggested adjourning to the Bolsover. 'I've got to work tonight,' Lucas said, 'can't say when I'll get back. But don't you worry. I don't pay a week's rent in advance for nothing.'

As soon as she left the house, he packed his suitcases. Before he took them downstairs, he thought of checking the money in his belt. It was all intact; so was the scrap of Grete's note from Alcantara. The sight of her handwriting reminded him of the letter which she'd given him in Dublin, which he'd slipped in his pocket. He unfolded it and read the scrawling Swedish script:

My dearest Lucas, Trust me I
do not write against my will
Give up trying to escape.
Work with my friends. Surely you
with all your skill in mining, will.
Otherwise, I fear that I may find
something terrible happening to me.
Skorzeny is a very good friend in
emergencies, if you are loyal. Peace
is something we all want but do
not see quite yet. But I trust
that if you pull things off in
London, nothing bad will come to me.
These are *my last words*. Yours

Grete Carlson

It was a strange note until he read the last words in each line. Then whistling 'Lili Marlene', he made his way to deposit his suitcases at Euston Station.

But before he did so, he went down to the gentlemen's lavatory and changed into his tunnelling clothes, packing away his everyday wear. Then he had a meal in the buffet and went to Holiday & Greenwood's yard. There was still time for a drink in the neighbouring pub; and the first person he saw was Pascoe Lovelace, who clapped him round the shoulders as if they'd known one another all their lives. The rest of the 'boys' were with him, but Pascoe insisted on introducing them once again in words almost identical to those he had used that morning.

Then he turned to Lucas. 'Am I right in thinking, Mr Mitchell, sir, that this is the first time that you have ever worked on electric railway maintenance?'

'No,' Lucas said.

Pascoe was disappointed. 'Then you know as well as I do, the first commandment: Do not, repeat, do not pee on the live rail!'

Lucas forced a laugh. He looked at the four of them, Pascoe Lovelace, Al Farmer, Jimmy Biggs and young Freddy Cronin with the flushed cheeks, red hair and bat ears. 'Glad I met you all. I've been thinking. You four concentrate on Number One East. And go well up. Halfway to Tower Hill. I'll fix the fault in Number Two East.'

'Sure you don't want a hand?' Freddy Cronin asked.

'Sure. And go well in, mind.' The blast would go down Number Two West, blow a bit into Number One platform but the tunnels of Number One should be as safe as an air-raid shelter.

'Don't worry about us, boss.' Lovelace said. 'We can do this work with our eyes closed.'

30 . . . not murder – warfare

In Llewellyn Street there was not a single dimmed-out street lamp. It was the deadest of wartime London's dead ends. But in the abandoned yard, the van was standing ready loaded. Dacey, O'Leary, Macdonald and Carter were having a fry-up, good ninety-per-cent Irish pork bangers, thick rashers of bacon, and fried bread. They needed to stoke up for the long hours ahead.

Suddenly Carter said, 'D'ye hear that? Listen!'

Dacey stopped talking and O'Leary said, 'It's the old lady!' He got up and went into the inner office. 'Christ!' he said. 'Sean! Here! Quick!'

Dacey went over, still chewing, and looked at the grey-haired old woman tied hand and foot to the solid armchair. They had gagged her with a white-spotted red handkerchief when she started to whine. Now something had gone wrong. Her face was purplish-black like a sloe, and veins stood out on her temples.

'Untie it!' Dacey ordered.

O'Leary tried to undo the knot, but his clumsy fingers could not untie it, because she was shaken with paroxysms.

'She's got a fit,' Macdonald said from the doorway.

O'Leary opened a flick-knife and pulled back the handkerchief to cut the knot. Perhaps the extra tension was too much. As the gag loosened, there was a noise like water running out of a bath and her head fell forward.

Dacey went in and knelt on the bare wood floor. He slapped her on the cheek with his hand, but she didn't react. 'Get water!' he ordered.

Carter went back to where they had been eating, but the only container he could find was an empty Guinness bottle. While he was filling it, Dacey and O'Leary untied her wrists and ankles. As they did so, she crumpled. The bathwater noise went on, but as they laid her on the floor, it changed as if something else had broken in the machinery of her breathing. 'What can I do?' asked Macdonald. After all these days and nights in which they had taken no notice except to feed her, let her shit and pee, tell her to shut up or force her to record, now she was the centre of their attention. 'Fuck off, Macdonald!' Dacey said.

Macdonald went back to the table and sat clutching his fists.

Carter came back with the Guinness bottle filled with water, dark bubbles on the top. 'Pour it on her face,' Dacey said, with the fierce authority of a man who knew something must be done but did not know what.

'Her head's skew-whiff,' said Carter.

O'Leary held her head straight and Carter poured. The water and Guinness ran over her hair and into her eyes and mouth. Some of it went down her chest. But it did no good.

'I don't like this, boss,' O'Leary said.

'Do you think *I* do?' Dacey snatched the bottle from Carter. O'Leary grunted approval. 'Now she's aisier.'

The old woman did seem easier. The paroxysms had stopped. So, it seemed, had the pain. Her face was calm.

'Pretty,' said Carter.

Dacey took her wrist, felt for her pulse. 'What you mean?'

'When she was young.'

Dacey undid her cardigan and her blouse and put his hand over her heart. 'You feel, O'Leary.'

O'Leary felt. 'Ave Maria, Mother of God, Ave Maria, Mother of God.'

Dacey looked down. 'She could have been no more use, anyway.'

'But, Jaysus,' O'Leary said, 'what shall we do with the puir old body?'

Dacey walked out into the warehouse. It was dark now and he had to use his torch. The light was dimmed by blue paper, and he held his hand to prevent even that glowworm glimmer being visible from the yard. Carter and O'Leary watched him opening galvanized iron bins against a wall. Macdonald seemed better. He was sitting at the table, wolfing a sausage which he held in his fingers.

'Here,' Dacey said, coming to the fourth bin. 'Stuff her in before she goes stiff. We'll be in Ireland before she starts to stink.'

O'Leary crossed himself. Carter did the same. But having rendered to God that which was God's, they rendered to Dacey that which was Dacey's.

31 Grete *chez* Ohlsen

Lying in the little bedroom of the first-floor flat in College Green, Grete Carlson could not sleep. She was thinking of Lucas engaged on a mysterious mission from which it was improbable he would return. The money which he had given her released her from the shameful tedium of secret-service prostitution into which she had drifted through hopeless failure. The

143

past was dead but the future was clouded and the present most unpleasant. Through the thin party-wall, she could hear the Ohlsens quarrelling about her. Gustav Ohlsen had some indeterminate position in the Swedish Embassy in Dublin. When she had sought asylum there, Gustav – tall as a beanpole and as myopic as a corn dolly – had promised that his wife Ingrid would be delighted to put Grete up until her passage to Stockholm could be arranged.

Ingrid Ohlsen, whose hair was screwed into plaits and wound round her head like a turban, was less than pleased at the eagerness with which her husband plied their guest with *smörgåsbord* and *akvavit*. 'You may say that woman is in danger,' she hissed, 'but don't think I haven't noticed your eyes following her wherever she goes. You never spring up to open the door for me – not now you don't; and plumping up the cushions in the best chair, *your* chair, so she can sit in it and cross her legs showing her knees, while you squat on the pouffe to see what more she'll show ... !'

'I can assure you that the interrogation at the embassy was very thorough,' Gustav Ohlsen said in his reasonable voice. 'She was held by *force majeure*, and just because she is a very attractive lady—'

'So you admit you are attracted?'

'She is a Swedish citizen and must enjoy the rights of citizenship ...'

'But why have *we* to have our privacy invaded?'

'Only till a Swedish ship—'

'And when will that be?'

'How can I, dearest Ingrid, say exactly when ... this war ... be reasonable.'

'And meanwhile you make eyes at the tart. Why should the Nazis be so interested in *her*? They've occupied all the brothels in Europe.'

'I've tried to tell you. Skorzeny used her to blackmail some English agent. Instead she fell in love with him. And so they want to hold her as a hostage. But she escaped.'

'You believe that?'

'We've checked her story with our people in Lisbon, back home and in Berlin. We haven't found any discrepancy.'

'But it might be a way of planting her as a Nazi agent?'

'We'll watch her. If she is, we'll turn her into a double agent; or feed her what we want.'

'So, even if you *are* interested in her, she isn't interested in you?'

'That's right,' he whispered, sliding his hand between her thighs. 'But aren't you?'

When she heard them gently snoring, Grete fell asleep.

32 Off Sheerness

The MS *Coonamara* lay at anchor, one of a score of vessels waiting for the tide to come flooding up the Thames. There was a thin mist rising gently from the sea. Every two minutes the man on the bridge sounded the fog horn, a short blast followed by a moan. The other ships sounding off in the darkness were like a herd of cattle lowing.

In her holds, the *Coonamara* carried meat and dairy produce. She was one of the neutral vessels licensed to enter the Port of London, passing through the narrow passage in the boom which ran across the estuary. The pilot would be coming aboard in about an hour's time, but already a wooden-runged rope ladder hung over her side. Her captain, Bob Flah·rty, walked up and down the passenger deck, talking quietly to a tall passenger with a scarred face. They were debating the feasibility of the U-boat which was lying submerged beneath the *Coonamara* maintaining its position on the voyage up the Thames without (a) running aground, (b) fouling the motor ship bottom, or (c) being detected by the radar of the other ships in the convoy.

'If any of these things happen, my dear Captain,' said Skorzeny, 'it will be their misfortune, not yours; and when you return to Cobh you will find that the money agreed upon has been placed to the credit of your account. You have nothing to lose by failure, even though you have twice as much to gain by success.'

'I still think you're mad.'

'The enemy consider us sane. So they are not prepared for madness. No one will be looking at the radar screens after you're through the boom.'

There was a cry, like a gull's, repeated twice. The two men stopped at the rail. They could see nothing until the mist parted for a moment. Then they both pointed at once to a launch in the prow of which a man in uniform stood waving. He grasped the dangling rope ladder as the helmsman cut the engine and swung the wheel.

Skorzeny shook Captain Flaherty's hand. 'The Führer will not forget you, my friend.' He swung himself over the rail and climbed down the ladder.

The two men in the launch wore the uniform of the Port of London Authority police; Skorzeny that of a chief inspector. As the launch pulled away, the little pennant from the mast revealed the letters 'PLA'.

Half an hour later a black Humber, looking uncommonly like a police car, bore Skorzeny from the sleeping village of Grain in the direction of Rochester. When they reached Stoke, he looked up at the lowering sky. 'Think it's going to rain?'

'Looks like it,' said Smith. 'Does it matter?'

'When it rains, drains flood.'

33 Hexite hesitation

Lucas parked the van in Fisher Street Hill. There wasn't a soul in sight in the City at this time of Saturday night. Apart from Stainton. Stainton saw them on to the job, told them to close the gates when they had finished and then toddled off in his Austin Seven to get a good night's sleep.

Lovelace and the boys were all a bit the worse for booze, but they lumbered down the Number One East with their clobber. Lucas himself then nipped back to the van for the box of hexite he had hidden under the seat. He had all his other equipment in his tool kit. He paced out fifty yards along Number Two East and left his main kit there. Then, choosing only what he needed, he paced the further distance for the Belmouth blow. This was an easy job, because he was working chest high. In half an hour he had the charge, detonator and wire fixed to his satisfaction. He made no effort to hide the wire, because no one would come along to see it before the explosion.

It was far more difficult to fix the charges which were to bring down the roof. He couldn't reach the top of the roof, so he decided on two charges, one either side, as high up as he could reach. He had never worked with hexite and he was uncertain of its implosive force. He decided to pack all the hexite he'd got into the two charges. After all, it would look bloody odd if the roof came down during an air raid without any sign of a bomb being dropped. If the road fell into the tunnel, that would really be convincing. He kept looking at his watch. Everything was taking him much longer than he had expected. The mixture of Paddy's Power and beer had slowed up his mental and physical reactions. His fingers were all thumbs and the faster he tried to work, the slower things went. By 03.15, the deadline Rainbow had given him, he was still only halfway through fixing the second of the roof charges. It wasn't completed until 03.47.

He ran the three detonator wires carelessly until he reached Monument platform. It was essential to hide the wires leading along the platform, otherwise the first person on the scene after the 'incident' would instantly see what had happened.

He got the wires unobtrusively behind some cabling which ran out of the tunnel and then highish along the platform wall. He was sweating like mad. It was 3.55 when he connected the wires to the air-raid siren. How did Rainbow know that it would be precisely 04.00 when the sirens went off? Anyone on Platform Two would be blown to buggery by the blast.

He had meant to warn the others that he was going back to the yard for more stuff, but there was no time. He had got to fetch his respirator from Holiday & Greenwood's and meet Dacey and the rest as soon as possible after the 'incident'. He got into the van, thanking God he'd remembered to ask for the ignition key.

The engine started at once. There was no traffic on the streets, but he couldn't drive fast. Low clouds hung over the city and the masked sidelights were useless. The only clues to the road were the dimmed street lamps. He steered between them, hooting at intersections and accelerating across. He saw an air-raid warden, heard 'Bloody madman'. His luminous watch dial read four minutes past four. He overshot the turning off to Holiday's, thought he could go round the block, found it was a dead end, had to turn round and go back.

As he did so, an air-raid siren moaned. Fifteen seconds later there was a *Boom*; a blast of air rushed down the street and there was the tinkling of broken glass. He ran into Holiday's and came out with his respirator. A sudden lightening of the sky reflected golden red on the undersides of the clouds; then came a noise quite different from the first explosion, a sort of *ThooUMP*. Christ! he thought, what've I done?

As he came to Finsbury Pavement, there was a vast glow ahead of him. Air-raid wardens were blowing their whistles and running. When he was halfway down Moorgate, he heard clanging bells – distant, then nearer – and suddenly in front of him a fire-appliance swung around London Wall from the west into Moorgate.

It was only then that the searchlights came on, cone-shaped pencils of light doodling on the clouds. Distantly he heard the noise of ack-ack guns and then closer the thud of a stick bomb exploding. What the hell would the plotters at ARP HQ make of a major explosion at the Monument before any plane had come over?

At the end of King William Street was a gigantic blaze against which the puny figures of fire fighters were silhouetted. Madness to try that way, so Lucas turned left into Lombard Street, right into Gracechurch Street and left to park in St Benet's Place.

Ten minutes before the City had been deserted; now figures appeared from everywhere, converging on the Monument: ARP, AFS, police, first-aid. This wasn't the panic Lucas had seen in Spain. This was a citizen army trained to deal with disasters, which efficiency and experience had reduced to the level of mere 'incidents'. Here was the urgent connection of hydrants, running out of hoses, concentration on what had to be done next; but someone at the brain centre must be saying, 'This is sabotage. Who? How? Why?'

If he'd been capable of rational action, Lucas would have driven back to Holiday & Greenwood, filled the tank and any cans he could find with petrol from the firm's pump and driven flat out to Holyhead or Liverpool. But he was drawn, mothlike, to the flames he had ignited. The southern end of Gracechurch Street was jammed with people and appliances. He put on his gas respirator and jammed the miner's helmet on his head. Perhaps he would be taken for a specialist: certainly his face could not be seen.

What puzzled Lucas was the position of the crater. He had reckoned the tunnel roof would be blown to the east of the station in Fisher Street Hill. But the fire was blazing in King William Street to the west of the station entrance. From a great hole in the road rose a vast pillar of leaping flames, in the centre of which could momentarily be seen the tail-end of a long loader; the cab end must have plunged into the platform below. Could one of Lucas's explosions have burst a gas main, which had turned the whole station into a gas bomb ignited by the merest spark, as the heavy loader was passing?

There was no chance of entering the station. Smoke was pouring out of the entrances. To go down was suicide.

Yet, as Lucas watched, a figure emerged staggering through the smoke. As he reached the air, his smouldering clothes burst into flames. It was the boy, Freddy Cronin. As the boy fell, Lucas started involuntarily forward to help an ambulance man who ran across with a blanket. But his wrist was gripped and Lucas jerked round to see a gasmasked figure, whom he knew from the physique was Dacey.

Dacey pulled him out of the crowd, down Eastcheap into Philpot Lane. There, in the shadowy entrance to an office building, the other three were waiting, their faces covered with scarves below the eyes.

'Bluddy mess you've made of it,' Dacey said, after he took his mask off. 'Only thing is to go in by Tower Hill.'

'OK.' Lucas said. 'Go ahead. I'll follow in my van.'

'O'Leary will go with you,' Dacey said. 'Jest to see you don't miss the way.'

Embleton, Nightingale and Hampshire sat in the firewatchers room at Pelican House, drinking mulled Algerian wine. They had volunteered to take over from the roster guard, because they wanted to discuss last-minute details of next day's operation.

The control room beneath the Mall HQ was linked by internal telephone to the despatch point – the north London warehouse – and the reception point – King George V dock. DODS had been given permission to use the rail system from 14.00 hours to 20.00 hours next day, but not the outside telephones, since these were reserved for communication with Eisenhower's HQ in Bushey Park and Montgomery's in St Paul's School, Hammersmith. The problem facing the three firewatchers was how to maintain contact between the control room at Mall HQ and DODS at Pelican House.

'For me,' said Nightingale, 'the only problem is why should Lady Virginia need to come here at all tomorrow? Serpent is a self-contained operation.'

'I can understand why Lady Virginia should want to stay in the picture,' Embleton said. 'After all, like Sir Hilary and you, Nightingale, she has been in on Serpent from the beginning. And God knows, without her, we'd never have got as far as we have. Her presence at DODS seems to me merely a sort of reward for services rendered. But *if* anything went wrong and we needed outside assistance, we'd need someone at DODS; and I can't think of anyone better than Lady Virginia. There isn't a government department or a service unit where she doesn't know someone by christian name because she played with them in the nursery, hunted with them with the Belvoir or danced with them at a coming-out ball. Talk about the old-boy network! She's got the young-girl network at her fingertips.'

'What about Audrey?' Hampshire asked. 'My wife, I mean.'

'What about her?'

'She'll be at a loose end, with me working. Suppose she goes to the Charing Cross Hotel, to write some of those letters to relatives she never gets down to, and have tea in the writing room. It's only a couple of minutes from Mall HQ. She could act as a go-between.'

'A very good idea,' said Embleton. 'And you wouldn't object to popping across to see her, Guy?'

Hampshire reddened. 'If Sir Hilary ordered me to.'

When they turned in, they took off only shoes and jackets. It was a muggy night and they did not fancy lying under the dirty army blankets. Embleton chose a bottom bunk, with Hampshire soon sound asleep above him.

When the alert sounded, Embleton was still awake. In a matter of seconds he had his shoes and jacket on and was climbing the ladder to the roof. But before he got outside he heard the muffled noise of a distant explosion. It was astonishing that the alert should have been sounded so late. The 'Moaning Minnies' were still wailing across the city when he looked around. No sound of aircraft, no searchlights, no ack-ack fire.

As Hampshire and Nightingale joined him, across the river from the heart of the dark city rose an expanding ball of flame. The black underbelly of the storm clouds glowed ember-red, and across the roofs came the boom of an explosion. In that first flash, Embleton could see the dome of St Paul's illuminated in profile on Ludgate Hill, and then the ball of flame collapsed like a pricked balloon. 'My God!' he said.

The three of them stood by the parapet of the roof while, as if in a firework display, flames began to leap in tongues from where the balloon of fire had been. They lit up the underside of new clouds of smoke – red and gold; blue in some places, and in others rose-pink.

'The air-raid siren didn't go off because of that,' said Hampshire.

'More like the other way round,' Nightingale agreed. 'But why ... ?'

Suddenly from across the river came a strange noise. It sounded like a great hornet, growing angrier and angrier as it approached. It was up in the sky, but hidden by the clouds. It was quite different from a bomber, not that awful drone which passed overhead and was away before its clutch of explosives and incendiaries was laid.

Searchlights leapt up against the baffling clouds. There were a few cracks of a-a shells fired blind. But the noise came closer – sounding, as it passed overhead, like a heavy lorry in second gear, and with a faulty silencer. Suddenly the engine cut out. There was silence, except for the ringing of fire-appliance bells, the crack of an exploding shell. Then, way to the north-west, there was the thump of a bomb.

No sooner had it fallen than there was another angry hornet aiming at the Houses of Parliament, a third towards Chelsea. The fourth was travelling lower, almost directly over Lambeth Bridge. It was below the cloud ceiling and Guy Hampshire, seeing the little plane streaming a comet tail of fire, said, 'That pilot must be a bloody hero.'

'Except,' observed Nightingale as the engine cut out, 'that there is no pilot. It's a flying bomb. My problem has been to find the right fuel.' There was a crunch. 'I've always thought of it as rather a sporting weapon. Gives you time to take shelter, when the engine stops.'

The three men pondered Hitler's secret weapon, each in his separate way.

Guy Hampshire said, 'Why are they aiming them at London instead of the invasion ports?'

'How do you know they aren't plastering Dover and Folkestone, too?' asked Bernard Nightingale. 'They may have thousands of launching ramps.'

'Cutting communications.' Embleton pointed to the holocaust blazing on the skyline in the direction of the river bridges at Blackfriars, Cannon Street or Monument. 'That may be part of the same operation.' His voice sank to a confidential whisper. 'I happen to know there was an attempt to blow in Rotherhithe tunnel three weeks ago; I wouldn't be surprised if they had a go at Sevenoaks and Redhill.'

35 An extraordinary inspection

They were playing pontoon in the guardhouse at St Katharine's dock. Sergeant Cousins had been five and eightpence down when the alert sounded; he had insisted on starting again when the raid seemed to fizzle out. He was half-a-crown up when Nobby Clarke on the gate came through on the blower. 'Sarge, there's an HQ car outside.'

'At this time of night! What the hell?'

'Says it's an extraordinary inspection.'

'Fuckin' extraordinary. Who says?'

'Never seen 'im before. There's a chief inspector. Identity cards look OK.'

'For Jesus Christ! In the middle of a fuckin' air raid. Hold 'em, Nobby. "Security reasons"! I'll be down.' He put the receiver back on its holder, picked up his winnings and said. 'HQ outside. Get them cards, bottles and glasses put away. Empty them ruddy ashtrays. And be doin' somethin' improvin', ready to drop everythin' on the command, "Report for inspection".'

'What d'you mean, "improvin'"?' Private Bean asked.

'Look at them books there,' the sergeant said. '*Lilliput, Picture Post*, them fuckin' ABCA pamphlets. Read 'em.' The sergeant was already slicking a steel comb through his hair, brushing dandruff off his shoulders, putting on his cap. He poked his swagger stick at Private Bean's flybuttons. 'Adjust your dress.'

Nobby Clarke swung back the dock gate, stood at attention as the Humber drove in, and then dutifully closed it.

The driver of the car got out and came over to Nobby, while the chap sitting beside him also got out but remained standing by the car. The chief inspector remained in the back seat with the window down.

'Looks like they've got it in hand now,' Nobby said, 'but I've never seen anything like what it was, not since the blitz, I mean.'

'It was a right old blaze,' said the driver.

Nobby looked at him curiously. Nobby's feet were terrible and his intelligence wasn't much better; but he had never heard anyone in the PLA mob talk like that. 'I ain't seen you before.'

'That is not surprising, as I am new. A "rooky", so to say.' Nobby said nothing, because Sergeant Cousins came down from the guard room, swagger stick under left arm, clicked his heels as he came to attention and threw up a proper bullshitting salute.

The man standing by the car gave a low order and the sergeant turned about and shouted, '*Guard! For inspection at the double, fall IN!*'

Nobby Clarke believed in Leslie Henson's advice to the conscript: Keep your bowels open, your mouth shut and *don't* volunteer. He had been born and bred to obey. His not to reason why. And yet something, the driver's manner, his standing so close, the chief inspector staying inside the Humber, made him uneasy. It almost made him break the habits of a lifetime.

But his four pals on the guard trotted out, old String-Bean as right marker, the other three eyeing right, shuffling into position, standing at attention like fucking ramrods. And if they and the Sarge didn't sense anything was wrong who was Nobby to open his trap?

The PLA man opened the rear door for the chief inspector to step out, as the sergeant turned about to face the Humber. But instead of the chief inspector came a stream of bullets fired from a sten-gun fitted with a silencer captured by the Germans from the British.

At that moment Private Nobby Clarke opened his mouth to scream a warning, the first individual thing he had ever attempted in the twenty-five years of his obedient life; but no words came. A twist of the driver's garroting wire had cut his windpipe. The last thing his eyes registered before they glazed was the back of the Sarge's head hitting String-Bean's face. He was dead before Skorzeny stepped out of the Humber.

They were all dead, except Haines, who was lying on the ground, holding his belly and convulsively kicking. Skorzeny went over to him and compassionately blew out his brains. Then he turned to the other two. 'Clear up this mess,' he said. 'We want no blood around. There must be brushes in the guard room.'

Then he walked down the dock to inspect the sluices and the opening and shutting mechanism. The dock hadn't been used since 1940. A sloppy people might have allowed them to rust up. But not the English, he noticed with approval. The threads were well greased. The wheels turned as easily as if they had been in daily use. 'Pity they weren't on our side,' he muttered. 'Between us, we would have mastered the world.'

36 A lesson for Lucas

To the north of London there were flashes and terrific booms. Lucas couldn't tell whether it was bombs or a thunderstorm.

Tower Hill station was closed, but the fire picket opened up, when Lucas rattled the gates. He was frightened but suspicious, until Lucas showed his pass. 'What's goin' on?' he asked. 'Can't get through on the blower. The line's dead.'

'God knows,' Lucas answered. 'Hell of a fire at Monument. Gas main gone, I think. Me and the boys are going in from this end.'

'I got no authority,' the fire picket said, as he opened the gates. 'I did ought to wait till the station master comes.'

'And get a bollocking for lack of initiative? Don't be a Charley. Give us a hand getting the gear down.'

'It isn't in the regulations,' the picket said, watching the accumulation of boxes, tools and haversacks brought in by the other four.

'Don't worry. I'll carry the can for you,' Lucas said. 'Now you take these and we'll go on down.'

'What about them gates? Them gates didn't ought to be open till the maintenance men's finished.'

'We *are* the maintenance men, mate.'

Grumbling, the picket helped them carry the gear down the emergency stairs, having insisted that the gates should be closed when everything was inside the station. 'The boys have got to park the vans off the main road,' Lucas explained. 'They'll need the keys to get in again, but they'll give them back when that's finished.'

'It ain't in the regulations!' But the picket handed over the keys to Dacey and O'Leary, whose first job was to park the vans unobtrusively up an alley and remove the number plates. Lucas looked at his watch. It was already 4.57. By their schedule, they should by now have already been inside the Belmouth outflow and ready to move. Things were proving him right. He had warned that there might be any number of hitches. But of course, if they failed to hijack the first train, there were still four more to come behind that.

On the platform he kept the picket talking. Lugging this stuff along the track to Monument was going to take a hell of a time. 'What we want is one of those hand-operated maintenance trucks,' he said. 'You haven't got one here?'

'Aldgate, that's the nearest. It'd take you—'

O'Leary and Dacey had come up with the last of the gear in time to overhear this. 'It doesn't matter,' Dacey said. 'The six of us can do it.'

It took a moment for the number to sink in on the picket. 'There's only five of you.'

'And you make six.'

'Listen, mister, I've already ... what'll happen if anyone wants ... ? I mean, when he knows, Mr Omes the station master will want to come ...'

'The station was to be closed until the maintenance men went off duty, so if you're giving them a hand—' suggested Lucas.

'No, mister. Enough is enough.' The picket was firm.

'Quite enough,' Dacey said impatiently. He took an automatic from his pocket. 'See this. Well, if you don't want to feel it, you'll do your share of carrying.'

'I ... I ... I d.d.d.don't understand.'

'Don't try. Get moving.' Dacey picked out the two heaviest boxes for him. Even with a pair of extra hands the load was enough to make their progress slow along the track, lit only by their helmet lamps. Lucas wondered what Dacey would do with the fire picket when they came to the Belmouth outflow entrance. He couldn't be let free or he would run back to Tower Hill station and give the alarm. But if he was tied up, the poor bugger might not be found perhaps until he was dead.

They could smell their approach to the blocked tunnel before they saw it. Some gas had escaped that side of the fall but had not ignited. Lucas had overdone his charges, and even if there had been no fire they would never have been able to get through from Monument station without God knows how many hours of excavation.

On the other hand, the passage through to the Belmouth outflow was a neat job: at the far end just big enough for even the burly Macdonald to wriggle through. Dacey dictated the order. Macdonald first, then Carter, then Lucas, then O'Leary. 'Now you won't be wanting me anymore,' said the fire picket.

'Oh, you,' said Dacey, as if he had forgotten all about him. 'You better go in third. I'll push your boxes in so that you can drag 'em up after you.'

'I won't go. I won't go, I tell you. You're not maintenance. I won't go!' He turned and started to run towards Tower Hill, but he tripped and fell across the rail. 'Get him,' Dacey ordered Lucas and O'Leary, flourishing his automatic.

Lucas did not move, but O'Leary made a dash and tackled the picket as he scrambled up. 'You heard my order,' said Dacey.

Lucas said nothing. Macdonald and Carter were in the Belmouth outflow. If he and the picket took on Dacey and O'Leary, it would be two against two. But *they* were armed.

Then he suddenly remembered. They wouldn't dare hurt him, far less kill him, until *after* the job was done. He brought his hand down on Dacey's forearm and caught him round the neck from behind. The automatic went off and as it did so Dacey shouted '*Hier! Schnell!*'

Lucas brought Dacey down backwards on top of himself. He was aware of the picket struggling with O'Leary, but now Dacey had got his teeth into the base of Lucas's left thumb. It was bloody agony and Dacey's heavier weight pinned him down.

Then suddenly it was over. 'Leggo, chief,' Macdonald said. 'I got him.' Dacey rolled over and Macdonald yoicked Lucas up by the scruff of his neck. 'Shall I clock him?' Lucas saw Macdonald's sledgehammer fist ready to strike.

'Not now. Later.'

And so, without a further struggle, they all crawled into the Belmouth outflow and rested for a moment on the platform which ran along the flowing drain.

The first to recover was the fire picket. 'You can't do this to me,' he said. 'You gotta let me go.'

Dacey was sitting on a box of tear-gas bombs. 'OK. You can go.'

The fire picket could not believe his ears. 'Honest?'

Dacey nodded his helmet light.

The fire picket started back to the hole leading to the underground tunnel. But Dacey held up his left arm, barring the way. 'Down there.' He pointed along the platform of the drain. 'That's where you go.'

'But it doesn't lead any—' He did not finish his sentence. Dacey's bullet landed almost in the middle of the forehead and he fell back into the drain. He did not move; because he had no life and because the water had not built up enough force to float him away.

'You bloody murderer!' Lucas said.

'*You* are the murderer, Mitchell,' said Dacey. '*I* would have tied him up. But you forced me to teach you a lesson.'

37 Belmouth to Fleet

As the materials were unpacked and parcelled out, Lucas kept one eye on the body of the fire picket. It formed a sort of dam across the outflow, which built up a body of water behind it, until the body floated and moved several feet downstream where it swung so that the drainwater could flow either side. But, at least in Lucas's opinion, the volume of water was increasing; which, if true, meant that somewhere in north London it was raining.

He looked at Carter, who seemed to him the most jittery of the gang. 'Ever been underground before?' Carter shook his head. 'What about the rest of you?'

Neither O'Leary nor Macdonald spoke. They looked to Dacey, who said, 'Don't worry about us, Mitchell. We'll manage.'

'You want me to go in front and show the way?' When he had first studied the map of subterranean London, Lucas had been bewildered. But, as Skorzeny had explained, the system was comparatively simple. The original structure of the city had been that everything – rainwater, slops, nightsoil – had been carried down the original streams and rivers which flowed into the Thames. Now these streams, and other man-made conduits were used purely to carry road-drainage into the Thames, where there were hinged traps which closed when the body of water, at high tide, exerted more pressure than the water in the outflow. An entirely man-made system carried *sewage* in an ultimately eastward direction along the northern outfall sewer to the main drainage metropolis and filter beds just west of Barking Creek. These two different systems each had their ventilation shafts which, for the convenience of the underground maintenance men, were interconnected by laterals. Anyone bearing this in mind was unlikely to be lost for long. Any sewer would be flowing roughly eastwards, any road-drainage conduit roughly south. With his underground experience, Lucas should be able to move faster than the others and, having given them the slip, find his way to the surface; with the cutting tools he carried he could escape from a ventilation shaft.

But Dacey was firm. 'O'Leary goes first.'

'And shows us the way?'

'You follow O'Leary and show *him* the way.'

'So long as he cares to take the risk, OK by me.'

'What risk?' asked O'Leary, suspiciously.

'I wouldn't know till I came to it. A rotten rung, slime, rats. Anything.'

'Shut up, Mitchell,' Dacey said. 'He's only trying to scare you, that's what.'

'You're the boss,' Lucas said. 'But keep your safety catches on. I'd hate to see you shooting yourselves. Or one another.'

'If anyone gets shot,' said Dacey, 'it'll be you.'

'Then you'll all be in the shit.' Lucas looked at his watch. 'We're already two hours and seven minutes behind schedule. Make it snappy, O'Leary. About seventy yards along, you'll find a ladder. Climb up it and if you don't fall down again, you'll know the rungs are sound. About twenty feet up, you'll see two laterals, left and right. Take the left one and give a shout.'

O'Leary moved gingerly up the platform, followed by Lucas, Carter, Macdonald and Dacey in that order. The current in the Belmouth was quickening and the depth rising. 'For Christ's sake, get a move on,' Lucas muttered, 'you aren't walking the fucking tightrope across Niagara Falls.'

Lucas had every excuse to force the pace, because they were so behind schedule. But the faster they moved with gathering confidence, the more he pressed them, with muttered comments like 'God, what a shower!' – and impatient assistance which rattled their nerves.

They went along the lateral as far as the Eastbourne ventilation shaft. They could have crossed over into the lateral running on to the Fleet, but Lucas forced them down to the Eastbourne, the volume of which made the Belmouth overflow appear a trickle. It was here Carter slipped and sprained his ankle. He managed to get up, but he yelled when he put his foot down. Lucas did not wait, he forced O'Leary on to the foot of the next ventilation ladder. They only stopped, because Dacey shouted. 'We'd best go back,' O'Leary said.

'Stay where you are. You'll need all your strength before you're through.' Lucas made his way slowly back to the other three. Dacey was saying, 'You've bloody well got to walk on it. We can't leave you here, you fool.'

Carter had not forgotten what had happened to the fire picket. He nodded. 'But I can't carry this stuff, boss, I jest can't.'

Davey asked, 'Mitchell, what can we drop?'

'Explosives and detonators for blowing the tunnel behind us. The rate we're going there won't be time to lay the charges anyway. We'll have to rely on smoke and tear gas. Macdonald'd better go ahead of Carter. Tie a rope under Carter's armpits and Macdonald can take the strain as Carter climbs.' Another quarter of an hour was wasted and their progress was slower than ever. 'God,' said O'Leary, 'think we'll ever make it?'

'Don't blame me. I told Scarface and Dacey we needed more time, more men, trained men. And now we're saddled with walking wounded.' They waited impatiently until Macdonald appeared at the lateral. When O'Leary helped Macdonald with the rope that supported Carter as he climbed, Lucas was free. He could have made his way quickly and silently along the lateral to the Fleet; or he could have charged O'Leary and Macdonald from behind in the hope that he could shove them both into the ventilation shaft. But he did neither. He had to know where his mother was and only *they* could tell him. O'Leary was the one to work on. There would be a series of these pauses while they waited for the others to catch up. He remembered a trick which Skorzeny had been proud of. When they were trying to find out where Mussolini was being held, Skorzeny or one of his chaps had bet a peasant that Musso was dead, and the peasant had pointed to the dictator in the grounds of a villa. What if he said to O'Leary, 'I bet my Mum's dead'?

But when they looked down the Fleet ventilation shaft, they could see that the river was over the platform, and that was all O'Leary could talk about. It was pouring down in spate. O'Leary was scared and called Lucas to join him.

Lucas flashed his torch down the river. Thirty feet away there was a bridge over to the other side and the handrails projected a couple of feet above the brown flood. 'It won't come up to your knees,' Lucas said.

'I don't like it.'

'Then I'll go first.'

'And what'll Dacey say?'

'Wait and ask him.'

They waited till the others reached the shaft. 'Don't be a fuckin' cissie,' Dacey shouted. 'Don't you realize the bastard just wants to get away.'

O'Leary put his foot down and as Lucas had said the water did not reach his knees. O'Leary made his way warily towards the bridge, but hugging the side of the tunnel for fear of stepping off the platform.

He had only gone halfway when a breeze started to blow, which suddenly became a gale. There was a roar and the river suddenly started to rise. O'Leary turned towards the ladder. In the light of his torch, Lucas saw the man's face, the mouth open in a yell, eyes starting from his head. Then O'Leary was lifted from his feet by a great wave which rose and rose. Lucas clutched at the ladder with both hands. His whole body was below the roof of the tunnel. As he tried to climb, the torrent tore his legs from the rungs. He clung to the ladder, his body streaming out like a pennant in a gale. He filled his lungs just before the tidal wave engulfed him. One hand was wrenched away, but he got another grip. It seemed as if the water was trying to strip him. His lungs felt as if they were going to burst. Blood throbbed in his temples. Before his closed eyelids appeared explosions of light. Consciousness began to ebb. He longed to loose hold and go down the drain like O'Leary.

Then though he was still submerged, the force of the torrent seemed to slacken. He got a foot on a rung, pushed himself up, grasped the rung above. Air burst from his lungs, but with a last tremendous impulse, he thrust his head above the water and clung, sobbing, weak and gasping for breath.

38 A good meal

The U-boat lay submerged in St Katharine's dock. All preparations had been made. The steel door leading to the disused warehouse had been opened with oxyacetylene blow lamps. The passage had been cleared to the subterranean terminal. Each supernumerary had rehearsed his action. Now was the time to rest. In the hours to come, there would be no time to eat. So everyone was having a good meal.

In the captain's cabin, Leutnant Heinrich Lustige was entertaining Major Skorzeny to a breakfast-lunch. They were drinking real coffee, the gift of Dom Rosario, instead of the *Kornkaffee* on which the Third Reich had subsisted for the last four years. There was good rye bread, salami from Italy, *bratwurst* from Germany, camembert from Normandy and from Mainz that transparent cheese which looks like fungus, smells like feet and is delicious with sliced Spanish onions and Cayenne pepper. '*Gut Geschmack!*' Skorzeny said. 'Tastes good.'

Leutnant Lustige looked at the clock. It was 11.55. 'How long do you reckon it will take for the train to get here?'

'I keep telling you. It's scheduled to reach the East India dock at 15.45. But that's with the electric engine. The maintenance engine isn't as powerful. But it hasn't as far to go. With luck, it might reach here about the same time, which gives us two and a half hours to load before high tide.'

'If we don't get it all stowed, we leave the rest. We go down on that tide, you understand?'

'Don't you worry, my dear fellow. Skorzeny may think up "lunatic schemes", but he isn't mad. You and I will live to fight another day.'

Lustige poured two liqueur glasses of schnapps. He passed one to Skorzeny, held up the other and they solemnly clinked. 'I drink to that,' he said. *'Prosit!'*

39 Hijack

Thanks to the rest, to Dacey's threat or Lucas's warning, Carter managed to keep up with the others. Considering the tough going, the slime and rats in the Westminster sewer, and the difficulty of opening the grille into the secret railway, they made good time.

But when they dropped on to the permanent way, it was 14.50 hours. The time had come to split up. Lucas's job was to steal the maintenance engine, while Dacey jumped the treasure train and rode on it until the alarm was given and the current cut. Then he would have to wait for the maintenance engine to arrive.

In the original plan, O'Leary was to go with Lucas and lay the smoke and tear-gas screens. Carter begged to take O'Leary's place. 'With this ankle, I'll never jump that fucking train.'

Carter had only to say this for Dacey to order Macdonald to go with Lucas. Maybe sheer cussedness. Maybe he distrusted Carter, because he had volunteered just for the money. Lucas was glad. Macdonald made up in strength what he lacked in brains. He was obviously shocked to hear Dacey say, 'If you

can't jump the train, Carter, you'll have to fucking-well walk.'
As they went towards the station, Lucas ahead with both arms
weighed down with bomb boxes, Macdonald covered him with
his automatic. 'He ain't no bluddy Irishman,' he apologized to
Lucas. 'Hans is his real moniker – *herp-hup!* – a bluddy kraut.'

From the moment they entered the tunnel, they heard the
hum of the rails. But now it was growing louder and louder.
The plan had been that Lucas should be already in the maintenance engine before the bullion train arrived, everything tested
ready to start. 'Jaysus, it's comin'.' Macdonald said, panicking.

'Don't worry, Mac,' Lucas said. 'If we go through to the
siding as the train passes, nobody will notice us.'

The noise of the train's wheels drowned the hum of rails. As
they waited at the end of the platform, Lucas said, 'Dacey shot
my old lady, didn't he?'

'I can't hear you,' Macdonald said.

Lucas could see the lights of the train. He shouted, 'I bet you
five nicker it was Dacey killed the old lady.'

'You're bloody wrong, Mitch,' Macdonald said. The train
came out of the northern end of the tunnel into the station and
the noise suddenly billowed out. Macdonald cupped his hands
and shouted, 'Carter'll tell you. *Herp-hup.* She died natural.'

It didn't matter how she died. His mother was dead, as he
had known in his heart of hearts. And he was free. Free to fight
against these bastards, no holds barred.

The train clanked and rumbled into the station.

'Now!' shouted Lucas; and as the engine with five heavy-
laden trucks, carrying God knew how many millions, trundled
by, Lucas and Macdonald slipped along the nearside platform,
unnoticed by the watchers in the control room.

Macdonald seemed panicky when they reached the siding.
Lucas dumped the smoke and tear-gas bombs in the back of the
maintenance engine. He gripped Macdonald's arm and helped
him up. He felt a bit sorry for the dumb bastard. Then, seeing
that the train was out of the station, he switched the points and
climbed into the cab.

But he did not start up the diesel.

Now was the perfect moment if he decided to surrender. He

had only to pretend that he could not get the diesel to fire, to leave the treasure train to move on its determined path to the docks, to reason with Macdonald when he came forward, threatening him with his sten-gun ... and then the whole nightmare which had begun in Kimberley would be ended. His skin would be safe and, if he played his cards right, he would be forgiven his desertion for his betrayal of Honeycomb.

But he knew the bloody army. There'd be a court martial. Weeks, months would pass before it was held. Even if he didn't get Jankers, Grete would have gone to Stockholm or somewhere. A beautiful woman, with money (*his money*) was very desirable. How long would she wait?

Macdonald leaned over from the back of the engine. 'What the fucking hell's wrong?' he asked. Lucas started up the diesel. He saw the tank was full. 'Just warming it up, Mac,' he said.

Macdonald came forward to the cab. He was holding a smoke bomb in his hand. 'How the hell do you start this fucking thing?' he asked.

The noise of the train was receding. All the better. The nearer it got to the junction between the two dock tunnels, the less distance the maintenance engine would have to shunt it.

Macdonald had his sten-gun over his shoulder. 'Take that off,' Lucas ordered. 'You can't do anything with that in your way.'

Macdonald gave him the sten and Lucas put it in the engine cab. Macdonald still had a haversack of hand-grenades, but he was at Lucas's mercy. Gently Lucas took him back to the rear of the engine. 'Didn't Dacey show you how to set these off?'

'It was O'Leary's job,' Macdonald said, 'God rest his soul!'

'Amen to that! And all of us.' Lucas set off a smoke bomb so that Macdonald saw how to do it. Then he made Macdonald do a second bomb on his own. These they set on the back of the engine.

By this time the ex-pug had become so jittery that Lucas had to lead him to the cab of the engine. He placed the smoke and Adamsite tear-gas bombs on Macdonald's side of the cab, keeping the sten-gun on his own side.

By this time the two smoke bombs in the back were going

full blast and the smoke was beginning to fill the siding. Lucas let in the clutch and the diesel engine moved slowly forward in a cloud of smoke.

When they came into the station itself, the smoke quickened with the pressure of the air from the second treasure train. Lucas waited with his eye on the panel of the control room.

As soon as he judged that the smoke could be seen, he accelerated. 'Two more smoke now, Mac,' he said. 'But don't drop 'em till I say when.'

Macdonald set off one bomb, but when Lucas reached the eastern tunnel's safety, he noticed something was very wrong with the big man. He was grasping the smoke bomb, as if for dear life.

40 A way with rats

After the treasure train had trundled through – which, Embleton thought, was frankly no more interesting than a load of coal, apart from the preciousness of its freight – they all turned to Carstairs at the control panel.

Apart from the screen which showed the traffic on the railway (the second train beginning its journey from the warehouse the moment the first entered the tunnel to the King George V dock), there was a formidable assembly of switches and knobs: switches to control the lights along different sections of the tunnels; switches to activate the sections of live rail; and knobs to control the speed of each engine. As Carstairs was explaining the system to the Brigadier, Nightingale heard an odd noise and walked over to the observation window.

The tunnel was for some reason filling with smoke, but he could see the maintenance engine and a glimpse of two men. 'Quick! All of you! Look!'

Embleton was by his side in a moment, then Hampshire. 'Sir Hilary! It's a hijack!'

'What, what?' Sir Hilary did not react quickly, but Carstairs rose from his swivel-chair, took one look, and then reached forward and cut the current from the whole live rail. 'KGV! NLW! Don't worry. I've cut the juice. It's not a power failure. Looks as if some jokers want to take the first train. At least, someone's gone off with the maintenance engine. Using smoke.'

There was a scramble of voices.

' . . . No. I don't know more than that. Have a think your end. No need to panic. We've got twenty-five or thirty minutes at least.'

'NLW here,' a voice said. 'Can't you jam on Number One Engine's brakes?'

'That's the bugger,' Carstairs said. 'They said it wasn't necessary with remote acceleration control. I warned them.' He turned in his chair. 'Well, Sir Hilary, what do we do now?'

The Brigadier turned to Embleton. 'Any ideas?'

'What about Hampshire and me taking the bren and going in after them?'

'Which is probably the first thing they thought of, dear boy. Anyway have you ever tried firing with a respirator on? I did with a Lewis-gun on the Somme. Once. Sheer waste of ammo. Nightingale?'

'If they want to take the train, sir, the only outlet is the St Katharine dock. They should be forewarned.'

Sir Hilary turned to Carstairs. 'What about it?'

'Never been connected, sir. St Katharine's has been out of commission since the system was installed.'

'What about Audrey?' volunteered Guy Hampshire.

'What?' thundered the Brigadier.

'Audrey, that's my wife, sir. She's at the Charing Cross Hotel. She could telephone Lady Virginia to alert St Katharine's if I popped over and told her.'

Hampshire was too eager. 'First things, first,' Sir Hilary said. 'The way with rats is smoke 'em out! What's the ventilation system on this railway, Mr Carstairs?'

Carstairs swivelled back to his control panel. 'This is the fresh-air injector fan at NLW.' He switched the dial to Maximum. 'This is the Westminster injector.' It was at Off. He turned it also full-on. 'There are two foul-air expellent rotor fans.' He switched one off. 'That ejects at the King George dock. This one ejects at St Katharine's—' He switched it full-on. 'It won't be long before that smoke starts moving down to St Katharine's as fast as the maintenance engine.'

41 Enemy in need

'You all right, Mac?' The train was not yet in sight, and Lucas could afford to spare a glance. Macdonald was clutching his fists and nodded 'Yes'. But he couldn't speak. No good asking him to lay the tear gas. Something terrible was going to happen to him. His right arm began to twitch horribly.

Lucas kept the accelerator pedal gently down to half speed, and very carefully adjusted his respirator. The tear gas was Adamsite, deadly stuff which penetrated chinks impermeable to smoke. If it did, it made you retch; and then it was a choice between choking on your own vomit or tearing off the respirator and taking the Adamsite into your lungs and eyes. That could mean immobilization; even death. As he flung the first tear-gas bomb behind him, he saw Macdonald's face. It was as dark as a thundercloud. He took a second bomb and, as he set it off and dropped it beside the tracks, he thought – If I was in that control room, I'd use the expellor fan if that was possible.

Macdonald began to shake. His arms and legs drummed so hard that Lucas felt it in his own body. Then suddenly the overhead lights went out, though they remained on ahead of him.

There must be a reason for that, but what was it? Had they sent a party out from the Mall station through the smoke and wanted to shoot them up against the illuminated background?

'Mr Carstairs,' Sir Hilary said, when K.G.V. control volunteered to send an intercepting party up to the Tower Hill junction, 'could you illuminate that junction, but keep all the rest dark?'

'Easily,' Carstairs answered. 'Every quarter of a mile is wired separately, for maintenance. It can be turned on and off in the tunnel, or from here.' He pointed to the little glowing red lights on the control panel.

'The station's clear of smoke now, sir,' Embleton said. 'Why not turn off the lights this end and let us get a pot at them in silhouette?'

'Do that,' said Sir Hilary, 'while I write instructions for Ginny to give the Chief about St Katharine's. The guard must be warned. And reinforced. You phone it, Nightingale, from Strand post office. Then come back here. Lady Virginia can handle this.'

Lucas put his hand out in the darkness but snatched it away, when Macdonald's teeth began to close on it. The ex-pug started to scream; and he went on screaming. In that tunnel which already throbbed with the noise of the engine and the hum of wheels, Lucas wanted to scream as well. After everything that had happened – the body of the dead fire picket floating down the Belmouth drain, O'Leary's yell of anguish as he was whipped down the flooding Fleet, and the casual news of his mother's death – he felt he could stand no more. He flicked his torch and shone it on Macdonald. He was stiff down the right side, his battered mug twisted to the right shoulder. Didn't seem to be breathing.

A screech of bullets whistled past. Lucas flicked off the torch. He could hear the whining ricochets. He groped for another smoke bomb and stopped the diesel while he set it off. He had to build up a curtain of smoke. It was his only hope. Smoke and tear gas.

But then Macdonald came out of the rigor. He seemed to be shaken with spasms, as if the devil had got him and was shaking inside him.

Lucas wanted to push him on to the track and leave him. But he had to keep the poor bugger to prove to Dacey that he was in good faith. He could hear the gnashing of teeth and, as they approached the lit section of the tunnel, Lucas could see bloody spittle frothing from the other man's lips and trickling down his chin.

Poor bastard, thought Lucas, as he cocked the sten-gun.

Embleton put a new magazine on the bren. 'I'm going to leave you to cope, Guy. I want to have a word with the Brigadier.'

'I don't imagine they'll be heading back this way,' Hampshire chuckled. 'With any luck they'll have laid down gas as well as smoke. But I'll give 'em a single round every four or five minutes.'

'Aim at the side of the tunnel about a hundred yards up,' suggested Embleton. 'It ought to ricochet round the bends, that way.'

42 Telephone exchange

Mr Nightingale went into the end booth in the Strand post office. He was armed with small change and noticed to his satisfaction that there was no one in the booth next door.

He got through to DODS without difficulty and told the switchboard girl that he wanted to speak to Lady Virginia in the DG's office. Sylvie was to go in there with her notebook and pencil to take down instructions on the extension. 'It's very urgent.'

After nearly a minute, Lady Virginia picked up the telephone. 'Has something gone wrong?' Her voice sounded anxious. Understandably.

'Is Mr Constantine in the office?' Nightingale asked.

'He may have been earlier,' she answered, 'but not now. What's happened?'

'There's an attempt to take the train.'

'But that's impossible. I don't believe it.'

'Please, Lady Virginia. We've contained them from the Mall; and there's an assault party coming up from K.G.V. The enemy is using smoke, perhaps even gas. But we've got the extractor fan working at St Katharine's. With luck they'll be knocked out by their own gas. Anyway they'll be slowed down by working in respirators. It'll take them an hour, maybe even two, to get the train to St Katharine's, even if they're not shot up at the junction.'

'But St Katharine's ... that's still open? You haven't phoned them?'

'Too risky. If the guard's been overwhelmed – which seems likely – it'd only warn the enemy. Is Sylvie getting this down?'

'Yes, Mr Nightingale,' Sylvie cut in.

'Good. Now this is the message, Lady Virginia. You're to ring the country and speak to the Chief. Put him in the picture. Tell him Sir Hilary's coming back to the office as soon as possible. Ask can the Chief lay on a raid on St Katharine's dock straight away?'

'But suppose everything's all right there? Won't we look pretty silly?'

'Leave that to the Chief. That's what Sir Hilary has written. You just do what he says, Lady Virginia; and stand by to hold the fort until Sir Hilary arrives to take over.'

A man had come into the telephone booth next door. He was wearing an old trench coat and had a brown velours hat pulled down so that his face was shaded. He was flicking over the S to Z directory at the Smith pages. He was running a finger down the columns, but he was bent towards Mr Nightingale's booth as if trying to overhear what he was saying. 'Everything clear? Good!' Nightingale said, and put down the receiver.

43 The odds are even

Lucas laid the sten-gun on the floor of the cab. It was a gamble, but he wagered that Dacey would not try to kill him till the train had passed the Tower Hill junction into the St Katharine's branch. Carter did not know enough about trains to manage the points.

Macdonald was suddenly silent. Lucas looked down, thinking the fit had passed. But something else seemed to have happened. He stopped the engine and got down on to the track. Screening the torch with his hand, he shone it on the big man's chest. A dark stain was spreading across his jacket. Lucas touched it:

it was warm and sticky – like blood. Lucas wondered how many people in the centuries of human warfare had been killed by a stray bullet in the middle of an epileptic seizure.

Dacey's voice boomed down the tunnel asking what the fucking hell he thought he was up to. Lucas could see the two men silhouetted against the illuminated section behind them. Neither of them was wearing a respirator.

An idea came to him. He went to the front of the engine and knelt down, using it as a shield in case the bren-gun opened fire again; then he flashed S-O-S with his torch.

They did not understand his message. Lucas could not shout because of his respirator. With the bright torch in his hand, Lucas waved them to come back to the maintenance engine. He could see the smoke drifting towards the back of the engine, which meant that there must be a heavy concentration of Adamsite between himself and the other two. Once they took it into their lungs, putting on a respirator would only make it worse . . .

Lucas could see the two men arguing. Dacey had a gun in his hand and he jerked it to emphasize what he was saying. Carter left him and began to walk towards Lucas with slow, reluctant steps.

Suddenly there was the whine of a bullet ricochetting down the tunnel. Carter flung himself forward on to the tracks, as the sound of the report reached them. He lay flat, as if expecting further bullets.

After a time Dacey shouted, 'For Chrissakes, Carter, you aren't hit, are you?'

Carter rose to his knees. Lucas could hear him coughing, then saw him get up and start running, or rather staggering, back towards Dacey.

Dacey tore open his respirator case and started to run as fast as he could towards the lit section of the tunnel. Carter could not follow him. A stream of vomit spurted from his mouth. He sprawled on to the tracks. He tried to crawl on all fours towards the light. But the gas was in his eyes, his nose, his lungs. He struggled like a fly sprayed with insecticide.

Carter was out of the struggle. Once sure of that, Lucas could feel pity for the poor bugger, the luxury that can be afforded to an enemy when defenceless. There was nothing he or

Dacey could do about Carter. Lucas turned to Dacey himself, who had stopped on the edge of the lit section of the tunnel and was fitting on his mask. Carter had provided him with advance warning against the Adamsite.

It was four against one to start with, Lucas thought. Now the odds were even. Apart from the fight in defence of the fire picket, Lucas had played fair. *He* hadn't drowned O'Leary in the Fleet. *He* hadn't given Macdonald an epileptic fit and then shot him. *He* hadn't ordered Carter to walk into a cloud of toxic tear gas – though of course he could have warned him, even though he could not make himself heard through a respirator.

He thought: Dacey would kill me now without a qualm. But he doesn't dare to. I am his only chance of getting the train to St Katharine's. And if he doesn't get that train there, he'll never escape alive.

But what is Dacey thinking? he wondered. Anything I do he will be instinctively against. So I must pretend to want to do what I don't really intend – so that I can persuade him that he's forcing me to do what I've decided.

Lucas thought of his possibilities. He could go back towards the Mall station and try to find the grille through which they had all entered. But another bullet ricochetting down the tunnel persuaded him that that was too risky. He would have to use his torch to find the grille; and once he did, the man on the bren might rake the tunnel with bursts. Lucas had no desire to kill Dacey, but he was determined to avoid being killed, if that were humanly possible.

The future lay eastwards, along the tunnel either to St Katharine's or the King George dock. He hadn't yet decided which. He flashed his torch once and waved to Dacey to join him.

As he anticipated, Dacey shook his fist and waved to him to bring the maintenance engine up to the train which was halted just within the illuminated section of the tunnel.

Lucas again pretended that he wanted Dacey to come back. This time, he flashed the torch at Dacey and drew the beam back towards the engine. Dacey gesticulated wildly.

Lucas started to walk towards Dacey. That made Dacey only more furious. He kept pointing towards the engine. Lucas pretended not to understand. He knew that the moment the Mall station had seen the hijack, an interception party would be sent in from the King George V dock; but even the simplest military operations took time.

Dacey fired a single shot from his sten-gun, aiming deliberately to miss Lucas.

Lucas held up his hands as if to say 'All right, you bloody fool', and turned about to walk back to the engine. As he started it up, he assessed the possibilities ahead. They had always thought of it as a four-man operation. One on the back of the maintenance engine to cover attack from the Mall. (That man could be dispensed with, because they obviously intended merely to use harassing fire.) A second to cover attack from the King George V tunnel with smoke, gas and/or give covering fire: that defence would have to be dispensed with also. With only two of them still left, one was needed to go forward and change the points to St Katharine's, the other to drive the maintenance engine.

Beneath his mask, Lucas grinned. Such a two-man operation could be carried out only by a team which trusted each other. If Lucas was sent forward to change the points, he could pretend to change them, but in fact leave them as they were or shift them back again, so that Dacey shunted the train into the King George V tunnel. But if Dacey insisted on changing the points, Lucas could shoot him when he came back to see why the train wasn't moving.

Being averse to killing, Lucas decided that he would volunteer to drive the engine. The cussed Dacey would be certain to insist on his changing the points.

44 Sir Hilary afraid

Carstairs was alone in the control room as Embleton came in. 'Just heard from K.G.V.,' he said. 'They've mustered an interception squad: a corporal and a couple of o.r's, with a bren-gun ~d some hand grenades. *Not* Pioneer Corps. And a walkie-talkie. They ought to be able to cope; unless the enemy sends reinforcements up from St Katharine's. There's a subaltern laying on a more ambitious reinforcement: hand-driven truck, field telephone, so they can go into St Katharine's tunnel without losing contact with K.G.V. That'll take time, though.'

'Where's the Brig?' asked Embleton.

'Went off to find a friend with a telephone,' Carstairs said. 'The old boy will be on the mat tomorrow; *and* his apology for a security officer.'

A yellow light started to flash on the wall. Embleton nodded towards it.

'Enemy aircraft approaching the coast,' Carstairs explained.

Sir Hilary came in. His cheeks were an unhealthy colour – ashen with pink-salmon patches in the centre. 'Oh, there you are, Embleton! I've got a job for you. Let's go upstairs right away. Everything under control down here, Carstairs?'

'Except for St Katharine's, Sir Hilary.'

'Leave that to us.' Sir Hilary took Embleton's elbow as they went out of the room and up the concrete stairs, either from friendliness or to steady himself. 'I've got you a d.r., my dear fellow. I trust you won't mind riding pillion down to St Katharine's. I think we ought to find out for ourselves just what's going on.'

'What about your phone call, sir?'

'Couldn't get through. Tried the office. Tried the Chief. Both of 'em engaged. Talking to one another, I suppose.'

As they went up the stairs, red lights were flashing at each landing, and out in the streets the alert was wailing from every 'Moaning Minnie' for miles around.

'Report to you at the DODS, sir?'

'When you need to, Embleton; but you have my authority to use your own initiative. I'll back you.'

'Thank you, sir.' Embleton gave the Brigadier a salute far more respectful than those he had flung up for the Chief. 'Anything else, sir?'

'Just refresh my memory. Who was at that meeting in my office yesterday afternoon.'

'Apart from us, just Nightingale, Hampshire and Lady Virginia.'

'Not Mr Constantine? No?' Sir Hilary sighed. 'I was afraid not.'

45 Plan D

The telephone rang in the dockmaster's office. Skorzeny sat in the dockmaster's chair and Leutnant Lustige sat opposite him. It was not the first time that the telephone had rung. Indeed, there had been a succession of attempted calls, the phone ringing and ringing until the caller had given up, under the impression that there must be something wrong with the bell mechanism, which could not be repaired until the engineers came on duty after the weekend. After ringing three times, the bell stopped.

Skorzeny and Lustige looked at one another and Skorzeny took a gold-tipped Turkish cigarette out of his gold case.

The bell rang again and he put the cigarette between his lips. The bell stopped after the fourth ring.

Skorzeny lit the cigarette. 'Sounds like Rainbow,' he said to Lustige; but he did not pick up the receiver when it began ringing again after an interval.

There was no extension on which the Leutnant could listen. He stood up and went to the window, through which he could see his U-boat surfaced in the dock with its newly-painted conning tower on which no identification marks were visible.

As the phone rang a fourth time, Skorzeny snatched up the receiver.

'Is that you, Honey?' a woman's voice asked.

'Comb here,' he answered.

There followed a whispered communication, interrupted only by Skorzeny saying, 'You must speak up, I can't hear you,' and later, 'I'll ask him.' He put his hand over the mouthpiece. 'Plan D. What's the earliest?'

Leutnant Lustige had known that Rainbow would not have rung unless there was bad news. As always, Skorzeny had made a variety of plans to cover different contingencies. Plan D covered the abandonment of the raiding party, the submersion of the U-boat, the lifting of the sluices and opening of the lock gates before the tide was at full. With luck, it could be managed in fifty-five minutes. But Lustige did not believe in luck. 'An hour and a half,' he answered.

Skorzeny spoke into the mouthpiece and Lustige could hear the voice the other end raised in some emotion – anger maybe, or desperation.

'I know you'll do your best, Honey,' Skorzeny said and replaced the receiver. 'It doesn't really rest with her,' he explained. 'It depends how long the others take to organize.'

In the distance was an angry buzz. It grew louder when they went to the head of the outside stairs. Skorzeny saw, as Leutnant Lustige signalled the retreat to the *Unter-Offizier* below, a flying bomb trailing fire across the river to the west. It was the earnest of the Führer's promise of victory, blazed across the sky. He raised his right arm in the Nazi salute; and Lustige, seeing him, did likewise.

Louder the noise grew, and louder. The seamen and SS Kommando men stopped what they were doing, stared and raised their arms in salute.

Then the engine cut out. Skorzeny silently counted the seconds. At thirty-five, the boom reached them. The men immediately sprang into action.

Lustige turned to Skorzeny. 'You will come with us?'

'I let you into this, comrade,' Skorzeny answered. 'I shall stay here with Schmidt and Thornton. I can find my own way home.'

46 Better to walk

Sir Hilary watched Embleton disappear through Admiralty Arch on the d.r.'s pillion. An o.r. said to him, 'There's no staff car, but shall I try to find you a taxi, sir?' The Brigadier shook his head. 'Better to walk.'

He chose Horse Guards rather than Whitehall. He wanted to see St James's Park, bursting into brilliant leaf oblivious of four terrible years of war, rather than sandbagged windows and shrapnel-pitted walls. Captain Hilary Fry, RN, his great great grand-uncle must have walked down Horse Guards', perhaps treading exactly where he trod, after collecting his prize-money for the Battle of Trafalgar. It was only about 140 years ago, which – to a man over sixty – did not seem so very long. But in those days, there would have been more life: not only people, but sheep and cows grazing in the Park, and milkmaids selling sillabubs.

When he reached Horse Guards' Parade, he heard a noise uncommonly like an angry bluebottle. It was one of those confounded robot planes. He looked up at it with disapproval. It was so noisy. And a stupid missile. It couldn't be accurately aimed. If only it could fall on him! But no such luck. It sailed over towards north London, futilely aggressive. Then there was silence. 'Pray God!' he thought, 'it falls somewhere silly, like a graveyard.'

Graveyards made him think of the late Earl Alaystair St Neots, poor wrongheaded chap, and that terrible funeral at Stansbury in the drizzling rain; and the vicar who made the gaffe saying, 'God, give him rest from his *friends*!' (which was curiously appropriate because most of them were Huns); and poor little Ginny, come from the convent at Ascot, crying her heart out. And that made him think of what at this moment he least wanted to remember – Lady Virginia, his own personal assistant, whom he loved, since his boy's death, more than anyone on earth, except his darling wife, once so beautiful and now so wildly practical, farming at Shepton Mallet.

He was shirking. He ought to get back to Pelican House as soon as he possibly could. But he paused beside the Foreign Office, hearing another of these horrible little buzzing monsters. It cut out somewhere in south London and he stood looking, as he prayed, for the last time over the lake towards Buckingham Palace, not yet completely obscured by greenery.

The bomb fell somewhere in the Park. There was a slight stir of air, as in the Underground when a train approaches. The young leaves scarcely rustled and none fell. The Brigadier resumed his walk towards Storey's Gate. Over on the right, up Birdcage Walk, was the Wellington Barracks. How many times he had paraded there before the changing of the guard! In the old days, which till now had not appeared such good old days.

Suddenly in the deserted park he heard the noise of an automobile. He turned and saw a taxi. It was driving full-pelt but the FOR HIRE sign was lit. Sir Hilary stepped out into the road and waved his swagger stick.

The taxi-driver did not slacken speed. He was bent over the wheel, peering through the windscreen. His face was very white, his eyes glued ahead. He paid no attention to the Brigadier.

'Bloody scandal!' muttered Sir Hilary.

Then, as he glared after the cab, he saw that there was nothing there. The back had been blown away.

47 Through Sunday city

The d.r. kicked the starter. 'I'd advise the tin-helmet sir,' he said, like a wartime Jeeves.

Embleton stowed his forage cap under the epaulet of his battle-dress, tightened the chin-strap of his helmet. 'Not that it matters with these bloody things,' he said, pointing skywards to a flying bomb. 'More like playing Aunt Sally. Know St Katharine's dock?'

'Not beyond St Paul's,' the d.r. said. 'Hold tight, sir.'

The heavy machine shot forward through Admiralty Arch. The lights were against them, but there was no traffic from Whitehall or the Strand. The d.r. jumped the lights, swung round Trafalgar Square, down Duncannon Street and along the Strand. According to the clock in Fleet Street, it had taken them minus three minutes to travel from St Martin's-in-the-Fields to the Law Courts: and it felt like it. The d.r. had the soul of a wall-of-death rider. There was nothing on the roads except fire engines, ambulances and a few buses with some cars, parked while their drivers were taking shelter. Every minute or so a flying bomb farted overhead.

At Mansion House station Cannon Street was closed. Seeing the diversion, Embleton remembered the explosion at Monument station (was it only early that morning? it seemed a week ago!). They sped up Queen Victoria Street to the Bank, swerved right into Lombard Street. Looking down King William and Gracechurch Streets Embleton saw the havoc – the teams of firemen and salvage men at work on clearance. But it was only a couple of glimpses before they roared up Fenchurch Street.

'Straight ahead,' shouted Embleton. 'Right at Aldgate East station.'

Coming towards them down Aldgate was a totter driving a pony and cart. Suddenly the pony shot up in the air and the whole street appeared to crumble. The d.r. flicked right into a side street. The blast struck the back wheel. The motor bike mounted the pavement and was heading straight for a lamppost, when the d.r. – 'Christ!' – swung back into the road. He stopped at the end of the road. 'Crutched Friars; Crosswall; or Cooper's Row: which'll it be, sir?'

'Try Crosswall,' Embleton said. 'Right when you get to the Minories; and then left of Tower Bridge. No need to go so fast. It's not far.'

'OK, sir,' said the d.r. 'Tell me when.'

A couple of minutes later, Embleton said, 'Stop. We're there.'

'Where, sir?'

Embleton got off the pillion and pointed to two large gates; beside them a small door, with three pint bottles of milk on the step.

Embleton walked over to the gates and listened. Then he beckoned to the d.r. to come over. 'Can you hear anything?' Embleton whispered.

The d.r. put his ear to the gates. Then he shook his head. 'I thought I did,' Embleton said. 'But I'm not sure.' He tried his weight against the gates. They were locked and bolted. So was the side door.

The gates were a good twelve feet high. No chance of looking over, even with a hoist. Opposite was a grim warehouse with sooty windows. If one could get in there, the whole dock would be visible. Embleton nodded and they walked back to the bike.

'Wheel it back about twenty yards before you start up,' he said softly.

'Then where?'

'There's a police station in Leman Street.'

48 Smoke without fire

Both wearing respirators, Lucas and Dacey had to communicate in sign language. But Lucas had misjudged Dacey's psychology; and his intelligence. Dacey was only too willing to let Lucas drive the maintenance engine. Dacey himself walked alongside with his finger in the trigger guard of the sten-gun pointed at Lucas. The train itself would act as a shield against any bullets coming from the King George dock tunnel.

Slowly, the massive train began to move; even full out, the maintenance engine could not make more than five or six miles an hour.

Lucas was sweating inside his respirator. Perspiration oozed down his neck and stuck his shirt to his chest. He had to work his lungs like bellows to get enough breath – with the blood beating in his temples it was terribly hard to think at the same time as driving.

Every now and again a stray shot came ricochetting down from the Mall. Dacey was more exposed than Lucas, but the chances of his being even grazed were not much higher than being run over crossing a road. The dangerous moment would be when changing the points. Whoever did that would have to leave the cover of the treasure train and would be a sitting target for the raiding party from King George V dock.

Leaning to the left, Lucas could see up the tunnel to a black hole in the casing. That was the Tower Hill junction. The mere fact that it was not illuminated meant that a raiding party was waiting for them.

Dacey is going to make me get out and change the points for

him, Lucas thought. If they get me, he won't care. But he'll still have to drive the engine to St Katharine's: and if they get me at the points, they'll certainly get him in the driving cab. Not that this was much consolation.

The smoke which Lucas and Macdonald had set off earlier was beginning to drift around them. Lucas could no longer see the opening of the King George tunnel. He bent down and felt in the smoke bomb box. There were two bombs left.

He and Dacey were enemies, like Hitler and Stalin. But for their own purposes, they might work a little longer together – a sort of Nazi-Soviet pact. He slowed down and waved to Dacey. Then he held up a smoke bomb and cut the engine. In dumb language, he suggested that they should set off one smoke bomb at the front of the treasure train and the other at the back of the maintenance engine.

For a time Dacey deliberated. Then he took one of the bombs and walked to the front of the train.

49 Retreat

Skorzeny and Lustige were standing on the dockside. The withdrawal was being made with quiet speed. A sergeant checked each man against his duty list before he went aboard the submarine. Only eight names remained unticked, of which two were those of the roof-watch. One of these came hurrying across to the Leutnant. A British officer and a despatch rider had ridden up, tested the gates and ridden off again.

Lustige and Skorzeny exchanged glances. 'Go up and bring Signalman Biedermeyer down with you at once,' Lustige said; then, turning to the sergeant, he said casually: 'I want all men aboard in five minutes.'

'What is your clearance when fully submerged?' Skorzeny asked.

'About eighty centimetres to the concrete base. It may be silted up, but that should not matter.'

They walked up the dockside to the lock gates. The level in the dock basin was two feet two inches higher than the river outside. They opened the sluices to the full.

As they walked back they could hear the low hum of the engines starting up. 'You should be able to open the gates before the levels are absolutely the same,' Lustige said.

'The outflow wouldn't make you foul the gates?'

'The engines can compensate for that. To get into the river without being seen: that is the important thing.' There was the buzz of another flying bomb; then silence. Looking back they saw the bomb dive into the river. Seconds later there was a great spout of water.

'It would be ironical,' Skorzeny said, 'if Field Marshal Hermann Goering dropped a depth charge on you.'

'But more probable, if it was the Royal Navy. I want time to reach, say, Woolwich under our own power and then drop down on the ebb-tide.'

'I'm sorry, my friend, Honeycomb has not proved to be one of my best ideas.'

'You will be very lucky,' answered Lustige, 'if you survive to have any more.'

The sergeant was waiting. 'All aboard, sir.'

Lustige and the sergeant climbed on to the superstructure and into the conning tower, the sergeant first, the Leutnant pausing to give the Nazi salute before he disappeared from view.

The hatch was battened down and in a moment there was the gurgle of bubbles escaping from the vents of the superstructure as the U-boat slowly submerged until the conning tower was hidden. Then the periscopes were retracted until they showed only six inches above the water.

50 Choice of evils

Lucas let in the maintenance engine as Dacey walked off to the head of the train. At five miles an hour, there should be no problem for Dacey to run forward and catch up with the front engine. It might make him short of breath, perhaps make him unable to think about anything else but setting off the smoke bomb. But that was all to the good. And after all, Dacey still wanted to get the treasure train to St Katharine's.

That thought made Lucas realize the difference between them. It didn't matter a fuck to him where the train went: into the King George tunnel would be better than St Katharine's, because it would provide cover from the raiding party.

Lucas envisaged Dacey's scenario. Having set off the smoke bomb in the front of the train, he would come back and cover Lucas with his sten-gun until just before they reached the points. Then he would order Lucas to go forward and change them. If he wasn't killed by the King George party while he was doing that, Dacey would kill him later and drive the maintenance engine through, himself.

Violence was what Lucas most hated. He had run away from, yet been pursued by it ever since the Spanish Civil War. But this was the moment of confrontation. It was kill now – or be killed later. Even more vividly than the murder of the fire picket, he remembered Dacey picking up the chicken caught between the bonnet and the fender of the car on the way to Dublin and pulling its head off. He bent down and picked Macdonald's sten-gun off the floor of the cab. He continued to drive, holding the sten down out of sight until he came nearly abreast of Dacey, who was holding his gun at the ready. If Lucas could have seen Dacey's eyes, it might have been different. As it was, he fired at the respirator: the eyepieces shattered. The arms of this robot-like creature jerked up as it fell back, and Lucas drove on, seeing the illuminated tunnel to St Katharine's open to his right, as the train switched into the King George V tunnel.

There was a burst of bren-gun fire. Bullets, striking the casing, were whining off at different angles. Lucas crouched down, trying to count the number of bullets and remember (was it thirty?) the number of rounds in a bren magazine.

They must be firing wild, because the smoke was dense, a cloud of gold. Should he get down and crawl? Or make a dash? From the direction of the Mall station came the sound of shots; but no bullets. They couldn't ricochet so far.

Lucas jumped, caught his foot on a rail or something, felt a shooting pain, crawled agonizedly forward. The firing from the tunnel started again. Lucas lay still.

He had suddenly remembered that he had no tools to work his way out. He was trapped.

51 Embleton at Leman Street

'With all due respect, sir,' said Superintendent Salt, 'this is hardly the province of the Metropolitan Police.'

'I am perfectly aware of that,' answered Lieut-Col Embleton, his tact and temper frayed at the minutes wasted in penetrating to his inner sanctum. 'But someone's in St Katharine's dock and it isn't the guard or they'd have taken in the milk.'

'I suggest, sir, that you notify the Port of London Authority police. It's their job to guard St Katharine's dock.'

'I'll do that, if I can use your telephone. But meanwhile can you get a constable into Rossiter's warehouse overlooking St Katharine's?'

'That won't be easy, sir.'

'Can you, or can't you? If you can't, will you sign a document to say that you refuse? I have to report to Downing Street; and Mr Churchill will want to know why you can't.'

Superintendent Salt was stirred. 'I *could* send Constable Cohn round on his bicycle . . .'

'In that case, my d.r. can take your constable on the back of his pillion. Give me the telephone number of the PLA police, and while you're arranging that, I'll phone them.' Embleton's anger was stoked by realization that the failure of Operation Serpent was due in part to his not checking DODS security as scrupulously as he should have done. The Chief would never take him back, even if he reverted to the rank of major.

At the PLA police, he got through to the duty officer. Yes, said the duty officer, they had made a telephone check on St Katharine's. The guard was seventy-two hours on, thirty-six hours off. But there was a bell-fault. Oh, they hadn't taken in their milk? That was certainly unusual.

Embleton sketched the outline of Operation Serpent.

'Yes, we knew there was a special movement from King George V. But St Katharine's? I don't understand.'

'Nor do I,' said Embleton. 'But my guess is there's some type of enemy craft in that dock, and you ought to do something about it.'

'The whole thing is utterly ridiculous. Anyway, how do I know who you are?'

'Ring up Brigadier Sir Hilary Fry at DODS and ask him.' Embleton gave the number. 'I've sent my d.r. round to Rossiter's warehouse, which overlooks the dock. I'll call you as soon as he reports back. But meanwhile, believe you me, it would be a good idea to send a PLA police launch to recce St Katharine's.'

When Embleton replaced the receiver, he saw Superintendent Salt holding a receiver on another line. 'No sign of any enemy in St Katharine's – Constable Cohn says.'

Embleton took the receiver. 'Is there any sign of *anybody*?' he asked.

'Yessir. There's two PLA officers at the bottom of the steps to the ... guard house, I suppose you'd call it.'

'Give 'em a blast on your whistle and see what they do. And tell the d.r. I want to speak to him.'

There was a silence for some time, then the noise of footsteps on bare boards. 'D.r. Howard here. You wanted me, sir?'

'That dock. Is it empty?'

'No – full, sir.'

Embleton could hear three blasts of a police whistle, but distantly. He turned to the superintendent, 'I'll need my d.r. What shall we do with Cohn? Tell him to hang on at Rossiter's?'

'The telephone's on the ground floor. To see what's going on in the dock, he's got to be on the first floor, maybe the floor above.'

'Got anybody else free?'

'Not at the station. Constable Sturt's on the beat; somewhere – Cable Street, East Smithfield, Ratcliffe Highway.'

'Bloody thin on the ground,' Embleton muttered.

'Wouldn't you be with half a mile of shop-windows blown in down Commercial Road?'

Embleton heard the d.r. handing the receiver over to the constable. 'Well, what did they do, when you blew the whistle?'

'Not a bleedin' thing, sir. Didn't look round. Just went up the stairs and into the office.'

'Didn't even start?'

'No. They might've been deaf, for all the notice they took.'

Embleton turned to the superintendent. 'I'd like the constable to stay watching those gates, if you can spare him.'

The superintendent took the phone. He explained that the d.r. was to come back to Leman Street at once; Cohn was to watch the dock and report anything which appeared to be suspicious. 'I *know* you can't be in two places at once; but you'll have to cope on your own, till I can pull someone in to help you.'

As Embleton waited for the d.r. to arrive, he said, 'Let's try the PLA police again.' He dialled, but the number was engaged.

There was an angry roar, growing louder and louder as it headed, it seemed, directly at them. Then the engine cut out. The superintendent flopped down behind his desk and Embleton threw himself on the floor in the protection of the wall below the window.

There was a thud in the distance; and, nearer to, the tinkle of glass shattering as it reached the pavements.

52 Nothing to sneeze at

Lucas thought: there must be a repair kit on the maintenance engine. The smoke was so thick that his torch was of little use, compared with fingers. He felt a metal box. It had a hasp, fitted over a staple. A padlock had been inserted, but was not closed. He was in luck. He lifted the lid and, bending down, he could examine the contents with aid of torch and touch. Corn in

Egypt! There was a portable oxyacetylene kit, a cold chisel, a metallurgical hammer, a clench, rust-dissolving oil, wire-cutters and pliers.

He put on the harness of the oxyacetylene kit, loaded the tools in his respirator case and bent down to tie up his boot lace, which had come loose.

Suddenly there was a flash, an ear-splitting roar, the *clink*, *clang, clunk* and whistle of shrapnel striking different surfaces or shooting down the tunnel. Two electric bulbs went out.

Dazed, but unhit, Lucas stood up. They wouldn't try another grenade immediately after the first. He started to hobble-run towards the darkness of St Katharine's tunnel. He tripped on Dacey's body, but he did not fall. He had left his sten behind; but bugger that! He reached the right-hand casing of the tunnel and felt his way along.

When he came to the point where he could see the trucks facing into the King George tunnel, he hesitated. There was so much smoke that he knew he couldn't be seen, but a blind burst from a bren couldn't fail to miss him. If he went fast, he would not be exposed for long. But with his bad ankle, he was liable to stumble and make a noise. So he edged slowly forward, clenching the tools in his respirator case so that they did not clink.

At last he was in the dead ground of the St Katharine's tunnel and he began to move faster, out of the glow of the light into the smoky darkness ahead. He did not dare to light his torch while he could see light behind him. The pursuing party would not wait long before they advanced to see what damage their grenade had done. They would find Dacey, with his riddled respirator: and that would prove that there was at least one survivor, perhaps wounded, perhaps unscathed, hiding either up the St Katharine's tunnel or in the section between Tower junction and the Mall. They would certainly tackle St Katharine's first.

He came to a recess in the casing, built for a maintenance man to shelter while a train passed on the tracks. He flashed his torch and saw a grille, like the one through which they had originally entered the secret railway. Thank God, he was used to oxyacetylene cutting! Within half a minute, he had a flame and was cutting through the grille-joints.

He had only one to do, when he realized that the darkness had grown lighter. He glanced back along the tunnel. The overhead lights had come on up to twenty yards away, where the track made a bend.

This meant that they must be in communication with the room controlling the tunnel lighting. They had probably cut the lights behind them (against which they would have been silhouetted if they had advanced into darkness) and were using light to expose each section while they moved forward in shadow. The next section would expose *him*.

He turned, cut through the last joint and with quiet desperation lifted out the grille. If he hauled himself up and left the grille on the ground, they would spot the hole and catch him in some sewer or drain. Deftly he fastened the end of the coiled wire to the top-right corner of the grille and cut off about four yards. Then he did likewise with the top-left corner. Holding the ends of the wires in his left hand, he tried to hoist himself up. But he couldn't. With his bad ankle, he hadn't the power to jump high enough.

He could hear the sounds of pursuit; there was a burst of bren fire, aimed to ricochet off the side of the tunnel round the bend. He twisted the two ends of wire into the strap of his respirator case. With the aid of his good leg and both arms, he hoisted himself into the ventilation shaft. He turned, sat on his bottom and wriggled his legs in. Then he caught hold of the ends of the wire and pulled up the grille.

Suddenly there was total darkness. He had to find somewhere to fix the wire so as to hold it in position. He flashed his torch upwards and behind himself. His heart was beating fast, even though he told himself not to worry. The pursuing party would not enter the section which had been illuminated until the section he was in was lit up.

Immediately that happened, he dowsed his torch. The ladder in the ventilation shaft had iron rungs. He fixed one wire loosely to a rung, while he got the other firmly into place. Then he secured the second wire.

He could hear noises and muffled voices. The grille, as he had fixed it, was merely a sort of flap which had only to be lifted up and anyone could shove a gun into the hole and fire blindly up the shaft. He had to secure the bottom so that he would have time to escape down some lateral and hide before they entered.

The trouble was that the wire was lighter in colour than the grille. He bent the last six inches of the coil of wire into a hook. He scraped the dust and grime of the ventilation shaft on the wire. It wasn't much good, but would have to suffice. Then he pushed the bent hook diagonally through a square hole in the middle of the bottom of the grille and, turning it ninety degrees, brought it back so that he could twist the end round the shank.

Then he heard a muffled voice say, 'Corp'l Donovan, this is taking altogether too long. Tell Control to light the whole tunnel as far as St Katharine's. We've got to move faster than this. Jenkins, you'll have to handhold the bren. Keep to the right side of the tracks to give covering fire to us on the left.'

Lucas, holding the bottom wire firm, could see through the grille. On the far side of the tunnel a middle-aged lieutenant wearing a tartan kilt plodded along with an automatic at the ready. 'Keep an eye to those manholes, Jenkins,' he called, pointing towards Lucas. And through the grille, Lucas found himself staring into the respirator glasses of the bren-gunner. In the draught of the ventilation shaft, he felt rising in him an impulse to sneeze into his mask.

53 Letter to a godfather

Nobody had thought to tell Pickersgill to come in on a Sunday, so the lift was locked. Under normal circumstances the Brigadier would have sworn – below his breath: since at his age it was idle to waste breath unless there was an audience. But he was rather glad to have the excuse of walking slowly up the stairs, resting at each half-landing. He was dreading what he would find when he reached the office.

When he reached the fourth floor landing, he found the folding iron gates, installed by Embleton in the interests of security, closed against him. 'My God!' he said. 'This is the blinking limit!' He shook the gates and shouted, 'Hullo! I say! You up there!' He couldn't remember the names of the girls in the front office, whom he always thought of as 'Frizzy' and 'Mousy' because of their hair.

Then he noticed that the key to the iron gates was lying on the step inside, from which it was quite possible even for him to extricate it. He opened the gate, closed it behind him and took the key halfway up the stairs, before thinking that if anyone like Nightingale or Hampshire wanted to come up he had better replace it. Embleton ought to have installed a push bell for an emergency like this. He would have to speak to him. Except of course there never would be another emergency like this.

As he went up the last flight of stairs, he felt the old ticker was a bit dickey. He really shouldn't have been pestered. Except that if he had stayed at Shepton Mallet, he would have been caught up in darling Candie's tireless Dig for Victory campaign and would have probably passed out tugging at one of her goat's udders. Since the flap was off in 1941, DODS had been a cushy billet, compared with front-line farming at Shepton Mallet, especially the geese: the way they stopped murdering grass and rushed honking at one, the moment one was within honking distance.

He rang the bell at the office door and Mousy came out and said, 'Oh, Sir Hilary, you're wanted on the line now. Could you take it in your office?'

Through the door of the outer room, he caught a glimpse of Frizzy at the switchboard. He nodded at her. She had an evanescent prettiness. Each time he saw her, he thought, Isn't she lovely? and about five seconds later, No, she isn't really. 'I'm putting you through, sir,' Frizzy said. 'Sir Hilary has just arrived.'

The Brigadier went into his office and picked up the telephone. It was a chap who said he was the duty officer at PLA police HQ. 'Just checking, sir. Somebody calling himself Lt-Col Embleton. Speaking from Leman Street police station. Rather an improbable story about St Katharine's dock. You know how overstretched we are at the moment. Wondered if it was the enemy ... a sort of diversionary effort.'

'Diversionary?' Sir Hilary said. 'Perhaps it very well may be.

I hadn't thought of that. I mean, in their overall plan . . .'

'Then I can ignore—?'

'No,' ordered Sir Hilary. 'The hijack of the train may be diversionary, but not Col Embleton. He is my adjutant, in this matter my 2-ic. We have reason to believe that St Katharine's dock may have been seized by an enemy kommando unit.'

'But how, Sir Hilary? Just tell me how.'

'I don't know, my dear chap,' Sir Hilary said irritably. 'That's your job to find out. All I can tell you is that a train routed for King George V was hijacked at Mall HQ. The only station it could have been switched to is St Katharine's. We have contained the hijack. At least, I trust we have. But the cargo vessel must be still in dock.'

'With all due respect, Sir Hilary—'

'I will not be insulted. Have you telephoned St Katharine's dock?'

'There is a bell-fault. At least that's what we're told. There very often is, these days.'

'Well, there'll be more than a bell-fault, if you don't do something quick, Mr Whateveryournameis. If it's not a court martial, it'll be whatever your equivalent is. Send a PLA launch immediately to watch St Katharine's dock. And if you want to cross-check, ring K.G.V. They've had an interception party up the tunnel to Tower junction for the last hour or more.'

'Thank you, Sir Hilary, for your help,' said the duty officer, 'insofar as I can call you helpful. You can understand, if I ring off.' The line went dead abruptly.

'Oh dear!' said the Brigadier, 'oh dear!' He replaced the receiver and stretched out to open the box in which he kept his panatellas. I will remember this day as long as I live, he thought, as he lighted up. He had had an active and successful life, in the army and later on the railways. But he had begun to feel that maybe he was too old. Now he knew it. He called out – 'Ginny!' She had carried him from the moment he took on DODS. He flicked the intercom. 'Ginny, please come in, dear.'

There was no answer.

He dialled the front office. 'Where is Lady Virginia?' Mousy answered. 'Didn't you see her, Sir Hilary? She went to meet you at the Mall. But she left a note. I'll bring it in.'

'Please do.' Sir Hilary stubbed out his panatella. It did not taste good. Mousy knocked and came in and laid the note on his blotting pad. 'Thank you,' he said.

When he looked down, he saw it wasn't the sort of note Ginny usually left, which would be typed 'The DG'. The envelope was handwritten, but formal. 'Brigadier Sir Hilary Fry, KBE, MC, DSO & Bar, Director General, Department of Overseas Despatch and Shipment.'

He did not open it at once. He looked up at Sir Thomas Lawrence's portrait of Captain Hilary Fry, a flattering portrait on which his ancestor had squandered too much of his prize-money after Trafalgar. Then he picked up the only other object which he had brought from Shepton Mallet to his office, a Damascene paper-knife of copper with a chased silver handle, his only legacy from great-uncle Wilfred – who, having journeyed to the Levant, never returned alive. With this he formally opened the envelope, which was of the fine paper Ginny kept for personal correspondence.

The paper on which it was written was headed with the family crest and had the address of Stansbury Chase, Wilts, her family home until it had been sold to pay death duties on the Earl's estate in 1938. The address had been slashed out with a thick-nibbed pen and in its place was written 'HERE' and beneath it 'NOW'. Sir Hilary put on his spectacles and read:

My dearest Bodgers,
You know how much I love you and always have, and will: more than anybody in the world, except Daddy. And after he died, perhaps even more than Daddy. Because you were so good to me, and kind; and of course also Candie. So you must know – no of course you can't know because you trusted me – but you must try to *realize* how awful, what a real *traitor to you*, I felt, being *loyal* to *Daddy's ideas*. Because he *foresaw* all this: the way poor Mr Chamberlain would get forced into this war. On the wrong side! I mean, the *Diktat* of Versailles. It was Lloyd George and Clemenceau did it. I know Hitler's *bad*, perhaps. But Stalin's *worse*. What did Poland matter? If only we had let Hitler and Stalin knock one another out! what a civilized peace we could have offered the German and the Russian people, Daddy always said. And he was *right*, darling Bodgers. As you'll see,

both you and Candie, if you live as long as I hope. I don't *believe* in any after-life; I wish I could because I'd like to be with Daddy, not with Mummy though. But in case there is one (after-life I mean), *pray* for me. Because I suppose I'll be with dubious characters like Brutus and Cassius, Benedict Arnold and that bugger Sir Roger Casement. Please, *PLEASE* forgive your Ginny.'

54 Water boatmen

When Constable Cohn had blown his police whistle, Skorzeny hissed, 'Take no notice.' His companion was the driver of the PLA car which had met him off the Isle of Grain two days before. His name was Thornton and, in the early days of Mosley, he had been one of the Blackshirt 'stewards'. But after the Olympia rally, where he had been 'over-zealous', the fascists had retired him to less conspicuous duties.

Inside the office was waiting the third member of that Isle of Grain landing-party; Henry Smith, born Heinrich Schmidt, an NSDP member since 1932, but a naturalized British citizen since 1925.

'You should have sailed with the Leutnant,' Smith said.

'I gave him my word,' Skorzeny answered, 'I would see he got away safe.'

'Will any of us?' Thornton asked. 'After the alarm has been given.'

'But how do we know that the alarm *has* been given?' asked Skorzeny. 'A policeman blows a whistle. Why? Not to summon reinforcements. If there were reinforcements to summon, he could have gone down into the street where we could not see him and waved. It was because he had no reinforcements that he blew the whistle. He wanted to see what we were going to do. If we were suspicious characters we would have been alarmed. But we were so intent on our business, that we did not even look round.'

'All the same,' Thornton said, 'he's still watching at that window. See him.'

The three men watched Constable Cohn clearing a still larger patch of grime, and peering through curiously.

'I could shoot him from here, easily,' said Thornton. 'I'm a first-class shot. I won prizes at Bisley.'

'But would you kill him?' asked Skorzeny. 'At this distance? Through glass? Not knowing how thick it is?' He lit a cigarette. 'Anyway, if you did, do we know he's alone? Mightn't there be someone downstairs at the end of a telephone? Or passing in the street?'

The flying bomb which had sent Embleton and Superintendent Salt to shelter on the floor became audible from across the river. It grew louder and louder. Skorzeny looked round. The office was a death-trap with windows on three sides. The engine cut out. 'This way,' he ordered and led them into a little kitchen with only a small window. They crouched on the floor under tables and shelves. There was a boom. We'll never win the war with that, Skorzeny thought, but he said, 'We'll use the Rowboat plan.'

If everything had gone right, they would have used the PLA plan in reverse and caught the *Coonamara* on the outgoing tide. But Skorzeny put his trust in alternatives. How could the enemy know what he would do, if he didn't himself know till the last minute?

The dock gates could be opened manually or by machinery from the control room. As they went back into the office, Skorzeny looked across to the warehouse. Constable Cohn was back on his look-out. Skorzeny decided to take a risk. He could see that the opening of the sluices had already lowered the level of the dockwater by some fifteen centimetres. If the dock gates could be opened by a few centimetres even, the water in the dock would level with the flowing tide faster. But it mustn't be so much that the constable would notice.

'You watch the policeman,' he told Thornton. 'Schmidt, change into waterman's gear, stuff your PLA clothes in the oven, and then take over from Thornton, while he changes.' He himself went into the control room and switched on the opening mechanism. The water level indicators showed that the dock

195

was still two and a half inches higher than the river. He swung the opening lever gradually until it reached Maximum. For a moment he thought that the gates wouldn't budge. He was afraid that the engine would seize up, but gradually the great gates started, minimally, to move. Then, with the pressure between the gates forcing its way through, they began to close again.

He realized that it was possible to put the full power of the engine to opening merely one gate. Now the body of the dock water flowing out sideways forced the opening gate inwards and he had to cut the power to prevent the outflow being too obvious.

Thornton came over. 'The bobby's still looking – I mean the policeman.'

Skorzeny didn't trust Thornton's mechanical ability. 'Relieve Smith,' he said, 'and tell him to take over from me. You look the real waterman. Very good!'

The secondhand waterman's clothes provided for Skorzeny were not so very good. He was too broad and tall to get a proper fit. Sea-boots concealed the shortness of his trousers. When he had changed, he went to the window overlooking the warehouse. The constable was still there.

Skorzeny smoked, trying to decide whether or not to shoot the constable. To ensure that he was killed would necessitate more than one bullet. It would make a great deal of noise and be likely to cause attention. But if the constable was killed, there would be, almost certainly, enough time to open and close the dock gates; so that after the submarine had left, the dock would not attract attention from any passing PLA patrol. On the other hand, if the constable was allowed to remain alive, he would be able to pass on information about what had happened in the dock. Knowing German policemen of similar rank, Skorzeny thought that the constable, if left alive, would cause more delay by misinformation, or uncertainty, than he would convey, if dead.

Another possibility occurred to him. Thornton was a traitor to his country. Supposing that Schmidt and himself, having opened the dock gates, made for the rowboat and told Thornton to join them as soon as they were closed? They could in fact leave him in the lurch. He rejected it, because Thornton, if taken alive, might give away dangerous information. He said, 'As soon as I open the dock gates and you see the constable has gone to report it, you and Schmidt will run down the dock and get into the rowboat. If a PLA launch comes past, row away upstream and then drop down to pick me up. If nobody appears, then wait for me and we proceed as arranged.' In attack, Skorzeny believed, lead from the front. In retreat, lead from the rear.

He repeated his instructions when he took over from Schmidt in the control room. '*Heil Hitler!*' Schmidt said, throwing up a grateful salute.

'*Heil Hitler!*' Skorzeny reassured him, with a wink. 'I'm going to open both gates now.' He took over from Schmidt and, first easing open the gate which had been shut, he gave them both full power.

'He's staring,' shouted Thornton. 'Can't believe his eyes! Now he's gone.'

'Off! Both of you!' Skorzeny turned his eyes to the dock basin. The forward periscope of the U-boat rose and began to ease forward, like the head of a grass-snake. It moved out between the gates and continued perilously projecting, while Schmidt and Thornton ran along the dockside to the river wall. Almost simultaneously, the periscope and the two men disappeared from view. Skorzeny swung the gate mechanism into reverse and slowly they began to close.

Before he left, Skorzeny looked at the warehouse window. There was, for some reason, no sign of the policeman; instead of running down the dockside, he walked to the river wall, like any waterman about his business, except taller than most.

55 Out of order

Constable Cohn hobbled across the warehouse floor and down the worn wooden stairs as fast as his flat feet could carry him. He dialled from the door-keeper's hut, in his excitement getting a wrong digit and having to wait for the dialling tone to come on, before starting all over again. In a career devoted to cases of assault and battery, breaking and entering, street accidents and bomb damage, this was his big moment. But when he succeeded at last in dialling the right number, all he got was the 'unobtainable' uninterrupted buzz. He tried again: same result.

What was he to do? Go up again to his second floor peephole? But that would waste time, even if it gave him further information. He went out into the street, looking for his bicycle. Then, remembering he had come on the d.r.'s pillion, he quietly swore and started off for Leman Street at an apology for a run.

'I'm going to try the PLA,' Embleton said. 'That duty officer should have rung back.' But when he picked up the receiver the line was dead.

Superintendent Salt tried the other line. That too was dead. 'Must have been that bomb.'

Embleton stood up. No point in staying at Leman Street. He called the d.r. But where to go? Back to the warehouse, from which he could report the latest developments to the PLA? 'No,' he said. 'We can phone Rossiter's from the duty officer's.' Then he turned to the superintendent. 'What's the quickest route to the PLA police?'

As he turned the corner into Leman Street, Constable Cohn saw the d.r. streaking off, with Embleton holding him by the waist. Cohn shouted, but the noise of the motor-cycle drowned his words.

56 Lucas underground

Lucas gritted his teeth. The bren-gunner was only four feet away from him. He seemed to be staring straight in his direction.

Lucas swallowed the sneeze and the bren-gunner turned away and started walking down the track. Of course! Lucas could

198

see the bren-gunner clearly through the openwork of the grille, because he was illuminated; all the gunner had seen through his respirator was iron mesh and holes of darkness. He hadn't noticed the wire.

But when the pursuit party reached St Katharine's dock and met up with the relief party (which by then must surely have occupied the dock), they would come back and examine each of the grilles carefully.

After waiting a couple of minutes for the bren-gunner to move out of earshot, Lucas turned on his torch and climbed the ventilation shaft until he reached the lateral. He went along this in the direction of the river until he reached another shaft. He shone his torch and could see water moving. He took off his respirator and began to breathe deeply. He had not realized what a tax the gas mask had imposed on his lungs. It was no more use to him, but it had to be disposed of without leaving a clue to his escape route. They might even get a scent for tracker-dogs, if they found it. He lay on his belly along the lateral, looking down the ventilation shaft. Holding the torch with his left hand, he dropped the respirator into the water below. It struck with a splash and then moved away to the left. Gone for good.

He stood up and examined the floor of the lateral with his torch. His footsteps showed up clearly. So when they did find the grille he had cut away, they would be able to follow him without much difficulty. He had hoped to be able to lie up somewhere until darkness fell – which, by looking at his watch, he reckoned would be in about five hours' time. Now he realized that he must keep moving to hold or increase his lead over his pursuers.

He started to climb down the ventilation shaft. To husband his battery, he turned off the torch while he was descending. His ankle gave him only an occasional twinge. Oddly enough, in the first stages of his escape, he had felt no pain: the anaesthetic of excitement or fear?

Even before he reached the platform, he could smell that this was a sewer not a drain. It would be flowing east to the main drainage metropolis at Barking. He switched on his torch and started to walk upstream, trying to take yard-long strides and counting each step.

'If you step on it, you may just catch 'em at Tower Pier,' said the duty officer. 'If they've gone, you'd better go back to Rossiter's. I understand Sir Hilary's trying to lay on something. But God knows how he'll do it on this day, of all days.'

Slowly, very slowly, the U-boat turned to face downstream. Leutnant Lustige raised the fore and after periscopes just above the choppy surface of the river. There was nothing visible. 'Quarter speed ahead,' he ordered as he lowered the periscopes.

'Quarter speed ahead,' repeated the chief engineer.

The U-boat moved gently forward against the flowing tide.

Skorzeny climbed down the iron ladder into the rowboat. Schmidt waited until Skorzeny was settled in the thwart amidships and had grasped his oars; then he let go the ladder and, sitting in the stern, took up the ribbons. Thornton in the bow pushed off with his right oar.

As he looked up from his first stroke, Skorzeny saw the dock gates were already half closed. The Pool of London appeared that Sunday afternoon to be utterly deserted. There was no launch at Swan Pier. But he could not see what lay beyond Tower Bridge.

Across the river, Schmidt saw that craft were tied up at Cherry Garden Pier. There seemed no sign of life there; but what lay hidden round the bend of Wapping Wall, he could not determine: nor what he would do if any boat appeared in sight. Watermen formed a closed community. Every man and his boat were familiar; the sight of three strange men in Water Gypsy 4 would provoke curiosity. The only thing would be to hug the shelter of the tethered barges.

The PLA launch was just casting off as the d.r. came down Tower Hill to Lower Thames Street. Embleton shouted and as the d.r. stopped, he leapt off and ran across to the Tower Bridge pier, waving.

As the launch edged back to the landing stage, the man in the prow reached forward and grasped Embleton's hand and pulled him aboard. Immediately, the launch reversed and then, as it turned downriver, it shot forward with a roar, the choppy waves slapping its prow and the brown river beaten into a frothy wake behind.

'Now tell me,' the launch captain said, 'what precisely it was you thought you saw in St Katharine's?'

'There were two men wearing PLA uniform: one of them very tall.'

'Could be Lofty,' suggested a man standing by the launch captain.

'Lofty's on compassionate leave. No soldiers?'

'None.'

The captain took a ring of keys out of his pocket and went below. He was not long. The launch was scarcely out of the shadow of Tower Bridge before he was back with a couple of sten-guns. 'Never thought we'd need these,' he said, 'but maybe we will.' He turned to the man who had mentioned Lofty and said, 'And there'd be no harm in mounting the bren.'

As they rounded Wapping Wall, Schmidt saw, coming round the bend, a tug. It was half a mile away, but he was taking no chances. He steered into the lee of a barge lying up against Wapping Wall. 'Ship your oars,' he said, 'something's coming.'

The gates of St Katharine's dock were closed. The launch drew in beside the iron ladder. 'Are you quite sure there were no soldiers?' asked the captain.

'None visible.' Embleton slung a sten-gun over his shoulder. 'Anyone join me?'

'We'll mount the bren-gun first,' said the captain. 'Then you and I will see what we can see.'

Between the barge and the wall, there was an iron ladder very similar to the one which the man with the bren-gun was beginning to mount. 'Tie up, Thornton, and have a look,' Skorzeny said. 'Perhaps this is where we disembark.'

Embleton and the launch captain stood against the wall, twenty feet apart, saying nothing, hearing nothing except the lap of waves against the launch. The whole dock looked dead. The bren-gunner had mounted his bipod on the yard floor and was standing with his feet on the ladder.

Embleton cupped his hands to his mouth and shouted, 'HullO THERE!' The walls echoed *O THERE*. But otherwise there was no answer. 'I'll go forward,' Embleton whispered. 'Just one's enough.'

He edged along the wall of the building, looking sharply, this way, that way, listening every four or five paces. Not a sound. Not a sight. He opened a green-painted door which screeched; inside just lumber and cobwebs.

More daring, he came away from the wall. He walked up the steps into the empty office; then into the control room. There was a red light above a lever which was turned to Shut. He moved it upwards and the red light went out. He opened the window and called 'They've been and gone, I think. But better search the place.'

Thornton leaned over the Wapping Wall and beckoned. Skorzeny grasped the iron ladder and climbed up. Schmidt followed, but before he did so he untied Water Gypsy 4 and with a thrust of his foot pushed her away, clear of the barge. If she drifted downstream on the ebbing tide, so much the better. It would put the police off the scent.

Skorzeny gave Schmidt his hand. 'So far,' he said, 'not so good, but could be worse.'

'Come to my place,' Schmidt answered. 'The sooner you get out of these clothes, the better.'

'Embleton! Here!' shouted the captain. 'We've found them!'

Embleton ran to the head of the steps. 'Who?'

'The guard.' The captain was standing by an open door at the foot of the steps. He looked a strange colour and, as Embleton ran down the steps, the captain turned away and walked to the side of the dock basin. Embleton stared through the door at what lay on the floor and the tarpaulin which had been drawn back. Then he turned away and looked at the captain, who seemed to be shaken with grief. But he wasn't sobbing.

He was vomiting.

58 In Westminster

Bernard Nightingale got off the bus at the bottom of Whitehall. He had good news as far as it went. If Operation Serpent had been a failure, the hijack had proved an utter disaster to the enemy. The treasure train had suffered no damage. Three of the hijackers had been found dead. A fourth had escaped into a ventilation shaft. He would have been pursued, if orders had not been received from on high to withdraw to the King George V dock area. He crossed Bridge Street and, looking up at Big Ben, he saw that it was ten past five: which explained why he felt so hungry, as he had eaten nothing since seven a.m.

As he entered Old Palace Yard, he saw Lady Virginia coming towards him from Millbank. He hoped that did not mean that the Brigadier had already left the office; though he could not blame the old gentleman if he had decided to call it a day.

Suddenly, almost as if she did not want to meet him, Lady Virginia turned and ran across the road in front of an omnibus. The driver jammed on his brakes and screeched his horn, swearing at her. But she took no notice of him or a Bedford fifteen-cwt army lorry coming in the opposite direction. 'She'll kill herself if she goes on like that,' muttered Mr Nightingale, as she vanished up Little College Street.

The sight of Bernard Nightingale was more than Lady Virginia could bear, his pale blue eyes blinking behind his rimless glasses, his thinning curly hair on a shiny scalp and his bashfully receding chin. It brought her face to face with the appalling realization of the blow which, out of blind devotion to her dead father, she had delivered to dear old Bodgers, the one person on earth she truly loved, the only one who loved her truly.

As she wandered in the back streets behind Westminster Abbey, she heard the noise of another flying bomb and instead of feeling the old exultation that the glorious Führer was dealing another blow against the stupid, blundering British, she was overwhelmed with a sense of futility at the damage sustained by buildings nobler than those who worshipped in them.

She found herself in the Abbey, so vast that it had withstood all the bombardment and the fires that had gutted the deanery, the Little Cloister and Dr Busby's library. It was too early for evensong, but here and there were people, mostly women, bent in prayer – reduced by the enormity of the edifice to the proportions of insects.

She went into a side chapel and knelt before an ancient Jesus nailed to an ancient cross. Her heart felt like an icicle, melting.

59 Somewhere in Bloomsbury

Lucas mounted the last step and looked out through the grille. There was a thicket of bushes, privet; and to the right a garden roller, a path, a rustic-work garden shed. To the left, he could see across grass to a long, slatted garden seat on which two old men sat, smoking pipes; and beyond, a road, traffic moving, a red bus, camouflaged vehicles, an army convoy.

By his watch it was 18.26. Apart from a four-ounce bar of reinforced chocolate and two packets of Freshets, he had had nothing to eat since the night before. He was terribly thirsty. And tired. It was thirty-eight hours since he had slept. He had some raisins somewhere, but he could not find them. It was all he could do to cling on.

He could climb down to the lateral and rest, perhaps sleep. He had always intended to wait until darkness before surfacing. But he had to cut his way out in daylight. The flame of the oxyacetylene cutter would attract attention at night. If he chose the panel of the grille facing the shed, he should not be seen. He'd tried the exits from four other shafts. Only one of these had been possible, and that was in a recreation ground where children were playing ball. The ball came bouncing towards the shaft. A dog followed it and saw him through the mesh of the grille and crouched on its hind legs, barking.

It should not have taken long to cut through the grille, but he had difficulty starting the oxyacetylene cutter and he had to keep changing his grasp, because his muscles ached so.

When at last the grille fell outwards with a thud, Lucas knew that he ought to go back to the lateral – stow his gear so that if he was followed up the main drain his point of exit would not be betrayed, and then wait till darkness before going above ground. But he had reached the end of his tether.

He stripped off the harness of the oxyacetylene kit and let it fall, clanging down the shaft. He emptied his respirator case of its tools, one by one – he was too weary to lift the respirator strap over his head. The noise of their landing below filled him with a curious satisfaction. It was like the clank of chains falling from the wrists of a prisoner, reprieved. Then, with the muster of all his strength, he hoisted himself out of the shaft and crawled towards the shed.

He lay for a moment, remembering there was something which he ought to do but uncertain what it was. Yes, of course. Replace the grille. He put his hand in his pocket, feeling for cigarettes, found instead the raisins, stuffed a few in his mouth and chewed.

God! he thought; Lucas, you're alive!

He stood up, winced at the pain in his ankle and then went back to the ventilation shaft. First he threw down his empty respirator case. Then he lifted the grille. If he tried to fit it into place, it might fall down into the drain. He looked round. There was a dead branch of privet half broken off. He snapped it to the length he needed, stuck it in the ground and propped the grille against it; the best he could do; which should be good enough.

He found his cigarettes and lit up. The first inhalation made his head whirl, but he was past caring. Light-headed, he came out from the privet clump into the square, shady with elms and maples. It could be any of a dozen London squares. He walked unsteadily over to a vacant bench and sat down, slouched forward, elbows on thighs, drawing on the cigarette.

He heard a little bell and looked up. The bell was below the chin of a King Charles spaniel. A lead was round its neck and at the other end was the hand of a middle-aged woman. The dog pranced towards him and he stretched out to stroke its head, then looked up at the woman, who was smiling. 'Nice dog,' he said.

'You look all in.'

'I am. That explosion at Monument station this morning. One hell of a mess. Been on it, ever since; without a stop.'

The women sat down and started asking questions. Somebody had told her it might be sabotage. Hundreds dead.

'I only saw one,' Lucas said. 'A young boy. Burst into flames. I'll never forget him, long as I live.'

'And then these horrible flying bomb things. What a day! I shan't forget it either.'

'And yet,' said Lucas, 'funny thing ... Suppose I'm tired ... But I've lost my way. Live near Euston, but I don't know where I am.'

'Oh, don't worry about that. Euston Station's quite close. I'll show you.'

60 A case of overwork

Sir Hilary sat at the desk of his study in Eaton Square. In front of him was a sheet of paper on which were written two words: 'Dear Winston'. In the wastepaper basket on his left were half a dozen crumpled balls of letter paper on which where written, 'Dear Prime Minister', 'My dear Winnie', 'I do not know ...', 'It is with the deepest shame ...', 'How can I ...', 'In tendering my resignation ...' On the desk at his right hand stood a half-empty glass of whisky and soda; and behind him, on an inlaid rosewood table, stood a salver on which was a quarter-empty bottle of Glenlivet whisky which had made its way from the Highlands to Washington, DC and thence in the diplomatic bag to Lady Virginia Chudleigh before reaching ('Your need is greater than mine, Bodgers, dearest') the Brigadier's flat in Eaton Square.

The telephone bell rang. Hoping that it was his dearest Candie, whom he had tried in vain to reach at Shepton Mallet, Sir Hilary picked up the receiver. 'Darling!'

'Could I speak to Sir Hilary Fry?' asked a strange voice at the other end.

'Speaking.'

'I'm sorry to trouble you, sir. This is the Charing Cross Hospital. It's concerning a Lady Virginia ... let me see ... Chudleigh, who was, I believe, a member of your staff ...'

'*Was?*'

'I regret so, sir. She was brought in an hour ago, sir.'

'An accident?'

'I'm afraid one could not call it an accident. She threw herself under a train at Westminster Underground.'

'*Threw?* Are you sure?'

'It was at the incoming tunnel. There was nobody standing near. And ... I don't want to go into detail, sir ... but the driver was emphatic and the nature of the injuries confirm ... she did not fall. "Dived" was the word ...'

'My God!' The Brigadier put his hand over the mouthpiece so that the chap at the other end could not hear him. Ginny! poor, dotty, traitorous child!

'Hullo! Hullo!' the voice at the other end queried. 'Are you still with me, Sir Hilary?'

'Um. Um.' Sir Hilary could venture no more. 'Um.'

'I know it is very distressing. But someone has to identify ... the next of kin.'

'Identify? Of course. It might not really be her. I'd better ... she was an orphan and I was her closest ...'

'Had you any reason to suspect, sir ... ?'

'She ... something went very wrong today,' Sir Hilary said. 'I think ... perhaps ... she blamed herself.'

'You might call it "a case of overwork",' the voice suggested.

'I suppose we might,' the Brigadier said. 'I'll be over ... as soon as I can manage it.'

61 Dublin, via Liverpool

The all-clear had not sounded all day. The air-raid warning system had broken down with the advent of flying bombs, which despite the counterattacks of low-flying Mosquito aircraft on the launching sites, continued to come over. Lucas had reason to bless them, because the presence of so many dirty and dishevelled ARP workers made his own condition less conspicuous. In the toilets at Euston Station, the lavatory attendant who opened the bathroom and provided his towel merely remarked, 'Looks like you had a busy day.'

'You won't recognize me when I come out,' Lucas said, as he took in the suitcase in which he had Philip Mitchell's best clothes.

'You're certainly right,' said the attendant, when Lucas emerged quite a time later, shaved, shining and relaxed. He carried, as well as the suitcase, a brown-paper parcel containing his working gear, which he dumped under a litter-basket already filled to overflowing. The only thing which he retained was the precious leather belt, containing his money.

He went over to the departure indicator and saw that the next train to Holyhead left at 20.00 hours. There was time to eat and drink, so he deposited his suitcase with the other one at the left luggage office and found the buffet. It was crowded, mostly with servicemen and their families. He fought his way to the counter and ordered a pint of bitter. 'Can't you see the time?' said the old-girl, nodding to the clock, which said five to seven.

'A pint of milk then.'

'We don't serve milk in pints.'

'Then two half pints.'

'One 'arf. Don'tcher know there's a war on?'

To eat, there was a choice of spam, spam sandwich, or spam roll. Lucas swallowed the milk in one gulp and ordered a spam roll with mustard. 'There ain't no mustard,' the old-girl said. 'Don'tcher know there's—'

He ordered a pint of bitter, pointing to the clock which now pointed to seven.

'That clock's fast,' the old-girl said. 'Five minutes.'

Lucas ate the spam and half the roll. He decided to buy his ticket and then find some pub nearby where they didn't say, 'Don'tcher know there's a war on?'

There were long queues at the ticket windows. Lucas ran his eye over them to see which was the shortest. Standing in the furthest queue was a very tall man. Something about him was familiar but his face was turned away. Lucas walked past the furthest queue and glanced round. The long scar running down the left side of his face was unmistakable.

Lucas turned away and went to the telephone booths. From there he could watch Skorzeny, while pretending to study a directory. He waited till Skorzeny was second in the queue and then went over to a timetable board, from which he could eavesdrop.

'A single, please, to Holyhead.'

'Where'd you say?'

'HOLYhead.'

'Oh, *Hollyhead*, you mean.'

Before Skorzeny had paid for his ticket, Lucas was in the inquiry office. 'Which is quicker for Dublin,' he asked, 'Holyhead or Liverpool?'

'Depends on the weather,' said the clerk. 'But I'd say Liverpool. The train's not till 20.30. But with any luck, you'd be in the centre of Dublin two hours earlier. If the weather's good.'

The weather *was* good. After sleeping all the way to Liverpool and halfway across the Irish Sea, Lucas found Grete through the Swedish Embassy, well before Skorzeny had reported to the German military attaché in Dublin.

They were married by special licence at the Swedish Embassy next morning, with Mr and Mrs Ohlsen as witnesses. 'Do you think that we'll be safe here?' asked Grete, when it was over.

'I think Major Skorzeny and his friends have other things to think about,' said Mr Ohlsen, producing the morning newspaper, with the banner headline: 'ALLIES LAND IN NORMANDY'.

Otto Skorzeny was too busy planning future triumphs to bother about clearing up the debris of his failure. The Molyneuxs flew unhindered to Lisbon and then rented an apartment in Estoril. About the time that Skorzeny foiled the Hungarian attempt at negotiating peace with Stalin by kidnapping Admiral Horthy's son, Grete gave birth to a boy whose features were the living spit of his unmemorable Dad's. The baby was christened Gustav in memory of Grete's father and Rosario in gratitude to the Brasilian shipowner who arranged a passage for them to Brasil; that same week a handful of Skorzeny's kommandos were assisting Rundstedt's counteroffensive in the Ardennes by parachuting behind the American lines in GI uniform, misdirecting the traffic and, on being captured, informing their interrogators that their numbers ran into hundreds.

Roosevelt and Churchill proclaimed 8 May 1945 VE Day eight days after Hitler and Eva Braun committed suicide in the bunker. Long before August and the destruction of Hiroshima, with the atomic bomb the Führer had tried but failed to make, fugitive Nazis were arriving in Rio de Janeiro and calling on Dom Rosario to surrender the loot they had entrusted to his cargo-vessels. Dom Rosario punctiliously handed over their treasures, having deducted freight charges. But he pointed out that he would have to be paid monthly instalments of silence-money to cover the risks involved in concealing their escape. Lucas was in charge of Dom Rosario's mining interests, extraction and prospecting; in addition, he undertook the shadowing of the fugitives: if they tried to escape payment, they were tracked down and the costs of finding them added to their monthly payments. Grete at this time helped Dom Rosario as his social secretary. The Molyneuxs, who had regarded Lucas's payment for Honeycomb as a fortune beyond their dreams, found it quite inadequate to their enlarged ambitions. So they rejoiced at the opportunities opened up by the Nuremberg Trials. Goering's Brasilian hoard was the largest, but not the only, prize which fell into Dom Rosario's hands. A new branch of Rosario Holdings was opened up, Carlson Fine Arts. Under

Grete's management, it contacted wealthy art-collectors avid to acquire masterpieces whatever their source of origin or to offset against tax the expenses of art-loving.

Lucas at first applauded the idea, because it gave Grete something to do during his absences from Rio. Later he grew more doubtful. For one thing, the money which Grete made from her commissions was more than he earned as mining director; for another, the second boy borne by Grete was the living spit of his mother, but bore no resemblance to Lucas. Though christened Lucas, he was given the second name of Bamberg after Frederick Z. Bamberg, the Minneapolis Cookie King, who was his godfather. Bamberg, having bought a Monet in the same month that Lucas Bamberg was conceived, came down for a Manet two months later and a Tissot 'Thames Riverside' after the boy was born. There was a jealous row between the Molyneuxs after he went back to Minneapolis. Nothing really came out into the open. But, after the sexual reconciliation which formed the climax to their quarrel, Grete held Lucas's head in her hands; looking at him with those eyes which, when he first met her, struck him as being gemlike – rather than humanly blue – she said, 'There is more to marriage than coming together.' Next day Rosario made him a gift of the two Leonardo da Vinci cartoons which Mussolini had presented to Skorzeny. 'For me, my friend,' Rosario said, 'they are already yours. But if Skorzeny, who has been acquitted at Nuremberg, comes to see me – I will tell him that you are holding them in trust.'

'How much are they worth?' asked Lucas.

'Anything by Leonardo is priceless,' Rosario said. 'You would get what the buyer was prepared to pay.' He shrugged his shoulders. 'I would not sell while Skorzeny still lives. Now he is a free man, perhaps he is already on his way to collect the cartoons. He may have forgotten them, though to me he is a man who does not forget – in that case, if you sell, he may remember: and what would you do then, my friend?'

'To put it crudely, you're frightened of Skorzeny and you're passing the buck to me.'

'Here I have many enemies already: Martin Bormann, others ... I do not wish to add Scarface to their number.' Rosario placed his large moist palm on the back of Molyneux's hand. 'In Honeycomb you outwitted Scarface and made some money. These pictures ... why not take them as your final payment?'

Lucas took them. 'I will wait as you suggest.'

'And when you sell,' smiled Dom Rosario, 'let Grete handle the transaction. She charges high commission. But she earns it.'

From this point onwards the relationship between Lucas and his wife and senior partner began to alter. Business became its main foundation, a business which gradually changed. Grete invested her profits from fine arts in a place on the Avenida Beira Mar. It served at the same time as her gallery and her residence. Displayed in the gallery were works of art legitimately acquired, or exhibitions by artists of international repute; in her private quarters were concealed her choicest pieces – revealed only to those of whose combination of discretion, wealth and good taste she was assured.

This caution became even more necessary when the loot of dead Nazis began to be exhausted and Dom Rosario decided to remit payment of hush-money in cash for contributions in kind. He pointed out to his victims that if they became his clients, he could secure for them higher prices for their plunder than they could get from other Latin American dealers in such merchandise. The Nuremberg Trials were a travesty of human justice, he assured them. After all, why should the Russians – whose economic system was founded on the exploitation of their Arctic resources by slave labour – or the Americans – who destroyed more Japanese by two atomic bombs than the SS at Auschwitz destroyed Jews in the gas-chambers in a month of Sundays – sit in judgement? To the Molyneuxs, Rosario added that the prospects of the Nazi refugees in the hereafter would be better if they served their term of purgatory on earth.

It was an argument which the ex-Nazis found unconvincing; and a joke which stopped being amusing to Lucas when one of his investigators returned with his left hand severed at the wrist and another did not return at all. The worms were turning, the hunted turning huntsmen. After the first reprisal Lucas's investigators demanded double wages, after the second, they quit.

Lucas discussed with Grete what they should do. He was

212

convinced that Skorzeny had come to Brasil and was organizing a kommando. Grete pooh-poohed the idea. Skorzeny's autobiography *Special Missions* had been published in German and she had obtained a copy. 'You don't understand Otto,' she said. 'He may have been a member of the SS, but he was never a real Nazi. He was a "Greater Germany" patriot;' and she translated passages to prove her point, omitting those which betrayed his reverence for Hitler. But she armed the security guards in the gallery and reinforced the doors and windows of her living quarters. Dom Rosario was shot at as he was entering his car in the Avenida Rio Branco. The bullet would have entered his heart, if he had not been wearing a bullet-proof vest. As soon as he heard of it, Lucas took the Leonardo cartoons to his bank with instructions that they should be lodged in a safe deposit in Mexico in the name of Leucas Ramoulian.

He did not tell Grete what he had done. Their son Gustav Rosario had left university and taken over the navigation section. Dom Rosario was loud in praise of the young Molyneux. 'When I am gone,' he would say, putting his arm round Gustav's shoulders, 'you will be my heir.' They could not leave the old man in the lurch, when millions were at stake. It was like Honeycomb all over again; or, more accurately, Honeycomb had not ended any more than the Second World War had with VE and VJ Days. 'Thank God,' said Grete, 'Lucas Bamberg is at Harvard and can stay with Fred Z. between semesters.'

Dom Rosario was not daunted by the assassination attempt. He did not report the incident to the police: what was the point when he was operating outside the law? 'Besides, the police are milking the same cows.' Instead, he wrote a letter to a gentleman in Vienna who had a long memory and a large number of filing cabinets. Two months later, as the ex-SS man who had cut off the investigator's hand came on to his verandah to savour the dawn of a new day, two Israeli gunmen discharged two magazines into his torso and were aboard an aeroplane before the hue and cry. '*Autres temps*,' observed Dom Rosario, when he read the news item in his newspaper, at the foot of page two, '*autres moeurs*.'

In this way discipline was maintained until 1970. With the

opening up of the interior and the massacre of aborigines in the Brasilian Government 'settlement' plan, Lucas spent more time in prospecting mineral deposits than in keeping track of Nazi criminals. This was highly competitive, and one evening Lucas flew in to Rio to report on rich deposits of uranium, for which a rival claim would be staked unless Rosario took immediate action. He drove straight to Dom Rosario's villa. The guard at the gate knew Lucas, but telephoned the house before admitting him. There was no answer. The servants had been given the evening off. 'Dom Rosario is entertaining, you understand,' explained the guard with a lewd wink.

'I will go up and wait,' Lucas said. 'I have business, very important.' He drove to the front of the villa. The door was not locked. Indeed, it was not even shut. He went into the living room where he poured himself a large Dimple Haig, with four cubes of ice.

As he rattled these round in the glass, he sensed a curious stillness. But he was aware that Dom Rosario had his 'funny ways' and he was not a man to interrupt another in intimate pleasures. He took a deep drink, lit a cigarette and then, seeing the record player open, he thought that here was a tactful way of announcing his presence. He switched it on, not looking to see the name of the disc lying on the turntable. It was one of Dom Rosario's favourites: *'Que sera, sera'*. The cheerful assertion of the old rogue's fatalism: 'whatever will be, will be.' He took another drink, watching the door of the bedroom for the emergence of Dom Rosario as soon as he was decently attired. When Rosario did not appear, Lucas turned up the volume, finished his drink and waited.

The record ended. The machine stopped. Lucas stubbed out his cigarette and strode to the bedroom door. No sound came from the other side. Lucas tried the door. It opened. But Lucas did not go in. Rosario was lying face upwards on the thick white carpet. He was wearing the dress of a waiting maid. The frilly, white-lace apron bulged with the protrusion of his bowels and was stained with blood and bile. It looked as if he had vomited as he died – but what crammed his mouth was a full scrotum.

Lucas went back into the living room and called the police.

He ought, he thought as he hysterically explained what had happened, to have looked to see whether it was Rosario's or another's. He began to shake. He could not speak. 'Come! Come quick! See for yourself!' Then he put down the telephone. He ought to call Grete. But his hands were shaking too much to dial. He had left the bedroom door open. He braced himself and went over and closed the door with eyes averted. 'Grete, Grete,' he kept saying to himself. 'Must call. She would know. Oh God! Oh God!' He held his right wrist with his left hand to stop the shaking. But he couldn't remember Grete's number. It had gone completely out of his mind.

There was a direct line to the lodge and the guard answered at once. Lucas heard himself explaining with a voice of extraordinary clarity that Dom Rosario had been murdered and the police were on their way and the reason why no one had answered the telephone was that the Dom was dead and the killer ... what had happened to the killer? Perhaps he was in the house still, or the grounds. The guard must stay on the gate to let the police in and see the killer didn't get out. 'No, don't worry about me!' he heard himself saying. 'I can look after myself. But call my wife. Please, call my wife and ask her to come over here as soon as possible. Tell her. Yes, tell her Dom Rosario has been murdered by a sex-maniac.'

He put down the receiver. 'A sex-maniac,' he repeated, 'yes, a sex-maniac.' He mustn't say Skorzeny to anyone, not even to Grete, least of all to Grete, who thought he was dotty about Skorzeny. 'Can look after myself,' he muttered. Yes, if it was a sex-maniac, but not if it was bloody Scarface. He needed a weapon. He never carried a gun, believing if you did you were more likely to get shot. But now he was likely to get castrated and disembowelled; yes, he needed a gun now. There was Rosario's desk, which was where he was likely to keep a gun. The drawers opened. They were crammed. Rosario's idea of tidiness was stuff in a drawer; perhaps dating back years. But no firearm – except perhaps the bottom right.

That was locked. And no key.

Keys for the others.

Tried them, but they didn't fit.

Maybe the old man had it on his keyring, which would be ...
he couldn't bear to face the bedroom again. There was a noise.
He looked round desperately, saw there was a paper-knife in
the pen tray. Sharp-pointed. Advert for Bethlehem Steel. He
seized it. It wasn't much good, but better than nothing.

He was still holding it when the police ran in. He pointed
with it to the bedroom door. He heard their exclamations, oaths,
horror, dismay.

Then a policeman came back into the living room. He began
asking questions and Lucas felt that he must answer them. But
suddenly he began to scream and as he tried to stop, burying
his head on his crossed arms, he remembered screaming like
this in the Cable Street kitchen when the scalding water cas-
caded down him from the saucepan on the stove.

The policeman poured a whiskey and came over to the desk.
'Drink this, senhor.' But Lucas could not drink.

Not till he heard Grete's voice; and Gustav's! He took the
glass, gulped down the neat spirit, choked and began to cough.
Grete ran over to him, Gustav hung back. Lucas tried to say
something. But all he could do was hold Grete's hand.

Grete was marvellous. It was as if she'd spent a lifetime coping
with the homicide squad. When Gustav drove his parents
home in the small hours, Grete explained everything to Lucas
as if he was a small child. 'There's nothing to worry about,' she
said. 'The police were very sympathetic. A crime of "perverted
sexual passion". We all agree on that. I'm seeing the Minister
the moment he comes to his office. The Government would not
want a scandal at the moment.'

She spoke as if Dom Rosario had passed away in his sleep.

Lucas was kept under deep sedation until it was all over. All
the nurse said, when he made desperate inquiries about what
was happening, was 'Not to worry', and she gave him another
jab. It was over three weeks before he really became himself
again and by then he was sitting under a sunshade at a table
beside a swimming pool. In front of him was a glass of black
coffee, beside him a chair on which was laid a bathrobe. In the
pool people were splashing and shouting, beside it they lay on

towels or chaises-longues, their skins the colour of dried bananas. It was no place he remembered, but nice; especially a girl outstretched three yards away. Her figure was perfect, her face hidden by a Spanish translation of a Mickey Spillane paperback.

Grete came up, towelling her back. Considering that she was in her late forties, she had a superb body: but not surprising, in view of the love she lavished on it. She took no notice of Lucas until he said, 'Hello!' Then she asked how he was feeling.

'Puzzled. Where are we?'

She snapped her fingers for a waiter, ordered a *café con crema* and sat down beside Lucas. 'Tehuantepec, Mexico, the Hotel Esplendido.'

'Esplendido!' It wasn't a good joke, but the first he had made for God knows how long. 'How come we come?'

'Oh, you're better. Listen!' She turned aside to sign the chit for the coffee and then drawing her chair close she told in a low voice what had happened 'while he was ill'. Rosario's murder had been reported as a natural death. She and Gustav had agreed that it would be best. As Rosario's heir, Gustav would stay on in Rio until he could dispose of the various branches of the business as going concerns. Grete would carry on the gallery for the time being and give Gustav moral support. Meanwhile Lucas, when he felt better, should look round for new premises in Mexico; there should be an office in Mexico City and a villa-gallery outside, like Grete's place on the Avenida Beira Mar, but on a grander scale. A sort of crypto-luxury hotel whose guests paid for their hospitality by buying works of art or alternatively crypto-art gallery in which works of art were included in the bill for board and lodging (whichever was more desirable tax-wise).

'A *Palacio do Sonho*?' suggested Lucas.

'Totally different!'

Lucas did not argue. 'Where am I to look?'

'Tehauntepec's too close to Mexico City. Taxco's too crowded in on itself. Cuernavaca would be best.'

Lucas nodded. Being given instructions was something new; but he guessed he could take it, until VS Day when

Skorzeny died and he converted the Leonardos into cash. 'What do we do for capital until Gustav settles Rio?'

'I've had a word with Fred Z. and he'll back us. His idea is that when Lucas leaves Harvard, he might start a US ancillary.'

'You've got it all worked out between you.'

'Not in detail, just the general outline,' Grete said. 'One has to evaluate potentialities. And, of course, let things grow.'

'Of course,' Lucas agreed. 'And when did you think of going back to Rio?'

'If you're feeling better, I thought tomorrow.'

The girl had stopped reading Mickey Spillane. Because of her dark glasses, Lucas could not be sure if she was watching them both, but when he smiled, she smiled deliciously back. 'I'm fine,' he answered. 'Quite my old self again.'

But he was not quite his old self. Partly it was the recollection of Dom Rosario as he had last seen him. Even more it was the conviction that Skorzeny had been behind the murder.

If he had been consulted, he would never have consented to Gustav staying on in Rio. But the boy was twenty-five, older than Lucas had been when he joined the International Brigade. If Gustav was prepared to risk death for wealth and power, it was more sensible than volunteering for a civil war which wasn't for any of the causes it was made out to be. He decided to cultivate, not his garden like Voltaire, but the girl he had seen reading Mickey Spillane.

Her name was Maria Molino y Abal y Queiroz. She was nineteen, untutored but eager to learn. When he asked for help in house- and office-hunting, she responded with pleasure and efficiency once she had made plain that this would involve the resignation of her job as receptionist at the Esplendido. Lucas proposed that she should become his personal assistant, offering her treble her salary, plus a living allowance when they left the hotel.

Maria had spent some years at school in the United States. Lucas had difficulty with Spanish which kept getting tangled up with Portuguese. They had fun correcting each other's grammar and pronunciation. Lucas, who had learned the habits of wealth the hard way, enjoyed a pupil adept at putting into practice herself what she had studied in others. In a building overlooking the Alameda garden and the Palace of Fine Arts, they found a penthouse which had its private lift and rooms enough for office and living quarters; in Cuernavaca they compiled a short-list of desirable properties from which Senora Molyneux might make her choice. Awaiting her arrival, Lucas bought for Maria the clothes they deemed necessary for his personal assistant. 'But what will *la Senora* say?' asked Maria, appalled but delighted at the expenditure. *'Esplendido!'* Grete commented after looking her over. 'Fancy finding all this in Mexico City!'

Grete chose the Villa Moctezuma in Cuernavaca. Too large for a private residence, too small for an hotel, too costly for a boarding house, it exactly suited her requirements. The gardens, sloping down the hillside, had interrupted views of the eroded mountains in the far distance. Laid out in terraces, each enclosed by walks of trees, shrubs and banana palms, the grounds provided sites for the chalets, or casitas, which over the years became the topic of admiration and of gossip, often lubricious, among those amateurs of painting, sculpture and love privileged to be the guests of Grete 'La Fabulosa'. In surroundings so priceless, millionaires travelling in search of rare delights, from the Middle West or Middle East, from Athens, Greece, or Athens, Tennessee, were never so vulgar as to query bills rounded down to the nearest grand. *'Optimum Nobis Sat'*, ran the Latin motto across the billhead: 'The best is good enough for us' – perhaps Lucas's major contribution to the success of Grete's venture.

In Mexico City, he remained on his own, until Maria moved into the penthouse to become his personal assistant at night as well as day. He fell in love with her; and to her alone he confided his fear of being pursued by Otto Skorzeny. Though so much younger than Lucas, Maria was at first delighted and astounded at his indefatigable pursuit of love. He was ready at any time and for any length of time. But when a rich young Mexican, nearer to her in temperament and culture, began to pester her with proposals of marriage, she began to hint that as a wife she could serve her employer better than his lady in Cuernavaca, who treated him more as her employee than her husband.

Lucas pleaded that he was a comparatively poor man, except for what he earned as Mexico City manager of Molyneux Empresas, the joint directors of which were Grete, her two sons, and Frederick Z. Bamberg. When, but only when, Skorzeny died, he would sell the Leonardo cartoons, now removed from safe deposit and gracing the walls of his office. Having received the fortune they realized, he would ask his wife for a divorce and make an honest woman of Maria.

The great day came on 8 July 1975. Maria brought him the copy of *Noticias* as if the headlines were all he needed to see. But before he telephoned Cuernavaca, he read the obituary through twice. There was not a mention of Honeycomb, unless the words 'Not all his schemes were notable' was an oblique reference.

Grete was some time before she came to the telephone. 'Is it important?' she asked, when she heard his voice, 'I'm very busy.'

'Skorzeny's dead,' Lucas said, 'I want you to sell the Leonardos for me.'

'Those cartoons!' she said. 'You don't think a four-flusher like Mussolini would part with originals. They're only "School of". You'd be lucky to get ten grand the pair. And you can't expect me to handle that sort of merchandise.'

Lucas said 'Oh!'

'If it's Maria you're thinking of, you'd better let her go. A nice girl like her wants children as well as marriage. You'll need a new assistant. Drive over any time, my dear, and take your pick. The best is good enough for you.' Grete put down the receiver and returned to her client from Houston, Texas.

Thomas N. Scortia and Frank M. Robinson
The Nightmare Factor 90p

It began with an isolated incident : a convention of war
veterans at a San Francisco hotel decimated by a mysterious
deadly disease. Calvin Doohan, epidemics expert, finds his
investigations hampered by the very authorities he is trying to
help – news blackouts, military intervention, hints of the most
evil weapons in the armouries of the super powers. Who is
the enemy ? Who can be trusted ? Only one thing is certain –
everyone is a potential victim.

'Spine-tingling to read and terrifying to ponder'
PUBLISHERS WEEKLY

Warren Adler
Trans-Siberian Express £1

As the Trans-Siberian Express journeys across six thousand miles
of frozen rail from the Moscow skyline through Asia's plain and
onward to the Pacific coast, Zeldovitch, KGB commandant and
confidant of the Soviet Premier, watches and waits for his moment
to strike . . .

'Packed with intrigue, violence and surprise' PUBLISHERS WEEKLY

Leslie Thomas
Ormerod's Landing 90p

1940 : only months after Dunkirk Churchill is determined to
set Europe ablaze. Detective-Sergeant George Ormerod of the
Metropolitan Police looks like being the first match !
Investigating a murder in Wandsworth, he suspects one Albert
Smales of the crime ; to apprehend him Ormerod travels to the
heart of Hitler's Fortress Europe, where Smales – a casualty of
Dunkirk – is safely inside a French hospital.
With his dog called Formidable and a delectable and ruthless
French lady agent, Ormerod makes his landing and finds
adventures of more kinds than one !

'Ingenious . . . funny . . . his best book yet' FINANCIAL TIMES

Wilbur Smith
Hungry as the Sea £1.20

Through shipwreck and hurricane, through the ice-world of
the Antarctic and the thundering surf of the African coast,
in the arms of the lovely Samantha and on the bridge of his
powerful *Warlock*, Berg is a man in his element. Deposed as top
man in a huge shipping consortium, he's running a debt-ridden
ocean-going salvage outfit – fighting back against the ruthless
ambition of the arch-rival who stole his wife and son and
robbed him of an empire – hell-bent on retribution . . .

'Surges forward with a bone in its teeth'
TIMES LITERARY SUPPLEMENT

Sandy Gall
Gold Scoop 80p

From one of Britain's top TV newsmen – high adventure in crisis-
torn Africa.
A journalist covering the African crisis, a sensual beauty
at the British High Commission, a sadistic General, a *coup d'état*
that rakes the streets with gunfire, tough mercenaries, and the
age-old lust for hoarded gold . . . a powerful and authentic
adventure of turbulent times.

George Fox
Amok 95p

He lives like a wild beast – kills like a professional executioner:
they call him the Amok . . .

When the Japanese forces evacuated the Philippines in the last
bloody months of the war, one man was left behind – a renegade
giant capable of nightmare violence and terrifying brutality,
armed with a razor-edged Samurai blade, and ordered to delay the
enemy advance as long as possible. Three decades later, he is
still killing – a murderous spectre haunting the lives of every man,
woman and child in an isolated island community. He's the reason
that two men have returned to the Philippines – one has come to kill
him, the other to save him.

Michael Booker
Danger – UXB 80p

The bombs that crashed down from the Luftwaffe raiders turned
the Home Front into a battleground in 1940. But for the men of
the Royal Engineers Bomb Disposal Company, the ones that
exploded were the ones you *didn't* worry about. When they went
into action they faced a sleeping mechanism that could explode
in their faces at any moment. Deft fingers, iron nerve and chill
courage were their weapons – and their battle-signal was : Danger –
UXB.

John Buchan
The Thirty Nine Steps 70p

When Richard Hannay offered sanctuary to the man he found
on the doorstep of his London flat in the middle of the night,
he took the first step in a trail of peril, murder and conspiracy,
a trail leading through one of the most famous thrillers ever
written.

'. . . Terse, taut, endlessly inventive, and as delightfully fresh
as the day it was written' NEW YORK TIMES

John le Carré
The Honourable Schoolboy £1.25

'The ultimate espionage novel. London. Hong Kong, Vientiane
are the settings and George Smiley and company are back . . .
It is hard to see how even le Carré could surpass himself
after this' PUBLISHERS WEEKLY

'One of the most effective thrillers we have had for years. His
command of detail is staggering, his strightforward, unaffected
prose is superb. In short, wonderful value' SUNDAY TIMES

'Compassionate, distinguished, terrifying' COSMOPOLITAN

J. D. Gilman and John Clive
KG 200 95p

They flew Flying Fortresses. They wore American uniforms...
but they were Germans! KG 200 – the phantom arm of Hitler's
Luftwaffe. From a secret base in occupied Norway these crack
pilots plan their ultimate mission, the raid that would bring Allied
defeat crashing down from the exploding skies...

Inspired by the best-kept secret of World War Two, this is one of
the most enthralling novels of air warfare, espionage and manhunt
ever written.

'Shattering' TELEGRAPH

Jack Higgins
The Eagle Has Landed 80p

The order: 'Bring me Churchill out of England' – Adolf Hitler
16 September 1943.

The plan: To kidnap the Prime Minister during a quiet weekend at a
country house in Norfolk.

The people: Kurt Steiner and his handful of crack paratroopers,
an embittered woman spy, an IRA gunman and a Free Corps
traitor.

The date: 6 November 1943 – the most audacious mission ever
conceived is poised to strike...